UNFATED MATES

LEXIE TALIONIS

CETERIS PARIBUS
PUBLISHING

CONTENT WARNING

This story includes strong language, some graphic violence, and scenes that might just have you reaching for a few pearls...

PART I

1

NAT CLIMBED OFF THE BUS, turning her hooded face at the last moment to block the incoming snowball. Her head snapped a bit to the side from the force before the icy globe slid down the worn fabric of her jacket to plop back in the snow.

"Haha—yeah, hide your face, Medusa!" The boys jeered at her as the bus driver closed the door and rolled away. The only other girl who got off at her stop chastised the boys for being mean, but she was giggling as she walked with them to their homes.

Nat adjusted her backpack and trudged along in the opposite direction, tensing when a couple more snowballs hit her. One of the boys must have added a rock, because it stung even through the hood of her jacket. Thankfully she'd been able to find the puffy type this year—seventh grade had been so much worse. She hadn't been quite big enough yet to earn enough money for anything beyond school lunch, and everything had soaked through. And the rocks had left bruises.

She wanted to rub the back of her head, but she wouldn't

give them the satisfaction of knowing they'd hurt her. For so long she'd dreamed that maybe when she grew up, she'd be pretty and they wouldn't pick on her anymore. But it didn't look like that was how it would turn out. Her body had gotten so much bigger this past year, blowing up in places that had always been flat before. She was suddenly taller than most the other girls, almost 5'6 now. Big and lurching. As good as being bigger was for working, she knew she was grotesque.

Frizzy long brown hair, always going everywhere. An ugly mouth with lips far too big for her face. Boring almond shaped brown eyes and a nose she hated. And horrible clothing that never fit her properly and someone else had already worn out. At least she was thin, so the *fat Nat* nickname they'd tried using never really caught on. There were some benefits to her mother constantly forgetting to buy food.

Her feet slowed as she neared the end of the lane where their trailer was parked, held up on cement blocks. Their neighbors had normal houses—she was the only kid at school who lived in a trailer. But it was better than the trailer park they'd been at when social services took her away. Safer. Except for when her mother's latest boyfriend-supplier showed up. Like today.

Nat came to a halt and stared at his truck in their drive. If her mother were awake, it would be fine. But if she'd already taken her pills…

Her eyes turned toward the woods far behind the trailer. It was cold today but not the worst it had been, and Missouri had plenty of hills and trees to block the wind, especially if she were deep inside the woods. She didn't need to think further and snuck around her neighbor's house, just in case *he* was looking out the window, before racing toward the line of trees.

The snow crunched beneath her sneakers and found its way into her socks, numbing her toes by the time she made it to the trees. She glanced behind her. No one seemed to be stirring from the trailer. Should she just hang out at the perimeter? Coyotes roamed the hills out here, and every now and then someone's dog got dragged off, although she hadn't heard of anyone having a problem with them this year.

A screen door slammed far behind her, and her eyes flew back to the trailer in a panic.

"Natty..."

Her stomach lurched, and she abandoned all thoughts of coyotes as her feet raced through the woods, desperate to put as much space between her and the smiling man calling her name.

———

Ten minutes later and she stopped, putting a hand on her knee and one on her side, her icy fingers digging into her as she dragged the painfully cold air into her lungs. Her PE teacher was always getting on to her for being lazy in class, but Nat didn't know how other kids managed to run the track so easily. She ran out of breath so quickly, and her side always hurt.

Better keep going.

She stood up to start forward once more, still holding her side and wheezing while she walked over the fallen pine needles. The snow wasn't too deep in here. The trees had caught most of it, so at least her feet weren't getting any more wet than they already had. She tried stepping in the areas without snow, but she couldn't completely avoid leaving tracks.

The scent of the pine finally began to feel pleasant to her lungs again, and she sighed as she walked. He wouldn't really chase her all the way in here, would he? The forest around her was silent except for the occasional bird or squirrel and the sounds of her feet crunching the snow and bits of forest floor below.

Perhaps another thirty minutes passed before she stepped into a clearing, and her breath caught at the beauty. The trees grew in a circle around a space ten or twelve feet wide, their branches leaning over and creating a canopy that kept out most of the snow. Pine needles filled the area, producing the driest spot she was likely to find.

Dropping her backpack beside her, she sat down to pull off her shoes and socks. Was it cold enough out to get frostbite? Her toes were going to hurt either way once she could feel them again. She unzipped her jacket and pushed the hood off her head, gently feeling where she'd been hit. A groan escaped her, turning quickly into a whine. Life sucked sometimes.

At least flexibility wasn't a problem for her. She pulled her feet up on her legs, keeping them off the forest floor, and leaned forward to warm them against her midsection as she tried pulling the coat around her. It wasn't the most comfortable position in the world, but warmth seeped through to her feet, so it was worth it.

Leaning forward across her legs, she stretched her arms up above her. There was some yoga name for this position, but she couldn't remember what it was. Her memory was terrible. She held the position as long as she could before leaning back up with a groan.

Her body froze halfway through the movement.

In the distance, a bird cried out. The wind whistled through the trees in soft whispers, and the sharp, sweet smell of pine filled the air. Nothing else stirred.

And at the edge of the clearing, only five feet in front of her, a pair of amber eyes watched her above a long black muzzle and snarling white fangs.

The blood pounded in her ears, the air around her vibrating with each beat of her heart. Stay still. Don't panic. Think.

She knew almost nothing about animals, but this didn't look like a coyote to her. A deep, ebony black coat covered it from head to toe—or paw. Huge paws and terrifying jaws that looked large enough to bite off her entire head. Its ears stood straight up as a low growl began rumbling in its throat.

Nat's entire body jolted inside at the sound, but she forced herself to be still. Tears stung her eyes, but she tried not to blink. Tried not to break the stare. Afraid it would be the trigger that made it attack her.

So she stayed very still, half bowed, her vision blurring until the tears wouldn't be contained and they spilled down her cheeks. What could she do? Everything she could think of seemed wrong. She didn't know animals. Or even people, really. Not enough to prevent them from attacking her. But if this was it, if this was her death, she had to at least try something.

"Hi," she whispered.

The wolf's head perked up, and it stopped snarling. Hope sprang inside her. Maybe if she kept talking calmly…

"I'm Nat." Her heart raced, and she struggled with each breath. But it wasn't coming after her. "I didn't mean to come into your space. I was just trying to get away from…" She didn't want to say it even to herself. "A bad man," she whispered at last.

The wolf growled, and her stomach clenched, tears springing to her eyes once more. Why did she think she could talk to an animal? Her body ached from the position she was in, but she would hold it until the last moment. It was the only thing she could do.

Keeping her gaze locked on his, she struggled to control her fear. Her tears. But she didn't speak, and the wolf grew silent once more. They stared for what felt like hours but couldn't have been more than a few minutes.

Eventually the wolf lowered its head…and stepped forward into the clearing.

Panic shot through her, but once again she held herself still. She wasn't able to control her trembling, though, and her bare hands shook on the ground in front of her.

The wolf approached slowly, its eyes never leaving hers, until it stood directly in front of her, its head low and so close she could feel the warmth of its breath flowing across her cheeks.

When it leaned in close to sniff her, she closed her eyes at last, biting back a whimper of fear. The wolf pulled back, but she couldn't make herself open them again. Was this what they did before they ate? Checked their food?

Tears choked her. She didn't know why she cared so much about dying. It's not like she had such a great life. But maybe one day, if she just kept going, she would be alone. Free.

When it didn't attack her after what seemed a very long time, she opened her eyes and her breath caught. It hadn't moved. Her heart raced when it leaned in once more to her face. Would it rip her skin off? Did they do that to the face? Or was it trying to reach her throat?

The warmth of its tongue lapping her cheek gently nearly made her collapse. Was it tasting her?

"I'm sorry I don't have any food." She couldn't control the tremor in her voice. "But please don't eat me."

The wolf whined, a small, short sound, but continued licking her cheeks. What did that mean? It wasn't biting her. Maybe... maybe it might not kill her.

She began leaning up slowly, very, very slowly, but it didn't stop licking her. Her heart hammered in her chest as she exposed her throat. Calm down. Animals could smell fear, right?

It whined again, and she jumped when a cold nose touched her neck as it lapped at her skin.

"Are you...really not going to eat me?" she whispered.

It rubbed its head against her, and her hands came up instinctively before she could stop herself. They both froze the moment her fingers touched its fur, and she stopped breathing, every muscle in her body locked in place as warm air flowed across her neck. Any moment now it would sink its teeth into her skin. Any moment.

Instead, it began licking her again.

She remained still, so afraid of being stupid. It couldn't

actually like her, could it? It was a wild animal. And she was…her.

But the licking didn't stop.

Taking a shaky breath, she tentatively began petting the deep black fur. Warmth flowed into her fingers each time they slid through the thick coat, and amazed relief began thawing her rigid muscles. It really wasn't going to hurt her!

Eventually she decided to risk leaning her head against its body. When it didn't pull away, she sank her fingers deep into its fur with a sigh.

Her brow furrowed immediately. The coat was very thick but underneath, its body felt far too thin. She pulled back to eye the wolf more carefully, petting it gently. Petting *him*, based on what was hanging from his body, she realized. Heat rushed to her face as she suddenly felt unaccountably rude for having looked. But at least she could stop thinking of him as an *it*.

"When was the last time you ate?" she murmured. He whined again, and she stroked his fur. "I can bring you food, but I don't know what wolves eat. Maybe I can find something about it at school tomorrow. They have a computer in the library."

He growled, and she snatched her hands back. What had she done wrong? But he whimpered and licked her.

It took her a while before she risked petting him again.

"What am I going to do," she sighed. "I can't leave you to starve out here."

He growled again, but this time she only jumped a little. Then frowned.

"Are you growling because I'm talking?" He kept licking her. Stupid. Wolves can't understand people. She sighed again.

"I wish I could stay here with you." She looked up at the darkening sky. "But I better get back now. The creep should be gone, and I still need to figure out where *I'm* going to find food if he cleared the cabinets out again."

The wolf stepped back, his eyes bright on hers, and she wanted to cry. This was the most special thing that had ever happened to her. The only special thing really. How many people could say they had pet a wolf? She couldn't tell anyone though, not that they'd believe her. She didn't want a hunting posse coming in here.

"You be careful, okay? And thank you for not eating me."

The wolf growled again, but it didn't seem like an actual threat. She wiped her wet eyes and started putting her damp socks back on while he stood beside her, watching. The warmth of his body flowed into her in waves, and she wanted to stretch the moment out longer. But it was late, and the long walk back would just be colder the longer she delayed.

The wolf didn't move when she climbed to her feet, and she blinked in surprise to find his eyes nearly at her level. He really was huge.

"Can I hug you goodbye?" she whispered, so unsure of how to indicate her question to an animal. She hoped her body language and voice inflection somehow managed to do it.

Evidently it worked because he stepped in to rub his face against her chest, and she wrapped her arms around his neck, leaning in with a sigh. This moment needed to last in her mind forever.

Wetness filled her eyes again as she pulled back, but she turned away to start walking—only to stop again when he followed her to the edge of the clearing.

"Well...bye." A hesitant smile touched her lips before she set off through the trees, but when she felt the heat of his breath flowing over her neck a minute later, she stopped once more. "You shouldn't follow me, you know. Someone might see you and they'll send hunters in here after you."

He growled and pushed her forward with his head. She continued walking but started to worry the longer he followed her.

"I wish I could make you understand me. It's dangerous for

you. They go after even little coyotes—I can't imagine what they would do if anyone saw a wolf."

He just butted her again, and she kept going, trying to think of how to get him to go away. She wouldn't dare risk yelling or throwing something at him. Maybe he just wanted to make sure she got out of his territory.

She walked on, periodically stopping and trying to get him to turn around, but he never did. Eventually they reached the edge of the wood, and Nat paused.

"That's where I live." She pointed toward the trailer. "So you can stay here." She held her hands up, hoping it was some universal sign of *stay*. He hit the ground in front of her with his paws, and she sighed. She didn't understand him any better than he understood her.

He bit down on her backpack, holding her in place when she tried walking out, and she groaned.

"I have no idea what you want. I can't stay here. I'm human. I'll freeze."

He whined.

"I can bring you food…"

He growled.

"But I have to go! I don't want to. The guy I was running from is gone, and I need to see if he left any food for me to eat or go try to find some."

The wolf whined, licking her again, and she put her arms around him once more. Maybe she'd see him again. Maybe he'd stay in the area. But her stomach sank. If he did, he was sure to get killed by one of the crazy yahoos out here waving their guns around in the woods.

"Please, please be careful," she whispered. "These people aren't all the nicest people in the world."

But he finally let her step out into the clearing, watching while she walked away. Her vision blurred, and she turned to face the trailer once more, her shoulders sagging as the weight of everything waiting for her came back.

When she at last made it to her door, she looked back at the woods. His dark coat was barely visible against the dark backdrop of the trees, but he was still watching her. Watching over her? She scoffed at herself as she went inside.

Don't be ridiculous. He probably just wanted food after all.

2

WOLVES PREFER to eat large hoofed mammals such as deer, elk, bison, and moose. Adults can eat 20 pounds of meat in a single meal.

Twenty pounds of meat… Nat sat back in her chair, staring at the computer screen with wide eyes. How had he survived this long? And what on earth could she possibly bring him? The only meat she usually had around was Spam.

Her brows lifted. That was pork. And she could maybe get a hold of a lot of it. Would it make him sick? That much Spam… Her stomach turned over.

It's not like he was even going to be there anymore. With as thin as he was, he must have roamed far from his normal territory searching for food. And she wanted him to go. He could get hurt if he stayed near.

But her heart raced hoping that somehow he'd still be there when she got home.

The bell rang, and Nat got to her feet, pulling at the arms of the shirt she was wearing, as if that would somehow make it fit her. At least animals didn't care about clothing.

"Heads up!"

Nat didn't look up but buried her face in her books as she walked down the hall, ignoring the laughter and his sound of disappointment as whatever had been thrown whizzed over her head. It was the same boy who was always picking on her. Preston Taylor.

She didn't know what his fascination was with bothering her in particular, other than that she was unlucky enough to have the same bus stop. He wasn't even one of the popular kids. Everyone at her bus stop lived on the wrong side of the tracks, although she was on the worst side. She guessed she might be the only one he *could* pick on.

She sat down and opened her math book, trying to quickly cram as much information in her brain before the test as possible. She'd been so busy thinking about the wolf, she had completely ignored her homework and test prep. Failing the test wouldn't be ideal, but her mother wouldn't even notice, and she wasn't close enough to flunking yet for it to be a major concern. But missing her homework for the third time this week...

"Natalie, you have something for me?"

Nat looked up, groaning inside. Why did this teacher always have to remember?

"I forgot it, Mrs. Smith," she said in a small voice. Forgot to do it, that is. Again. Although even that wasn't exactly true.

Mrs. Smith sighed loudly.

"Then I have no choice but to place you in detention. You really need to learn to take responsibility for yourself, young lady. Life won't always be as easy as it is when you're young."

The students around her snickered derisively. This wasn't the first time the three strikes and you're out policy had struck. But she had no intention of going to detention today. A simple nod and a small apology would have to do until Mrs. Smith could manage to hunt her down after school. And Nat had grown fairly good at dodging her.

When the last bell of the day rang, she hurried to her locker, keeping her head down and hugging her books close. A silent groan went through her when she saw the girls hovering around it, whispering and giggling.

Trying to avoid their eyes, she opened her locker.

"It's so sparkly!" one of the girls said, eyeing Heather's ring. Probably a Valentines Day gift from her boyfriend.

Heather was the most popular girl in school, and her locker *would* be beside Nat's. She always looked so pretty, with her long blonde curls and perfect face. She was a nice girl, too, but her friends weren't.

"Ex*cuse* me! Trying to talk here!"

One of the girls bumped into her as Nat crouched putting her books in her bag, and Nat mumbled an apology while the girl rolled her eyes and turned back to the group.

She hurried and shut her locker, racing away and toward the exit before Mrs. Smith caught sight of her. The school wasn't very big.

———

"Hand me my pills before you go, baby." Her mom was lying on the couch watching tv, and Nat exhaled. Refusing was pointless. She'd just get up and get them herself, hurting her back more. Then she'd take more pills than what Nat would give her.

Nat brought her a couple and refilled her water.

"You're so sweet to me, baby. Don't let the boys steal your sugar."

Her mother still seemed to think she was a pretty little doll. She used to dress her in doll clothes, which Nat only knew from the pictures and the stories her mother would tell. Used to tell, that is. She got clean for a while to get Nat back from foster care, and for about a year Nat really thought life might be different. But it hadn't lasted.

She didn't seem to noticed when Nat opened the front door and left.

The snow fell in big, loose flakes that got stuck in her eyelashes only to melt quickly. She wished she hadn't outgrown her boots, but at least today she was prepared. Her eyes fell to her feet. Trash bags wrapped around them, secured with tape, keeping her sneakers and socks inside nice and dry. She looked ridiculous, but what else was new.

Her pace quickened. The corner store wouldn't have much Spam, but they always carried at least a couple cans. And if the wolf liked it, she would make the longer trip to the grocery store and get as much as she could afford. Her summer earnings were already gone, but she'd recently figured out how to manage her mom's bank account. It was constantly overdrawn from her mother's checks, so she hid her checkbook and kept a careful eye on how much money was going in and out. They could afford a couple cans of spam for the wolf, even if she had to have a few lighter meals herself to compensate.

An hour later and she had trudged through the wood again, armed this time with food. A knot grew in her stomach as she approached the spot where the wolf had been. Had he already moved on? What if he'd forgotten her? Or what if he'd just been in a good mood the other day and today he'd decide to eat her?

She swallowed when the clearing came into view. Empty.

That's okay. Maybe he was just off doing something else. He hadn't been there when she'd first arrived before, either.

This time she sat close to the edge, trying not to intrude into his space too much.

The wind blew the canopy above her, and particles of snow and water fell through. She drew her knees to her chest underneath her coat, huddling in a small ball as the minutes crept by.

Every sound made her jump and look up, hoping to see him. But nothing was there. And the evening grew dark.

Nat stared at the bag of Spam at her feet, her eyes filling with tears. Of course he'd moved on. And he should have. It was safer. She should be happy for him.

She buried her face in her arms, silent sobs shaking her body, and didn't look up the next time she heard a sound. Until the warm breath warmed her and a nuzzle nudged her head.

Her startled wet eyes flew up as his tongue slipped in to lick her cheek, and she threw her arms around him, crying even harder. She didn't let go for a long time, and he didn't pull away.

Finally she pulled back with a shaky laugh.

"I brought you food!"

He growled immediately, and a frown tugged at the corners of her mouth. Had he been growling every time she said food? Maybe he recognized the word from other humans somewhere? If he'd been watching them from the woods, maybe he'd seen people eating.

She pulled out one of the cans and opened it, and he jumped away.

"Oh, come on. It's not that bad." She smelled it. Okay, it wasn't like steak, probably, but he ate raw meat. How bad could this be? Maybe it's because it wasn't fresh. "I'm sorry I can't afford real meat. I know this sucks, but I just…I don't really have a lot."

Her voice ended quietly as she stared at the open can. What a waste she was. Any other kid could have grabbed all sorts of food from their home for him.

He whined and walked over, leaning toward the can and sniffing it. She started to pull it back.

"Wait, don't lick—" But it was too late. His tongue reached out, and the edge of the can sliced it.

The can fell from her hands at his yelp.

"I'm sorry! I'm so sorry!" she gasped, her hands reaching for him. "The edges are sharp! I was going to take it out for you!"

He was sitting back on his haunches and pawing his mouth,

his head snapping back and forth, and she slowly pulled her hands back to herself. The last thing he'd want now is for her to touch him. She was surprised he wasn't growling.

His head shook with a small snort one more time before his eyes met hers again. But he didn't move away. Or growl.

Nat hesitated before reaching for the can again and turning it upside down until the meat slid out enough for her to grab. She broke off a piece and held it out to him, her eyes uncertain.

"Do you still want to try it?"

The wolf sat still for a moment longer but then leaned forward just enough to take the bite from her hand, licking her fingers. She saw the thin red line on his tongue, and a small sound escaped her. He flattened his tongue against her skin, licking more slowly. Maybe it didn't hurt him too much.

She ended up feeding him both cans and then pulled out the bottle of water she'd brought. He must have a water source somewhere, but she didn't know how far away it was. And Spam was salty.

"Drink?"

He sniffed it and nudged her hand toward her.

"You don't want it?"

He nudged her again, this time causing the bottle to come close to her face.

"You…want me to take a drink?"

The wolf sat back and watched her. She shrugged and took a drink before holding it out to him again. When he didn't move, she took another and tried again.

"Do you have water around here?"

He nodded, and she fell back, the bottle falling from her hands. He cocked his head at her.

"There is no way you understand me," she breathed. When he didn't react, she sat up on her knees, staring at him intently. "Do you understand me?"

For a moment he didn't move, and she started to laugh at

herself. But he nodded again, and she blinked. Maybe he was just doing it no matter what she said.

"Did you like licking the can?" His head jerked to the side with a snort. "No way…" She stared at him wide eyed. "Sorry for bringing up the can. I just wanted to check. You really understand me?"

He nodded again, and a small laugh escaped her. This was so weird.

"Then I…I guess I should ask you if I'm bothering you. To visit you. Is it okay…if I come back?" Her voice shook a bit, a sickness settling in her stomach. Of course she was bothering him. She was a clunky girl who just stumbled into his home and acted like she lived there.

He whined and began licking her face again, and she realized she'd dropped her eyes.

"Sorry. Answer again? Do you want me to stay away?" His head shook immediately before going back to licking her face. She buried her hands in his coat, the warmth stealing into her icy fingers. "This is so crazy…"

Drowsiness was beginning to seep into her, and she wanted nothing more than to curl up on the ground beside him. Her mother probably wouldn't even notice if she stayed out all night.

But her eyes fell to her body and the bags wrapped around her legs, the slippery material of her puffer coat…she would be about as cuddly as…trash.

She sighed once more and leaned down to clean up the mess she'd made. Tomorrow. She would return tomorrow.

————

Nat wanted to run to the woods every single day after school and stay there as long as possible. Up until now, her life had been so lonely. Lonely at school. Lonely at home. Invisible or unliked.

Loved only by her mother who had drifted so far away Nat could barely find her anymore.

But something amazing had happened. Something special. To *her*. As if the universe was telling her she *was* worth something. And she needed to prove it wasn't wrong. She needed to take care of the wolf. Protect him.

So she couldn't go running off to the woods all the time. She had to find money.

"Hey! Girl! The stairs still have ice on them!" The woman's voice called out from behind the glass door.

"Sorry!"

Nat stopped shoveling the drive and hurried back over to the front steps to try and get the crusted ice off the edges. The porch light came on, and she glanced around in dismay. How had the night come so soon? She looked back at the dimly lit drive, still half covered with snow. If they wanted every last bit off, this was going to take a very long time.

The darkness grew while she worked as quickly as she could, the layer of previously melted and refrozen snow beneath the newest batch feeling more like part of the pavement than part of the snow. She thought she was finished multiple times, only to have the woman tell her she wasn't paying unless she finished the job.

Finally it seemed to be done close enough. Or maybe it was just too dark for her to see the bits Nat couldn't manage to get.

"This took you too long. I don't like having to keep an eye on a lazy girl. You're lucky I'm still giving you the full amount," the woman told her, handing her the two dollars promised.

Nat apologized wearily and headed off. She'd thought it would only take her half an hour and she'd have been able to do other houses that evening, but she had wasted her whole evening and blew her chance to help the wolf tonight.

At least staying out every day trying to get work kept the creep from getting his hands on her. She'd seen him drive by earlier, leaving their place, but she'd ignored him when he slowed his truck down to call her name.

The screen door slammed behind her, and she placed the shovel by the door inside. She couldn't risk someone stealing it if she left it outside. It was the best way she had to earn money this time of year.

Her mother was asleep on the couch, so Nat grabbed one of the cans of tuna she'd hidden and a can opener, filled a bottle of water for herself, stuffed them in her coat pockets and headed back out the door. She had hoped to be able to eat the tuna herself and give the wolf something better, but the corner store would be closed by the time she got there at this point. And it's not like she had enough to buy anything worth getting anyhow. Maybe tomorrow.

The door closed behind her, and she put her hands to her mouth, trying to warm them. They were pretty red and ugly now. Blistered, calloused, and dry. She kept breathing warm air on them, trying to get some feeling back before she had to work the can opener.

The wolf was waiting at the edge of the woods, and her eyes perked up as she hurried forward. Well, tried to hurry. The snow was pretty deep.

"Hey! I didn't mean to take so long," she said, stepping into the line of the trees. The wolf whined and began licking her hands, and she sighed at the warmth. "The house I picked today had sooo much ice all over the drive. If I were stronger, it wouldn't have taken so long. Or maybe I took too many breaks," she admitted, feeling guilty. It just felt so exhausting, but other people seemed to manage just fine. She was either weak or lazy. Maybe both.

The wolf was whining like crazy, and she reached into her pocket.

"Hold on hold on—I have to use a can opener on this one."

He darted back with yet another whine and a growl, and she looked up.

"You want us to go further in first?"

He jerked his head side to side before pausing and nodding, and she laughed.

"Okay, show me where to go."

He stared at her a moment before turning with his head hung low and walking them just a few feet farther before plopping down with another whine and putting his paws over his eyes.

She sat down gingerly, her body aching, and he looked up immediately.

"Sorry," she sighed as she opened the can. "It's not much, and it's tuna. I don't know if you like fish."

His whine sounded more like a cry now, and he buried his head under his paws on the ground again.

"No good?" she asked, uncertain.

The whining grew as he leaned up and crawled close enough to her for her to feed him. She smiled in relief, and began scooping some out when her stomach growled.

A bomb might as well have gone off with the way he jumped up and back. Growling, whining—even turning in a circle.

"Jeez! It's just my stomach! You don't have to embarrass a girl." She held her hand out with the tuna, waiting with a smile, and he stared, the whine in his throat almost a constant sound now. Her smile faltered, and she dropped her hand to stare down at the can.

"I'm sorry. I don't know what I'm supposed to do," she whispered. Her breath shook a bit as she tried holding the tears back. It was just because she was tired. She wasn't a crybaby.

He yelped, and she looked up through blurry eyes. He repeated the sound, only it seemed harsher, and his black coat seemed to be vibrating. She wiped her eyes.

The tuna fell from her fingers as she scrambled backwards until she hit the tree behind her, shock locking her scream in her throat. All she could do was stare in horror as her wolf's coat grew shorter and shorter, his muzzle disappeared, and a terrifyingly gorgeous black haired *naked* boy, who might have been a year or two older than she was, stared at her with frustrated eyes.

"I don't want you going hungry for me! I know how to hunt, and you *don't* need to bring me food!" he exploded.

3

CALEB HAD NEVER BEEN so frustrated in his entire fifteen years of life. Of all the ridiculous, aggravating, nonsensical things he had ever seen, watching this girl practically kill herself just to bring him what barely amounted to a snack for his wolf body was the worst. He had been ready to start actually howling, and *that* would definitely have gotten him the wrong sort of attention out here.

He should never have approached her. Not the first time he saw her, when her pale, terrified face struggled so hard to be brave. Not the second time when he'd watched from the trees while she sat waiting to feed him—*feed him!* Like he was a dog! Only to then see her shaking quietly as she cried for him when she thought he wasn't coming. It had been nine years since he'd felt anything as miserable as he'd felt in that moment—the only moment worse in his life being the big one: the crash that killed his parents.

But she kept bringing him scraps of food, day after day. If he'd eaten them as a human, the way he'd been eating all his food out here, it would have actually done some good. But he couldn't very well change in front of her to eat. And he didn't *need* it, and she did! Winters were always lean. He might be bigger now and need more, but he was also a much better hunter. As his dad had always said, life was a series of tradeoffs.

And he'd traded his comfortable, completely independent, private existence lately for stealing food from a girl! Out of her hand! Bare hands without any fur to protect them that she kept using to do things so she could bring him scraps!

He wanted to howl again, but he couldn't. Because he wasn't in his wolf form anymore. Because no amount of growling or whining or *anything* seemed to work with her!

He'd been watching from the edge of the wood, making sure that guy in the truck didn't get near her. She'd called him a bad man, and he didn't like the look in her eyes when she'd said it. It reached something deep inside him—he might have even growled.

But she'd barely even come to see him for the past two weeks! He'd hunt while she was at school and then found himself dancing around the perimeter the rest of the day. Excited. Like a pup. Only to wait and wait and wait, worried something might have happened to her. Worried about the bad man. Worried to the point of howling so much he had to shift to his human form sometimes, just to control it.

And when she'd finally show up, she always looked ready to fall over. He just couldn't take it anymore.

Never mind how much he'd liked licking her face…her fingers as she fed him. How much he'd enjoyed her hands buried deep in his fur or stroking him. Never mind how much he was never, ever, *ever* to shift in front of a human according to his parents. He'd honored that rule faithfully his entire life.

Until now.

"You are the most frustrating, stubborn girl!" He paced back and forth in front of her, his hands buried in his hair while he avoided looking at her horrified eyes. "A growl means no! No no no no no! No, do not bring me food! No, do not spend every single day torturing yourself for something I don't even *want*!"

He had worked himself into a full rage now.

"Wolves aren't dogs! We don't want collars or little bowls with our names on them that you fill with food and water!"

He glared at her only to have the air sucked out of his lungs immediately.

She was fighting back tears, and he knew that expression far too well by now. He slid on his knees as he dashed to her and dropped down in one move, hesitating when her body stiffened in fear.

"I didn't mean it like that," he breathed. "I just meant...I meant I didn't want to take from you. I liked it. And I liked..." He clenched his fists. This wasn't something he wanted to say out loud. It was too humiliating. "I liked you feeding me."

Her eyes were twin pools of alarm. Confusion. Uncertainty. Hurt. But it looked like the horror might be slipping away a bit.

"I just..." He hesitated but slowly reached his hand out to brush her long bangs out of her eyes, pausing for a moment when she jumped a bit. Her beautiful, warm brown eyes were so huge in her face right now and so often hidden behind her hair. It was so nice to be able to see them fully at last—this was something he couldn't do as a wolf. A sigh of contentment escaped him as he brushed them back and kept petting her. "I just didn't want you hurting for me. I hate it."

Her lips parted, and he blinked at the unfamiliar sensation in his gut. It was uncomfortable, and he shifted his weight, trying to make it go away. It didn't help. He frowned, and her lashes fell as she turned her head aside. A whine scratched at his throat. *Look back at me.*

"What's your name," he whispered, his hand still stroking her hair.

Her lashes lifted to look at him briefly out of the corner of her eye before she dropped them again. He did whine then, and her eyes flew back to his. A smile spread across his face, and she swallowed.

"Nat."

His smile turned into a frown. Her parents named her after a bug?

"Or Natty. Or Natalie. I don't really care."

His gut hurt again, but he knew this pain. He'd felt it a lot the last two weeks. Although…it felt a bit different in human form.

"Which one makes you happiest?" His eyes felt as soft as his voice as he looked down at her.

She shrugged.

"None of them. All of them."

Hesitation stilled his tongue. He wished he could name her. A name that said something about her quiet strength. Her soft, beautiful eyes. The delicate line of her body that she couldn't hide no matter how hard she seemed to try.

The deep, aching loneliness he'd seen in her. Recognized. Because he felt it, too.

"I like Nat," he breathed, his stomach clenching again when she looked up at him with glistening eyes.

Because he did. He liked her very much.

"I'm Caleb."

———

Caleb kept stroking her hair, so happy to be the one to pet *her* now. Maybe she'd let him feed her, too. His eyes searched the ground, following the scent of the fallen can. It didn't look as if the food inside had gotten dirty, so he reached for it with his free hand. The Shift had cleaned him, and he grabbed some and held it out towards her mouth. Would she lick his fingers?

Her eyes widened even more, and she leaned her head back into the tree, her neck stiff. A whine escaped him, and he tried again, holding it closer to her lips. Soft whispers of air floated around them as the wind blew, but his body radiated heat, nestling them in a cocoon of warmth. Her lashes fell to the food in his hand before lifting again to stare at him as wide as ever, her brows drawing together.

"Eat," he breathed. "You're hungry."

A small sound came from her throat that he couldn't interpret, and his own brows pulled together and lifted. What had his mother told him to say?

"Please?" He didn't care for the wobble he heard in his voice, and he was about to clear his throat when she made another sound—this one more like a groan—and parted her lips.

A smile lit his face, and he carefully slid the small bit between her lips. Their lashes both blinked rapidly as her mouth closed, her tongue grazing the tips of his fingers. The pain in his gut returned, more intense this time, and he withdrew his fingers slowly, watching her swallow.

"I can do it," she squeaked.

Confusion furrowed his brow, preventing him from arguing, and he handed her the can to sit back and pull his knees up, crossing his arms over them while he watched her. The pain didn't go away, but the intensity level seemed to fall after he put some distance between them.

She ate quickly and wiped her mouth on the back of her hand before pulling a bottle out of her coat pocket and guzzling it down. Her scent had changed slightly. He couldn't quite figure out how, and he wanted to shift again to investigate.

When the water bottle was empty, her hands gripped it while her eyes looked everywhere except at him. Her cheeks were even redder than they'd been when she showed up, and he wondered if she was too cold now that he'd moved. His body generated a lot of heat when he wanted it to.

He sat back up to lean into her again only to jump a bit when she yelped and scrambled back away from the tree.

"What are you doing?" She sounded panicked, and he frowned.

"I'm not going to hurt you. I would never hurt you."

That sound came from her throat again. A whimper?

"Come back. You're cold, and I can keep you warm," he said, starting to crawl towards her.

The sound she made then was much stronger, but it was her mad scramble away from him as she pushed herself to her feet that let him know what it meant. She really was afraid of him.

Sadness filled his eyes, and he stood to face her, but she yelped again when her eyes fell and covered her face. He frowned and looked down. It's not like he'd only half shifted. That wasn't even possible, his parents had said. Not for more than a second or two. He stared down at his body, lean and muscular, with a bit of dark hair on his broad chest and a soft dark line along his abdomen that disappeared into deep dark curls. The large appendage he used to urinate hung low on his thigh, and his legs continued, strong and lean to the ground, the hair increasing again as his gaze lowered. Nothing unusual.

He looked back up to see her still covering her eyes.

"Do I...look wrong?" His voice sounded far too timid, and he wished he hadn't asked. But her eyes peeked over her hands in surprise.

"No..." Warm. Reassuring. He relaxed. "But...you're naked," she finished in a tiny voice.

A frown touched his lips again. He'd been naked since she met him. Although his parents had always had the rule that they wear clothes when in human form. It had been so long, he just hadn't really thought about it.

He scratched his head.

"Do you want me to shift back?"

"No!"

Alarm rang out in her voice, and he hesitated. Was she afraid of his wolf form again?

"I don't have clothes," he said.

She was the one whining now, her hands back over her eyes. Then her body stiffened suddenly before she began unzipping her coat.

His feet flew to her faster than she could react, and he grabbed her wrists as she yelped once more.

"No way! It's freezing out here, and you can't control your temperature like I can. Just don't look at me if it's unpleasant." He frowned down at her wide eyes, keeping her hands pressed against his chest even when she tried pulling them away. They were so cold.

"It's not unpleasant," she whispered with a feeble whimper.

"Then why won't you look at me?"

She swallowed, her eyes locked on his now, and her lips parted as if to speak, but no sound came out.

His gut clenched again, frustrating him. Was he getting sick? He never got sick, but he never went around humans, either.

The scent grew stronger. Beautifully sweet and musky. His own eyes felt like closing now, and he wanted to lean closer and breathe her in. But she wasn't comfortable with him right now. He needed to convince her again that he was safe.

"Please don't be afraid of me," he whispered.

A shudder went through her, but she didn't turn away. And her hands were beginning to feel warm against his chest.

"I didn't know it was possible for...what are you?" Her eyes were tentative on his.

"I'm a wolf," he answered.

"So...wolves...can do...this?" Her eyes were wide again, and he laughed a bit.

"No. I guess I'm human, too. I don't really know. My parents died before they explained very much to me—or maybe I just forgot."

Her eyes had grown soft at his words.

"I'm so sorry," she whispered, and he blinked again, his heart beating harder.

"It was a long time ago. I was six."

A deep line formed between her brow.

"Are you on your own?"

He nodded.

"Ever since then?"

"Yeah. They wanted to put me in foster care. Human foster care. So I ran away to the woods."

The sound she made was full of pain. Pain for him. And her hands flattened against his chest, causing the pain in his gut to flare up once more. He ignored it this time. His heart was beating too quickly.

"I was in foster care," she said. "Some families are fine. But yeah...if I could have run, I think I would have, too."

The pain in his middle was overwhelming now. He didn't think she realized she was stroking his chest, but he was afraid if he moved, she'd stop. So he stayed very still and let her pet him.

"Did your parents live around here?"

"No. We were a lot farther north in the hills. I just came down this season for food."

She grew very still, and he forced himself not to whine when her hands stilled as well.

"So you're leaving again?" she whispered.

His chest tightened at the thought. He hadn't thought that far ahead. But once warmer weather set in, he wouldn't be able to stay here safely. The woods weren't thick enough here for him to hide.

A sound of frustration made its way up from deep in his throat. He didn't want to go. Who would look out for her? And how could he take not having her pet him anymore?

"If...if you wanted to...I mean, it's not much...really not. It's really terrible. It's...it's...never mind." Her voice disappeared to nothing, and he pressed her hands harder into his chest.

"Tell me."

Her brows were pulled together and raised as she looked up at him, a shuddering breath escaping her before she spoke in a husky voice.

"Well…if you wanted…you could…stay with me."

———————

Stay with her. She meant…in her house. Trailer. Which he couldn't do as a wolf.

He'd have to live as a human.

He stumbled back from her, dropping her hands at last and shaking his head as his heart pounded against his chest painfully.

No. No no no. He would never live as a human. *Never.*

The urge to shift was almost overwhelming, and he spun around, pacing back and forth as he tore his hands through his hair again.

What was she thinking? Didn't she understand he was a *wolf?* He wasn't domesticated! He was wild! Free! How could she think he could ever be pinned up inside that tiny prison? To have to walk around in those hideous things she wrapped herself in. To be *trapped*.

He would run. The food around here was too scarce anyhow —he should never have delayed this long. His body bristled, the change pulling at him, stinging his skin when he resisted. Why was he resisting? He was a wolf! The forest was his home! And it called to his blood.

The burning sensation in his gut flowered out of him as he shifted, the release from the agony a wave of pure pleasure that flowed through him as he flew across the ground, racing racing racing away from a face he didn't dare look at again. The scent of pine filled his nostrils, and he breathed it in deeply as he fled, expelling the last remnants of the sweet scent of *her*.

His paws dug up the earth as he tore through the trees, the

power of his body replacing every bit of the softness of his human form. He jerked his head with a fierce snort as he ran. Yes, every bit. There was no room for softness in a wolf. No room for being *petted*. For having small, fragile hands *feeding* him. He'd only felt sorry for her. Nothing more.

On and on he flew through the night, reveling in the crispness of the air, the wind whistling through his thick fur, the glow of the moon shining through the trees and tying him to her in an age old pull far stronger than his pull to *her*.

His head jerked yet again, his snort even more fierce. He did not have a pull to the girl! She was nothing—nothing!

His claws dug into the earth as he jerked to a halt, panting.

Nothing. Just what she believed. That she was nothing.

He looked behind him, an ache inside that had never been there before.

She would have gone back home by now. And the bad man would be back eventually.

A long whine welled up from deep in his throat, the sound carried away on the wind.

She would be alone. All alone. Taking care of her mother. Of herself. Even though she was so delicate. So small.

He took a step back in the direction he'd come from, and a snort overtook him as he shook his head, jumping back. He was a wolf!

But a wolf could protect her...

A whine left him again as he took another step back to her. And another. The sound grew and grew until he could no longer resist, and he leaned back and howled into the moon, the long, mournful tones filling the night sky.

When the last of the feeling disappeared, he lowered his head once more. And began running.

4

NAT WATCHED NUMBLY while the water pooled around her feet, the rust stains appearing and disappearing as the suds from her shampoo streamed by. The bus wouldn't be here for another hour. For once, she'd woken up in plenty of time. Too much time. Too much time to think.

He'd run away. More horrified of the idea of being with her than she'd been at finding out her wolf—no. Not hers. At finding out the wolf was a human. She couldn't blame him. But that didn't stop the feeling of a knife slicing into her stomach.

Her hand reached to turn off the water, and she pulled the ripped plastic curtain aside to grab a thin towel. Time to do the laundry again. She'd been a bit remiss the last couple of weeks, but life was back to normal now.

She swiped the fog away on the small mirror over the sink before turning her head upside-down to wrap the towel around her hair. When she stood back up, she stared at her reflection for a moment. She'd grown a little too thin lately. Her eyes loomed hugely in her small face, her protruding lips a stark contrast with the sharp lines of her cheeks and jaw.

She reached up to touch the full, soft flesh, remembering the feel as they'd wrapped around the tips of his fingers. As he'd slid them back out. The way he'd looked at her, his own lips parting. Her pulse quickened, and her body responded as it had when he'd touched her. She stroked her lips softly back and forth, lost in the memory.

Caleb. He dwarfed her with his human size nearly as much as when he was a wolf, towering over her maybe eight inches with a well muscled body he moved so gracefully.

His hair was pitch black and shaggy, falling onto his forehead in silky dark locks. Thick, dark eyebrows arched cockily or furrowed in concern while deep black eyelashes framed his beautiful amber eyes. He had the perfect nose, straight and not too sharp or flat. It squared off at the tip, the strong line echoing his wolf form. A square jaw and chin gave him a far manlier look than other boys his age, and his lips...

Nat's touch paused on her own lips. His lips were full and wide, pulling to the side in a charmingly smug smile or parting gently in thought. They were perfect on him, his every feature in harmony, creating the darkest, wildest, most gorgeous boy she had ever seen. She'd thought her own lips too full, but they would be perfect under his.

A sound beneath the trailer made her jump, and she dropped her hand hastily, heat flooding her face. Probably another raccoon. She'd have to take a look once she got home from school before it chewed through any wires. They couldn't afford the repairs. She blinked at her flushed cheeks in the mirror, her lashes tangling with the scraggly line of her bangs. Caleb's touch had been so soft when he'd brushed them from her eyes...

Stop it!

The towel fell to her feet, and her hands reached for the scissors. She trimmed her bangs before flipping her head upside down to cut the long strands in a straight line across as high up as her arms would reach. The website said it would give her a layered look, but she hadn't tried it before. She reached for her blowdryer, drying her hair with one hand while cleaning up with her other.

When she stood up again, her eyes widened. She looked like a lion, with her brown hair poofing out all around her like a huge mane. She stared a moment before turning to finish getting ready. Her hood would hide it. By the time the bus got to school, it would probably have calmed down...or give everyone yet another reason to mock her all day.

Her mother lay passed out on the couch as usual. At least she managed to shower herself frequently enough. They might be poor, but they were clean.

Nat grabbed an egg and cracked it into a cup to microwave it, scarfing down the rubbery mess quickly once done. Eggs were cheap for a meal. Maybe the wolf could eat—

Pain hit her when she remembered she wouldn't need to worry about that anymore. And evidently she hadn't been helping anyway.

Egg stuck to the sides of the scratched up plastic cup while she washed it, and she scraped it carefully before setting it to drain in the plastic dish rack beside the stained sink.

The clock on the microwave said it was time to go at last. She skipped the bags on her legs. They would have still been nice, but she couldn't afford to waste them when she didn't need to be walking through the heavy snow. So she wrapped the heavy coat around her and left the trailer.

Her footsteps crunched over the snow, her toes freezing almost immediately. A sound beneath the trailer pulled her gaze back as she walked away, but she didn't look too carefully. It seemed a little late for a raccoon to still be awake, but whatever it was, she didn't have time to deal with it right now. So she headed to her stop without looking back again.

———

Nat stepped off the bus, straight into a snowball planted right in her face. The bus driver at least had the decency to yell at Preston while he and the other boys laughed uproariously. She wiped the snow away, her eyes stinging from the blow and tears. At least there hadn't been a rock in it.

Her mother had always told her to ignore bullies and they'd go away when they realized they couldn't get under your skin. The advice usually worked, but not with Preston. Maybe it was because it did get under her skin. She might not be able to hide it as well as she thought.

The new fallen snow crept into her socks again as she walked home with heavy feet. Hopefully this weather would end soon. She was so tired. So very tired.

Keeping her head down as she walked, she only vaguely registered the sound of the screen door as she approached the trailer and lifted her eyes wearily.

Adrenaline shot through her, gluing her to the spot where she stood at the edge of the drive. His truck. Why hadn't she checked!

"Natty! Sweetie, I haven't seen you in forever! Come give your uncle a hug."

Her stomach lodged in her throat while the smiling man who most definitely was *not* her uncle approached. Could she run? The cops had given her to him once when she had. He'd told them she was going through a rebellious phase, and they didn't seem interested in listening to her trying to tell them anything. *Aw, he's just a good ol' boy*, they'd told her. He'd known too many of them since they were kids.

Her eyes flew to the door behind him as she backed away, hoping that somehow her mother would walk to it. Through it. To be up. But no one came.

"Now Natty, don't go running off again," he said pleasantly, now only a few feet away. "Your mom and I might have to have another talk."

Her heart hammered in her chest. She knew what that meant. The bruises he'd left last time had taken weeks to go away.

Sickness curled in her gut, and she bit down on her tongue, desperately trying to keep the tears at bay. She would never let him see her cry.

"Now why don't you come inside, honey, and get those wet clothes off," he murmured, reaching out for her.

A blur of black fur flew out from under the trailer a moment before he was thrown to the ground, his body shaken like a rag doll by monstrous jaws clenched around his neck. Strangled sounds came from the pasty, fleshy throat, and Nat threw her arms around Caleb with a cry, whispering in his ear frantically.

"If you hurt him, the cops will come! I know you can get away. But I can't. Social services will take me."

Her heart pounded in terror against him. Terror that someone would see him. That someone would grab their shotgun and race outside to help the disgusting, bloated man making strange bleating sounds from the ground.

She could feel Caleb's heart pounding even faster than her own, the tension in his enormous body radiating into hers, and she hugged him tightly. If anyone came out, maybe they wouldn't shoot if she was holding him.

Caleb slowly lifted his head, and a trickle of blood leaked onto the snow. The man didn't move, and Nat's stomach clenched in fear that it was too late. If he'd killed someone, they'd hunt him down and he'd have to run so far away she would never see him again.

She leaned over to check while Caleb growled low and menacing, his teeth not far from the punctured throat. Punctured —but only slightly. Breath filled her lungs once more.

"Get out of here," she hissed, looking down into the terrified eyes locked on the bared teeth in front of him. "And don't come back."

When he didn't move, she kicked his side, even the small touch making her insides heave.

"Go!"

Caleb punctuated her words with a sharp snarl and snap, and the man twisted away at last, a mewling sound coming from his throat as he crawled on shaky arms toward his truck. He reached up and opened the door without standing, pulling himself up and looking ready to fall over each moment until it closed behind him.

Nat could see him fumbling with something before the engine roared to life. She breathed a sigh of relief that he'd left his keys in the ignition as usual. The tires rolled down the drive, alternately lurching and squealing, stalling in the snow before traction would kick in until at last the truck raced away far down the lane.

Nat looked around, panic setting in that someone would have heard the sounds and looked out the window to see Caleb.

"Hide!"

Her eyes flew down when he grabbed her wrist in his jaws and pulled her with him until he was under the trailer. She crouched low, blinking rapidly as he shifted.

"I'm going to need some clothes."

————

Nat unzipped her jacket and quickly wiggled out of it before passing it to him under the trailer.

"Maybe you could wrap it around your...waist." She finished with a squeak, jerking her face away, the blood rushing to her cheeks. He really wasn't shy at all.

A moment later he crept out to stand beside her, and she glanced up, ready to rush them inside—and completely forgot what she was doing.

He stood so close, his muscles rippling as his hand clenched the coat around his waist while he scanned the area slowly. Her breath caught in her throat when his dark fringed amber eyes suddenly dropped to hers, his thick black locks falling onto his forehead while he stared down at her, his expression alert. Focused. Until his eyes began to soften and his lips parted, one corner of his mouth pulling up. She swallowed. And froze completely when his gaze slid down her body, a light growing in his eyes until he frowned and pressed a hand to his stomach, turning away.

Her heart jumped, remembering where they were.

"Will you come inside?" she whispered.

He glanced at her, and his tone was a bit wistful when he answered.

"Unless you want to run away in the woods with me."

Her heart leapt again, but this time from something else.

"I wish I could." Her voice sounded very small to her ears, so very small to hide the feelings that were so big. He had rescued her. He had come back. He would let her run away with him…

"I'll come inside," he said softly.

Her eyes grew wet, and she looked down to hurry toward the trailer…trying not to think of how warm his own eyes had just grown.

She opened the door quickly, hoping no one was peeking out, and moved to the side once indoors to wait for him to walk in.

He hesitated, pressing his lips together while his eyes searched the dark, enclosed space. Her heart caught, torn between melting at the endearing, beautiful image in front of her and fear that he would change his mind. That he would be miserable. That he must be horrified at what he was seeing.

Matted carpet that no amount of vacuuming could fix. Linoleum peeling away on the kitchen floor. Rust stained fixtures. An old TV with an actual dial on it and a rough, sticky couch, where her mother lay oblivious. And worst of all, a musty odor that choked *her*—she couldn't even imagine what it must be like to him.

Was she being selfish? He could go far away from here. Keep his freedom. There was nothing she could provide for him that he needed. That he couldn't get for himself and in a much better way.

He had done enough for her. So much more than enough. It might even keep the creep away from her forever. And she was going to reward him with *this*?

She drew in a breath and opened her mouth in the same moment he stepped through the doorway and reached for her, closing the door behind him.

Her lashes fluttered rapidly when he wrapped his arms around her and buried his face in her neck, breathing deeply and filling his lungs over and over. It took her a moment to be able to speak, and her voice quavered when she finally could.

"I keep the window cracked in my room. It's easier to breathe in there."

His head perked up immediately, his eyes bright on hers.

"Show me!"

Nat took a quick look at her mother, making sure she was breathing okay and looked normal, before leading Caleb down the very short hall, past her mother's room that was almost never used and the tiny bathroom directly across from it, to her room at the end.

Opening her door, she barely had time to move before he'd bounded past her, the coat falling to the floor as he shifted and began sniffing everything. His wagging tail beat against the walls while she quickly shut her door, her heart pounding.

He was almost too big for the room. It was only a nine by nine foot space, and Caleb was easily five feet from front to back. Adding on the extra two or three feet of tail, and the room didn't stand a chance.

She rescued her TV tray with the cup on it before they flew

into the wall, only to yelp as the modular metal grid shelving she'd put together for her clothes crumbled in on itself, pieces scattering and clothing falling as she grabbed it.

"Caleb!"

But he was too busy digging through her pile of dirty clothes now, sniffing everything, and she shrieked, dropping the shelving, tray, and cup to dive for the clothes, bundling them up as he rammed his head between her arms and her body, still trying to sniff everything.

"Would you stop!" her cry was a bit strangled, and she buried the clothes in a tight ball beneath her, trying to keep them away. He bounded away to her mattress on the floor, pouncing on it and burying his nose under the covers as he finally stilled, watching her.

Her heart was hammering against the clothing underneath her while she stared at him lying on her bed, her breathing slowly beginning to return to normal when he remained still. Okay. He was finally calming. Or... Wait. Was he... Her eyes widened as she realized he was sniffing the pillow she slept with between her legs, and she lunged forward across her clothes, reaching out to snatch it. He grabbed it with his teeth, pulling back and jerking his head side to side, trying to tear it from her.

"Caleb—you can't—would—you—STOP!" she choked out, struggling to hold on as he growled, still shaking the pillow fiercely every few seconds until he finally tore it from her grasp. He turned quickly in the bed, plopping down with it buried under his front paws to continue sniffing, and she climbed into the bed beside him, shoving at his body and trying to pull it away.

She might as well have tried moving the entire trailer. A long whine sounded in her throat, and she collapsed on the bed, hiding her face in her hands and making mewling sounds while he lay beside her, continuing to sniff for a painfully long couple of minutes. She didn't move when she felt him get up. Or when he began sniffing her. Until his muzzle went right between her legs.

She sat up instantly and hit his nose hard.

"NO!"

He yelped and jumped back, shifting immediately and rubbing his nose.

"What'd you do that for!"

Nat's face was on fire, but her voice was furious.

"You do not sniff...people's...private things!" she finished with a raised voice, pointing her finger at him.

"Why not!" he shot back, thoroughly disgruntled.

She threw a blanket at him.

"And cover up!"

He snatched it, glaring at her as he put it around his shoulders. And left his *appendage* completely exposed.

She smacked her hands over her eyes.

"Not that part!"

"Well what part then!" The frustration in his voice couldn't quite disguise the hurt, and she peeked out, a whine coming from her throat again.

"Caleb...don't you...I mean..." Oh god. Was she really going to have to say this? She covered her cheeks with her hands, trying to cool them as she spoke. "Caleb...the parts we use to..." HOW WAS SHE SUPPOSED TO SAY THIS?

She closed her eyes and tried again, blocking out his gorgeous, disturbing confusion.

"Caleb, your penis. Please cover your penis. And your butt. Those two things, you need to keep covered." She opened one eye to see him frowning at her before he opened his mouth to speak. "AND—" she cut him off—"never never never try to sniff or touch or look at...this." She gestured with her hand around her breasts, and he blinked. "Or this," she gestured between her legs, and his frown deepened, "or *my* butt. Or *anything that has touched these parts!*"

He stared at her for just a few beats of silence.

"HOW AM I SUPPOSED TO DO THAT?" he exploded. "You are sitting on the bed and you sit on the ground sometimes and you've even hugged *me* and then your chest is on *me* and now I'm not supposed to even smell myself?"

She gave a mini scream and turned to take her shoes off, her cold wet socks a welcome distraction.

"You are impossible! Just...just...oh. Just stop embarrassing me!"

She whimpered as she peeled off the fabric sticking to her skin and held her toes in her hands, warming them. When he didn't say anything, she snuck a peak under her lashes. And her heart turned over.

He looked so lost. What was she doing...

"Caleb," she whispered, crawling over to sit beside him. He didn't look at her but stared down and away. "I'm sorry. It's just...you're...very attractive." Nat was sure she was blood red, but his eyes darted to hers in surprise.

"Then why don't you want to look at me?"

Her body tightened and her lips parted, but she didn't have an answer.

"And why does your scent change like that sometimes," he said, his voice softer, and she was sure her body was flaming so badly now she would melt right through the floor.

"I think it's when...I think you're...attractive," she managed to choke out.

He blinked and smiled, turning toward her more and alarming her when he leaned in closer to breathe her neck.

"But I like that scent," he murmured, his lips brushing her skin. A shiver went through her, and his hand went to his stomach.

"But...it makes me...uncomfortable," she whispered.

He leaned back immediately, his eyes wide.

"It does?"

She nodded. Vehemently.

"Very. Very very very very very. Very."

He frowned, but he didn't look hurt anymore.

"I don't want to make you uncomfortable."

Relief flooded her body.

"Good! Then…will you just…cover up like you see other people doing?"

He looked down and pulled the cover around himself, hiding everything this time. She sighed.

"Better?" he asked, uncertain.

"Much." And she smiled.

"And I won't put my nose between your legs again."

A choked sound came from her throat, but she drew in a deep breath. His eyes were so earnest.

"Thank you," she said at last, only the smallest wobble in her voice.

He frowned suddenly.

"Are you attracted to my wolf penis and butt?"

A coughing fit seized her, and he stroked her back in concern until she finally leaned up, wheezing.

"No. No, I do not feel attraction to your wolf body."

His eyes brightened.

"So I can be naked as a wolf?"

She stared at him a moment, her lips parted and her brows pulled together and raised.

"Yes. Yes, Caleb. It's…yes."

He let out a little yip before shifting and suddenly he was licking her all over her face, her neck, little chirping sounds coming from his throat while she alternately groaned and laughed until she finally collapsed on him, her arms around his neck and her hands buried in his fur.

Her eyes closed, and she breathed him in. He always smelled so clean. Like the wind and the trees. She leaned a bit more heavily, drowsiness stealing over her. She needed to get up. There was laundry to do. Homework. She needed to clean up the room. Eat.

Sliding down into his fur as he laid back, she fell asleep.

————

Nat awoke to the feel of fingers running softly through her hair, and she reached her hands up to stroke Caleb's fur, starting to burrow her face into him more deeply. And froze at the feel of bare skin.

Her eyes flew open to find her cheek pressed against his naked chest and her bare leg crossed over his under the covers.

"What's wrong?" Worry filled his voice as small, high pitched sounds came from her throat. "I'm still covered! If you look down you won't see anything, and I didn't touch the thing on your chest or your butt! I did everything you said!"

His sincerity only stole what little voice she had remaining, and her breath came in small, wheezing gasps.

"I had to change back. I couldn't pet you with paws," he complained. "And I didn't want you to be uncomfortable on the floor. And those clothes—I *know* those are uncomfortable. I was just trying to help."

A whine crept into his voice, and he started to curl up into her.

She bolted up off the mattress, tearing the blanket from him to wrap it around herself only to gasp again and throw it back at him, covering him as he sat up with wounded eyes.

Her eyes flew down to see her body clothed only in her underwear and bra, and she tore the blanket back again halfway, dropping to her knees to cover herself and squeezing her eyes together tightly.

"You didn't say anything about the rest of the parts," he said petulantly.

Nat wished she knew a prayer right now. Any prayer. Something to recite. Anything.

She started rattling off the pledge of allegiance.

"What are you doing?"

"And to the republic for which it stands..."

"Nat..." His mournful tone pierced her hysteria, and she slowly opened her eyes to find him staring at her with growing distress, the muscles of his arms and chest a mixture of light and shadows in the moonlight streaming through the window.

"Caleb," her voice was hoarse. "You also can't put your... parts near...my parts."

He looked down, twisting the blanket in his hands.

"Why are there so many rules," he mumbled. He swallowed and looked over at her. "I thought it was just if you saw me."

She shook her head. And once she started, it kept going. Back and forth, over and over, until she had to reach up and press her cheeks together with her hands to stop it.

"When I see you. When you touch me. When I touch you. When you look at my body..." She trailed off in a whisper.

He swallowed and pressed a hand against his stomach as a deep line formed between his brows.

"So I'm not supposed to touch you? Why can't I pet you, too? It's not fair." He sounded like such a child...but a very lonely child.

Tears stung her eyes. He must not have been held in human arms since his parents died. She was so panicked at how gorgeous he was, she forgot how deeply hurt he'd been.

He was so innocent. Genuine. And trying so hard to be good to her. And she was making him feel bad.

"Oh, Caleb..." She looked around for a shirt and saw her cubby organizer—all put back together. Her eyes drifted back to him, deep warmth and remorse filling them. She quickly threw a long t-shirt on and moved back to sit by his side.

"Please pet me," she whispered, looking up at him.

He glanced over, uncertainty clouding his eyes, and she leaned her head into his arm.

"Please. I love it when you touch me. So much that it makes me a little crazy. I'm so sorry. You didn't do anything wrong. You've been…" A deep sigh drifted from her as she searched for the words. "You're my hero. I've never had a hero. I didn't think someone like me could ever get one. I didn't think someone like you even existed."

She raised her head. He still looked so unsure of himself, and her stomach clenched in pain.

"I don't mean because you're a wolf. That's…crazy and amazing and wonderful. I mean *you*. You are so brave. So bold. And so, so kind."

His eyes were warming at last, his hair falling forward on his forehead and making her stomach clench again. But differently.

"And unfortunately for you, you are also *sooo* cute that it's really hard to be close to you without going crazy."

A little smile finally tugged at a corner of his mouth, and she remembered his fingers on her lips and swallowed when he finally began stroking her hair again.

"Honestly," she whispered. "You have no idea."

His lips parted, and he stared down at her for a long time, his eyes growing heavy. But he pulled his brow together and looked away with a frown, pulling his hand back from her hair and rubbing his stomach.

"Are you hungry?"

"No…I just—does it hurt?" He looked back at her. "The way you feel. When you think I look attractive. Does it hurt?"

Her breath caught as she considered the question. She supposed it did send certain…pangs to certain places.

"In a way, I guess."

His frown deepened as he looked at her.

"Then I think I feel that, too."

She stared up at him silent. And burst into laughter, wrapping her arms around him when he seemed hurt.

"No no—I'm not laughing at you. Just the idea of *you* being attracted to *me*!" She giggled, squeezing him harder. "Trust me when I tell you this: you aren't. I may not know wolves, but this is something I learned…"

Dark memories brushed through her mind for a moment, but she'd also learned how to not let them own her. And a wolf boy who had protected her was here, in her arms. She was as safe as she could ever be.

Caleb seemed agitated, and she released him. He was rubbing his stomach harder, and she frowned now.

"What is it? Do you feel sick?" Was it something in the trailer? Panic started to fill her again that she might have brought harm to him, but he was shaking his head.

"I don't know," he muttered. "It kept happening while you were sleeping, too."

She reached out to stroke his back, trying to soothe him, but it only seemed to agitate him more so she stopped.

"You're sure this isn't what it feels like?" He looked back at her, his eyes more intense than usual. "I mean—how can you know for sure?"

She hesitated, biting down on her lip, before sighing. She needed to get over her embarrassment with him. He was truly very innocent, and there was no one else to tell him.

"When a guy feels attracted, his penis gets really stiff and sticks out or up. The harder it is, the more attracted he is."

Caleb blinked.

"You've never gotten even a little bit hard with me. Trust me —what you are feeling is not attraction."

He stared at her intently, almost glaring, but finally turned his eyes away. His lips were set in a hard line, matching the line between his brow. But then he turned back with a cocky smile.

"I think you're wrong."

She stared at him, her lips slightly apart, a laugh stuck in her throat. He was so perfectly, confidently, charmingly, *totally* ignorant about human attraction. It was sooo adorable.

"And anyway, the pain goes away when I shift. So—"

"Wait!" she stopped him, grabbing his arm, and he raised a brow. "We need to figure out what we're going to do! How long do you want to stay? We need a story to tell my mom. And anyone else we might need to tell."

He blinked in surprise.

"I want to stay forever."

5

"HEY, NATALIE!"

Nat turned her head at the whisper as the teacher droned on about plants in Biology class, a required course for high school freshmen.

The girl at the desk beside her was leaning down with her book propped up in front of her.

"Does your brother have a date for the homecoming dance yet?" she whispered.

Nat shook her head and turned back to pretend to pay attention to the teacher.

It had been a crazy few months, and there were so many times Nat had been afraid they would get caught. Stopped. But her mom had really come through for them when Nat had explained the situation. Not all of it of course, but enough to work on her mom's heartstrings. Nat felt a little guilty about it though, since half the time she seemed to think Caleb really was her son.

But she'd needed her mom to get him in the system. Nat had asked her to pretend that Caleb's late father had taken him away from her when he was little to live out in the woods somewhere. She had wanted to keep the story as close to the truth as possible, since lies were easier when you didn't have to memorize too much.

Except between the lies and the drugs, her mom had confused Caleb with a baby she'd lost late in a pregnancy before Nat came along, so she had a tendency to cry and apologize to him every time she saw him. When she wasn't passed out, of course. And aside from the first few weeks when she was searching for a new supplier and getting Caleb in the system, she seemed to have checked out of life even more than before. Nat and Caleb managed everything in the house now except her drugs.

They had worked all summer together. Raking leaves, running errands—whatever they could find in the nearby neighborhoods. And Nat had never had so much fun in her entire life.

They laughed together constantly. Figured out how to do new things. He couldn't remember his exact birthdate, so they'd celebrated his sixteenth and her fifteenth on her birthday in June. She explained what she knew about the world, and he learned so fast that soon he was the one getting them jobs. People liked him so much better than they liked her—and paid him so much more.

They finally had enough money between them to buy everything they needed, from food to clothes. Her mom's disability checks just went to pay the household bills and for her prescriptions—including the ones that weren't actually prescribed. Nat wanted so much to just hide the money so she couldn't buy them anymore, but she'd tried that before. It was the only time her mom ever got really angry.

The bell rang, and Nat grabbed her books to hurry to the door, pretending not to hear when some girls called out to her. Her popularity hadn't suddenly increased. But Caleb's…

"Natalie, wait up!"

Nat closed her eyes for a brief moment as a swarm of girls surrounded her.

"Who is your brother asking to Homecoming?"

"Is he seeing anyone?"

"Since he made varsity, will he still go out with freshmen?"

Nat kept walking to her locker, staring straight ahead.

"Why don't you go ask him?" Her full lips thinned as she pressed them together, trying to keep her cool.

The girls tittered.

"Oh my god, I would die if he talked to me! Can you talk to him for me?"

It was the girl who used to yell at her for being in her way at Nat's own locker. Nat didn't answer her, and suddenly the chattering around her grew silent. She looked up.

Caleb leaned against the locker beside hers, staring down at her with a light in his eyes and that cocky half smile she kept telling him a brother shouldn't use on a sister. His body had filled out more, and the muscles strained against his t-shirt and hoodie. He was sixteen now, 6'2", and pure muscle.

It didn't matter how many times she saw him. Her body always responded.

His lips parted as he stared down at her for a moment before looking away, his hand on his stomach. He leaned his back against the locker, facing the group of girls who were still staring up at him in awe.

"Are—are you going to the dance?"

The squeak came from the girl who used to yell at her, and Nat shoved her books into her locker a little too hard.

"I don't know. Are we going, Nat?" He turned his head to her once more, tying her stomach in knots for a moment.

"You don't go with your sister!" The girls all giggled. "You have to take a date!"

He frowned back at her.

"Then no."

Nat closed her eyes again, wanting to whine in misery for being so desperately happy about his answer. *He's mine. You can't have him.*

She closed her locker at last and leaned her head on it for a moment. Caleb needed her to be a friend. A real friend. Someone who would help him do what was good for him. Not what was good for her.

But how could she do this when every time she looked at him...every time he looked at her...every time she had gone to sleep with him as a wolf only to wake up in his arms with him stroking her... She groaned quietly into the locker as a shudder went through her and felt him look over.

"Ready for lunch?"

Her sigh floated through the air, lost in the cacophony of trampling feet, loud voices, and banging lockers. She nodded up at him, and they headed to the cafeteria and the next group of kids who would spend the entire period trying to get Caleb's attention while she jabbed her food and avoided his eyes.

———

"Are you mad at me?"

Nat's gaze darted up to him in surprise as they walked home, her backpack slung over his shoulder, and she shook her head. They didn't take the bus home anymore since Caleb had to stay after school for tutoring and football practice. He'd wanted *her* to tutor him, but the school had required something more formal. As fast of a learner as he was, he hadn't been in school since he was six and there was a lot to catch up on before sports scholarships began rolling in, they'd said.

"Then why are you avoiding looking at me?"

Because I want to go to the dance with you.

Her gaze fell again.

"I just think you should go to the dance. With someone. Else."

"Why?"

"Because...it's expected. It will look weird if you don't."

She peeked up to see him frowning at her.

"Are you going with someone else?" he demanded.

A helpless laugh bubbled out of her.

"No! Nobody would want to go with *me*."

"*I* want to go with you!"

"That's because you don't know what you're missing yet." A weight settle in her stomach, but it was time to stop being selfish. "I'm serious, Caleb. Ask someone. Someone pretty. Someone you like."

"Okay. Will you go to the dance with me?"

She laughed up at him, her eyes full of helpless happiness, and a smile pulled at the corner of his mouth. But his eyes were serious.

"Someone who isn't your sister," she added.

"Will you go, too?"

"I can't! I don't have anything to wear. And I told you—no one would want to go with me." She quickly stopped and covered his mouth before he could speak. He rubbed his lips against her palm and leaned into her hand, staring down at her.

Heat rushed through her body. Everything stilled around them as she looked up into his deep amber eyes looking at her so steadily. Open. Serious. His gaze fell to her lips, and he leaned in further.

The sound of a car approaching broke through her fog, and she dropped her hand quickly and turned to continue walking. She saw his brow furrow out of the corner of her eye.

"Is your stomach hurting?"

"Yeah."

"Have you considered that you might be...allergic to me?"

His eyes snapped to hers again, but with a glare this time.

"I'm *not* allergic to you."

"How do you know? You don't," she cut him off. "And you should go with someone to the dance and…and…see if it happens with them."

She walked faster when his steps faltered, trying to breathe through the sick feeling settling in her stomach.

Her breath left her lungs when he grabbed her arm and whirled her around.

"You want me to touch someone else?"

The air stuck in her throat, so she only nodded. A very small nod.

He stared at her intently, his lips in a hard line. She felt like squirming under his gaze, but she forced herself to be still.

"Fine," he said at last, and the knot in her stomach grew. "But only if you go, too. We can get you something to wear."

Her lips parted to argue, but he was looking a little dangerous so she just nodded again.

He held her gaze a moment more and then turned back to walking. But he kept his hand on her arm, keeping her with him.

"Caleb…sister," she reminded him in a whisper.

"I've seen how other boys treat bratty little sisters." He glanced down at her, anger in his eyes. "I think this is fine."

And he marched her the rest of the way home without speaking to her again.

———

Nat stood against the farthest wall from where Caleb danced with yet another girl, never even looking her way. Nat's dress actually had flowers on it, tiny little daisies on a faded blue background that Caleb said reminded him of the forest. The soft, thin fabric fell just above her knee, so light she worried each time a breeze stirred when she walked. But old clothes were like that sometimes, and this had to have been made twenty years before.

Aside from when they'd gone shopping, Caleb had barely spoken to her all week, only thawing the smallest bit when he shifted into his wolf form at night and let her curl up to him. He was always up by the time she woke, though, getting breakfast for them and plopping down to eat in stony silence once she emerged from the room.

He hadn't asked anyone to the dance. They could all think what they liked, he said, but if she wanted to see if he was affected by other girls, he was going to test *all* the girls. He'd made it through about half of them so far, and some of the senior girls were really, really bold.

Nat looked away again as another one slid her hands down his body and pressed her chest against him. He didn't seem to feel sick. Not with any of them. The weight that had settled in her stomach days ago threatened to choke her, and she barely noticed a tall, lanky boy approaching her until he was only a few feet away.

"You look nice tonight, Natty," he mumbled, looking down at the ground.

Nat's eyes widened in alarm. What new game was this?

Preston cleared his throat nervously as she flattened herself against the wall and watched him. His eyes darted up to hers before dropping once more.

"I'm sorry—for last year. I was still…you know. A kid."

A kid who Caleb had thrown from the bus into the snow the first day he'd waited for her at the bus stop. He'd told him if he ever so much as looked at Nat again, they'd never find his body. Nat didn't know if he was serious or not, but Preston had stayed far away from her since then. Until now. Now with a thin line of fuzz above his lip after hitting a growth spurt over the summer.

"Sure. It's fine," she said, looking around for his buddies who were probably in on the gag.

"Do you…want to dance?"

So that was it. Get her on the dance floor and then make fun of her. Maybe worse.

She wrapped her arms around her body more tightly.

"No thanks. I'm good."

Preston stood shifting back and forth for a moment before walking to the wall beside her and leaning back to watch the crowd. What was he up to now?

"Dances are dumb," he muttered, scuffing his shoe on the ground. When she scooted away from him slightly, he looked up. "I wasn't the one who used the rocks—I didn't know he'd been doing that. I wanted to tell you sorry, but your brother's always around..."

His eyes looked almost like Caleb's when Caleb had done something to upset her. Her lips parted in surprise...an instant before Caleb's arm smashed into Preston's neck, pinning him to the wall.

"What did I tell you," he snarled, pressing harder when Preston grabbed at his arm, trying to breathe.

"Caleb, stop!" Nat wrapped her arms around him, trying to keep him from pressing any further. "He was just apologizing! Don't hurt him!"

His muscles strained beneath her hands, and Nat could see a teacher approaching. A growing number of kids on the dance floor were no longer dancing and staring their way.

"A teacher is coming and everyone's watching," she whispered. "Let him go! Please..."

The music blared loudly around them, the bass sending pulsing vibrations through her chest, accelerating her already rapid heartbeat. Caleb's eyes were narrowed and deadly, showing no sign of having heard her, and Preston was turning blue.

Her hand slid up slowly to wrap around Caleb's wrist, tugging gently.

"I don't want them to take you away from me," she breathed, hoping he could hear her. He glanced at her out of the corner of his eye a moment before finally stepping back, watching while Preston doubled over, gasping for breath. The teacher's voice called out to them, but Caleb grabbed her and pulled her out into the hall, ducking into the open doorway of a nearby dark classroom. He closed the door and pulled her against his chest to lean back on the wall, waiting until the sound of advancing footsteps disappeared.

Nat's heart hammered against her chest so hard she knew Caleb could feel it. This was the first time he'd held her as a human all week, and she ached to smooth her hands over the muscles of his chest beneath her palms.

Her lashes lifted to see his head still turned toward the door, listening, and her breath caught at the sight. His wild dark locks fell in disarray on his forehead, more tousled than usual from too many hands Nat had wanted to tear away from him. She reached up to brush them back but froze when he jerked his gaze to her. He was furious.

"Is that why you wanted me to go with someone else? So you could talk to him?"

Her eyes blinked multiple times.

"What?"

"I saw you. You parted your lips for him."

Her lips parted again, and she couldn't seem to stop blinking.

"You...you think—you think I like *Preston*?"

The revulsion in her voice was unmistakable, and doubt crept into his eyes.

"But you parted your lips..."

"Caleb...people do that sometimes just from surprise."

He stared down at her and swallowed.

"Oh."

Her hand still hovered by his head, and she tentatively reached out to brush the thick strands back from his eyes. Their faces were so close to each other, she could feel his breath with every rise and fall of his chest, his scent earthy and warm.

"Are you surprised now?" His tone was husky, and she realized her lips had parted again. She swallowed and shook her head, her pulse racing when his own mouth opened slightly.

His head lowered until his lips hovered right above hers, their breath mingling, and she breathed him in, a small sound escaping her. The line between his brow was as severe as she'd ever seen it, but he leaned in closer and touched his lips to hers.

Nat moaned into him helplessly, her hand dropping to tangle in the thick tufts of hair at the base of his neck. She stood on her toes, trying to get closer, and he made a sound of pain as his tongue reached out to lick the inside of her mouth, drawing a gasp from her. A sharp whimper came from deep in his throat, and he buried a hand in her hair and tilted her head to lick her more deeply, his tongue trailing her lips before sliding deep into her mouth.

The air felt empty and cold when he tore himself away, doubling over and turning to lean on the wall with his arms around his waist.

"Caleb! I'm so sorry!" she gasped, reaching for him but jerking away again when it seemed to make it worse. She stepped a few feet back as he turned and leaned his head against the wall, hitting his fist against it with a cry of frustration.

Nat held her hands to her mouth, tears filling her eyes. She had known there was something wrong with her for a long time. Why had she let him anywhere near her?

"It's not you, Nat," he said hoarsely, his eyes closed while he leaned his forehead against the wall. "You're not doing anything wrong."

Tears spilled over her cheeks. She knew that wasn't true. But he was so innocent, he just didn't understand.

"It is," she whispered. "I just…I've been selfish."

His head turned toward her, still leaning against the wall.

"Don't be ridiculous. You're the least selfish person in the world."

She gave a small laugh, but the tears kept falling. It was time for her to be honest.

"You don't understand…" Sickness clawed at her stomach. "I'm not…like normal kids."

A frown pulled his lips down as he turned to face her fully, worry filling his eyes when he saw the tears. But he didn't come closer.

"What do you mean?"

A shudder went through her.

"There's something wrong with me. It…it makes boys my age…not like me. Just gross old men."

His frown was severe now.

"That's the dumbest thing I ever heard."

Nat's head dropped, and she wrapped her arms around herself while she stared at her feet.

"It's true," she whispered. "It wasn't just…the creep you scared away. There was another one before him. It started when I was ten."

"What started?" Caleb's voice sounded dangerous, and she swallowed. Would he hate her for not telling him? For making him sick?

"He started…getting…stiff. And…you know. Putting it inside me." Nausea roiled in her gut, but she pushed it away. He deserved to know what she was.

Silence filled the room as she stared at her toes, her breath catching with each inhale. She flinched as he walked over to her.

"I'm so sorry," she whispered. "I didn't know it could make you sick."

His arms went around her and he pulled her close, putting her head in his neck and rubbing her back.

"Nat…" His voice was soft. "There is nothing—*nothing*—wrong with you." She shook her head against him, and he kissed her forehead. "Hush…listen to me. There is something wrong with *them*." For a moment, a snarl rumbled in his throat, fierce and terrifying, but he pressed his lips to her head again and it went away. "Not you. Never, ever you."

Her tears spilled over again, and she leaned into him, letting him hold her close.

"And I'm not sick. I've been trying to figure out what's going on, but I know I'm not sick. And I also know," his voice grew husky, "that it only happens with you because you're the only one who makes me feel anything good."

"You didn't…like any of the girls?" she whispered.

He did growl this time.

"No! Why did you want me to do that?" A bit of the anger from the week was back, and Nat looked up at him. His eyes softened again, and he stroked the tears from her cheeks.

"I was trying to not be selfish."

His hand stilled.

"Are you telling me you did that for *me?*"

She nodded, her eyes earnest, and a flame seemed to grow in his.

"Nat, do you really think I would have left the forest and hunting and running free to wear clothes—to sleep boxed in—to go to *school.*" His volume grew as he continued. "*For any reason except to be with you?*"

A whimper escaped her, and she buried her head in his chest, wrapping her arms around him tightly.

"I need time to figure this out. Just…don't push me away. Please." His voice was husky, and she breathed him in, nodding against him.

His lips brushed her neck.

"Now will you look at me again," he whispered. "So I can keep trying to figure it out?"

A shiver went through her, and she looked up, melting inside.

And he tried again.

6

CALEB CROUCHED low beside the house, his black fur shrouded in the darkness of the night, while he watched the man in the truck guzzling the last of his beer. The car door flew open a moment later, accompanied by a loud belch, and the man clambered out to stagger towards the front door.

He would have preferred a chase, running after him, terrifying him for a while first, rather than lying in wait. The thrill of the hunt wasn't something he'd indulged in lately, since he'd been trying to live as a human, but these humans lived too close to one another. The man would scream and someone would be sure to call the cops or—worse—try to help the man themselves. And Caleb didn't want to risk hurting anyone else.

The man fumbled at the lock, and Caleb's muscles strained with the effort to wait. He needed to silence him in his first lunge, but the man's head was down too low.

"Fuckin' bitch," the man muttered before grunting once he managed to jam the key in the lock. "That's right, open for daddy."

Caleb dug his claws into the earth, locking his snarl in his throat before it could escape. This was it. If he waited any longer, he'd have to go inside, and they might not dismiss it as an animal attack.

The man shoved the door open just as a bolt of darkness flew toward him, and he turned his head toward the side of his house for just an instant—but it was long enough.

Caleb's jaws clamped into his throat, capturing his strangled cry and crushing his windpipe while warm blood spurted into his mouth. The man's hands clawed at him desperately, ripping at his fur, and Caleb slammed him to the ground, dragging him back into the darkness where he'd been hiding.

Sickness filled his gut as the man's attempts to free himself became more feeble. This was too easy. Far too easy. His death should have been more painful. More terrifying and humiliating. He should have known exactly why he was dying and who he never, ever should have touched.

Caleb consoled himself by tearing his claws through the man's stomach, relishing the brief spasm that went through the body before the heart gave out at last. He shook the corpse viciously, hearing a bone snap when a leg hit the side of the house. Too loud. The limp form fell from his jaws as he spit him out.

His blood was disgusting, and Caleb wanted nothing more than to piss on him and leave. But that would invite curiosity. Questions. And Caleb's parents had told him they must always keep their existence hidden from humans. Of course, they'd also told him never to *hunt* humans, but some of their rules made more sense to him than others.

He bit into the body, tearing through it quickly. If he left it in enough pieces, hopefully they wouldn't notice none of it had been eaten. Coyotes in the area had been known to tear into dogs on occasion, so Caleb mimicked their behavior as much as possible.

A few minutes later, he darted back toward the woods, racing to the rocky area deep inside where he'd left his clothes. He wouldn't leave a trail showing the change in tracks, and his shift would take care of all the blood on his coat. It would mean walking a few miles on human legs back to Nat's, but there would be no sign to lead anyone back to her door. Nothing to link his female to the mangled body of the grotesque creature who had dared to hurt her. Nothing to take him away from her.

———

"It's two in the morning!" Nat hissed, pulling him inside and closing the door. The air of the trailer sat stale and sticky on his skin, and he leaned into her quickly to breathe, her warm, sweet fragrance a balm to his tortured lungs.

"I missed you," he murmured, nuzzling her as he picked her up to carry her back to their room. Caleb wasn't sure why Nat bothered whispering. Her mother was passed out on the couch as usual, and nothing seemed to wake her.

He fought with disgust each time he saw the woman. She'd helped him, and he was grateful, but she'd also abandoned her daughter for years, leaving her to fend for herself against predators far worse than anything Caleb had faced in the wild. He could never forgive that.

But now he was here, and no one would hurt her again.

"Would you put me down!" she whispered again, smacking his back while he kicked the bedroom door closed. Her heart was beating really fast, and her scent had changed to the one he loved so much, but she seemed mad at him, too. He looked down at her with a frown but didn't let go.

"You shouldn't have been waiting up for me."

She kept smacking him, her heart hammering against his chest, but she wouldn't meet his eyes.

"Why are you hitting me? I know you think I'm attractive right now."

Her choked sound was a mix of frustration and something he couldn't figure out, and she shoved her hands against his chest.

"You are the most ridiculous…cocky…would you let me go!" she exploded, finally looking up to glare at him.

Her face was really red, and he thought about telling her, but he'd tried that before and it never went well. Maybe she really did want him to let her go.

He could feel the sadness in his eyes when he released her.

"Don't you dare give me that look!" she fumed. "I've been worried for hours! You can't just come back and…and…"

Her high pitched little yip was too cute, and he couldn't help grinning. She grabbed a pillow and slung it at him, and he let her hit him, still smiling.

"Why were you worried? I'm a wolf! Everything else should worry," he said with a smug smile, grabbing the pillow mid-swing and reaching for her again. She jumped back, catching her foot on the edge of the mattress, and he pulled her into his arms to tumble onto the cushioned surface together.

His smile faltered as he stared down into her beautiful eyes. The pain was only getting worse, and some nights it wouldn't go away at all. He hadn't told her, but it had started bothering him even after he shifted, although it was different somehow. Less cutting and more…burning. And no matter which form he was in, it felt like a nonstop race between his desire to be close to her and the pain that always rose up to stop him.

Wait. Were her eyes wet?

"Nat…why are you crying?"

"I am not crying!" She glared at him while a small tear leaked out of the corner of her eye. He leaned down to lick it away softly, a whine sounding in his throat.

"Why are you sad? Please tell me…" He kissed her skin, his body tensing when pain shot into his gut. *No.* He wanted to kiss her. But his brow furrowed deeply as he continued pressing soft kisses along her cheek.

A whimper laced her groan, and her arms wrapped around him while she buried her face in his neck, stopping him from kissing her. He frowned.

"I thought…I mean, why shouldn't you…" she clenched him harder. "What if you get tired of coming back?"

He leaned up to glare down at her.

"You still think I would *leave*? What the fuck, Nat!" *Fuck* was a new addition to his vocabulary, and he thought it rather nicely captured his feelings.

"Well I know you hate being here! You said it—wearing clothes, going to school. How long until it's just too much? I'm stuck, but there's no reason that you should be, too," she finished with worry in her eyes. Guilt.

He glared harder.

"No reason? *You're* my reason!"

"That's a *bad* reason!"

"Don't you ever say that." He wanted to shake her. To kiss her. He did both before leaning back up, his stomach a hard knot in his gut as he looked down at her soft eyes. "Yes, clothes are stupid and so is school. Although some of the games are okay, I guess. And sitting with you at lunch. But yeah—a lot of it sucks.

"Being able to run and hunt and sleep under the stars was the best part of living for me for years. I love it. But…" Pain hit him again, but this time higher in his chest. His voice softened.

"But then something better came into my life. A lot better. And sleeping with you is so much better than sleeping under the stars, Nat," he whispered, leaning down to kiss her once again. Her scent rushed through him when their tongues met, and he dug his hands into the bed, struggling to hold on just a little longer.

Her moan plunged a knife through him, and he barely had time to pull back and tear his clothes off before he shifted. He turned in a circle a couple of times, frustrated. It was still there.

An ache. His whine pierced the silence of the room, and Nat leaned forward to stroke his fur.

"It was hurting? What can I do?" Her voice soothed him, and he crawled into bed beside her, curling up and laying his muzzle across her neck.

"Caleb," she coughed, pushing him a bit. "I need to breathe, you know."

He whined, shifting his position in the bed, needing to be as close as possible. She wouldn't let him put his muzzle where he'd really like, where he could drown in her scent, where the ache in his gut would somehow be better and so much worse at the same time.

He nuzzled her neck again, licking the skin until she giggled, and tried resting his head on her once more. This time she just sighed and turned a bit until he felt her relax.

He'd asked her to give him time to figure it out, and every day for the past month, he'd tried. But the only thing he'd figured out was that he couldn't bear being away from her and he couldn't bear being close to her. And it was getting worse.

At least he could take care of the threats in her life. One down and one more to go for now. And once both of the bad men were gone, he would start going through the list of everyone else who had hurt her, starting with that boy down the street.

The sound of Nat's breathing slipping into sleep pierced the burning pain in his gut, letting it spread throughout his body in a warm, deep ache. And his own breathing grew steady as sleep opened her arms to him at last.

———

"Man. Did you see Heather today?" The boy cupped his soapy hands around his bare chest while the shower head sprayed above him. "You can see all the way to here."

"Oh, I saw! But that's not even the best part. Did you see her skirt? I sit beside her in Pre-calc, and dropped my pencil a few times. No underwear."

"Nuh uh!"

"Swear to god. I was so fucking hard, I had to stop dropping it because it was getting too big to bend over."

The other boy snorted.

"You wish. Now if you were Caleb, maybe I'd believe you! Kid's only a freshman and already part horse."

The two senior boys turned their heads toward Caleb where he was just finishing his shower.

"Hey, Caleb, how big are you when hard?"

Caleb glanced at them while the locker room grew quiet.

"Still 6'2"," he grinned, and a few guffaws sounded around him, the noise level picking up once more.

He turned back to finish rinsing off, the smile falling from his face. His time in the locker room had proved almost as educational as the sex ed portion of health class they'd taken at the start of the year. And both worried him.

Was his body that different from theirs? He'd looked up the way wolves mated and their penises didn't just get hard—they emerged from behind the skin when they got excited and, unlike humans, their boners actually had a bone in them. Did he have another penis on the inside that needed to come out, and that was why he never got hard? Maybe his stomach hurt because something was stopping it.

Except his human body didn't differ from other humans in any other way that he could tell. He'd had to get a physical exam and shots to be allowed in school, and the doctor didn't seem to think there was anything out of the ordinary. Nat had been a nervous wreck about it, but he'd been too ignorant at the time to realize the risk he was taking. He understood more now.

But he didn't understand why he couldn't get hard. His parents had never explained anything about that, and Caleb didn't know anyone else like them he could ask. It had just been the three of them living up in the hills, and they'd always said they'd tell him about their families some other time. Caleb hadn't cared back then; he'd been too interested in running and playing or curling up in his mom's arms—or fur. If he'd only known how little time he would have before they were taken from him forever...

He shook off the sad feelings and walked out of the shower to grab a towel, wishing he could have just shifted to get clean. But it would look too suspicious for him to always be clean without joining the other boys in the locker room.

"Are you going to ask her out?" Shane, the team's captain—and starting quarterback before Caleb came along—looked over as Caleb pulled his clean clothes out of the locker beside him.

"Who?"

"Dude. *Heather*. She just broke up with her boyfriend."

"Oh. No."

Shane stared at him.

"You know she likes you, right?"

Caleb frowned, pulling his t-shirt over his head.

"I heard she likes everyone."

Shane snorted.

"Not like she likes you. And you hang out at her locker all the time. I just figured..."

Caleb's frown deepened. He certainly did not. The only locker he ever went to was Nat's. His brow cleared.

"Oh. Her locker is beside Nat's, isn't it?"

"Uh, yeah, like you've been fooling anyone. Nobody hangs out at their sister's locker that often, especially a sister that—" Shane stopped himself and turned back to his own locker quickly.

"That what?"

"Nothing," Shane muttered, stuffing his gym bag inside and closing the door. Caleb grabbed him before he could walk away, easily shoving him against the locker with one hand. Talk died down around them, and Shane swallowed.

"Look, man, she's your sister. I respect that. But come on… it's not like she's at your level."

Caleb narrowed his eyes, his hand holding the older boy firmly in place.

"What do you mean."

"I mean…shit…" His eyes darted around for help, but the other boys suddenly became very busy getting dressed.

His face broke out in a sweat as he looked back at Caleb.

"Look, she seems like a really nice girl. She's just one of those girls that doesn't care about…dressing cool or…her hair or… makeup," he finished weakly. "Which is a great thing! Girls are usually so shallow and—"

At Caleb's expression, he bit back whatever else he was going to say.

"What's wrong with how she dresses?" he demanded. He never paid much attention when they went shopping, letting Nat choose whatever they needed. It's not like he knew anything about clothes. But no one seemed to think *his* clothes looked bad. Had she been spending more on him? Fuck.

"N—nothing! She looks…fine!"

Caleb made a sound of impatience and shoved him harder into the locker as he released him. He wanted to tell him he was blind. Nat's big brown eyes could stop his heart with a look. Her pink, full lips tempted him constantly, teasing him each time they parted and her eyes grew soft. And when she was lying beneath him, her hair flowed around her like an angel.

Pain hit his stomach, and he turned away with a scowl. He couldn't say any of that. Grabbing his bag, he stalked out of the room while harsh whispers carried down the hall to his sensitive ears.

"Dude…" Multiple snickers and quiet peals of laughter met with a low groan. "You can't say shit about his *sister!*"

"I know, I know! I was all distracted thinking about Heather," he hissed. "Jeez…he should be glad she's ugly if he's that protective."

Caleb paused, his hand digging into the strap of his bag as he clenched it, but he stepped forward again after a moment.

She was *beautiful.* But if the stupid clothes they all wore were so important, he was going to make sure they were the right ones from now on. He just needed to find someone who knew how girls were supposed to dress to help. Maybe he would ask Heather out after all.

———

Nat's face lit up the moment she saw him waiting at her locker, and the bands in Caleb's chest began to ease. He leaned his head against the cold metal, certain if he moved toward her he would end up burying his face in her neck.

Her heavily fringed brown eyes sparkled while her cheeks grew pink and round, trying to suppress her smile. So fucking beautiful. She was wearing one of the few pieces of clothing that didn't bother him: a thin, faded dress that fell in a straight line from her chest to her ankles. He couldn't *see* her body very well, but he could feel everything when he held her close. And he desperately wanted to hold her close right now.

"Hi," she breathed once she was beside him, still sparkling up at him for a moment until concern crept into her eyes. "What's wrong?"

Everything but her.

"Long day," he said, moving to the side so she could put her books away. But the small group of girls who always seemed to be gathered at Heather's locker spilled into their space, bumping Nat back a few steps and turning with a gasp to Caleb.

"Oops—oh my goodness! I'm so sorry!"

Caleb glanced irritably at the girl, ready to pull Nat back, but then he remembered he needed help with shopping. His eyes turned to Heather putting her books in her locker calmly, and his gaze wandered down her body. She wore a long-sleeved top with a matching short skirt in some sort of soft looking sweater material that hugged every curve. Nat would look so good in that. He'd be able to see her figure for once and feel every part of her body when he pressed her close to him.

He raised his eyes again to talk to Heather and saw she'd turned a bright red. The girls around her were giggling, and he glanced back at Nat wondering if he'd done something wrong.

Her face was pale, and she dropped her eyes immediately. Shit. He'd definitely done something.

"You know," the girl who'd bumped Nat out of the way simpered up at him. "Heather was just saying how she needed some help getting our cheer equipment loaded up for the away game."

"Shut up, Megan!" Heather hissed.

"What? Caleb is strong and could load your, um, car for you really well, I bet," the girl smirked while her friends tittered around them.

Caleb frowned, looking back at Heather. If he helped her, maybe she'd help him.

"I can help."

Heather hesitated, her face still rather pink.

"Well, if you want to, I have my car parked out back. It shouldn't take too long, and I could drop you off after."

Shit. Now? His eyes went back to Nat, but she was staring at the ground and he couldn't see her expression.

"Or whatever." Heather shrugged and tucked her blonde curls behind her ear, turning back to her locker.

He just wanted to get home and bury himself in Nat's scent. But a temporary delay would be worth it if it meant figuring out how to buy the things for Nat that she should have.

"Yeah, that sounds good."

Heather swallowed and closed her locker, stepping back.

"Great. Well, it's this way…" she said, turning to walk away, waiting for him to walk with her.

Fuck. Couldn't he just meet her in whatever classroom it was? Nat didn't seem happy with him, and he wanted to talk to her first. But Nat moved in the opposite direction before he could think of anything to say.

"I'm just going to catch the bus today. See you at home," she mumbled.

"Wait—you need your coat!"

"No time," she said over her shoulder, hurrying down the hall.

Caleb watched her, frustration etching a line between his brow.

"Man, I wish my big brother looked after me like that! She is soooo lucky, Caleb," a girl crooned.

"She looks after me, too," he frowned, his irritation growing when the girls all giggled.

"Oh, if you were my big brother, I'd be looking, too."

"Megan!" Heather put her hand over her face.

"What! I'm just sayin'…"

Their chatter swirled around him while worry gnawed at his stomach. Was Nat upset with him? He wanted to go after her, but he had an opportunity here to do something for her and he needed to use it.

His choice made, he fell into step beside Heather to ask her about her clothes.

———

Caleb grabbed the box out of Heather's car.

"Thanks a lot, Heather!" He beamed at her from the sidewalk while she stared up at him in confusion, still in the driver's seat but no longer leaning over the way she had when she'd stopped the car.

"Do you want me to come in and show her which outfits go together...?"

"No, I think we can figure it out. See you at school tomorrow!"

He waved and turned toward the trailer, his pulse racing as he imagined Nat's surprise. The car behind him didn't move until he'd disappeared through the screen door, but he barely noticed, closing it behind him to hurry down the hall.

"Nat!" Bursting through the door, he found her sitting on the bed with papers spread around her. He grunted in frustration when she didn't look up and dropped the box to grab the papers and toss them off the bed.

She sat unmoving, watching his hands, but she didn't lift her eyes.

"Nat, I brought you something!" He grinned, dumping the box on the bed, waiting for her cry of delight. It didn't come.

Nat stared at the pile of clothes without expression.

"It's from Heather! She took me to her place and gave me so much stuff. You wouldn't believe how much she has! Her closet is bigger than this entire room!"

He looked at her expectantly, waiting for her to be amazed, but again he was disappointed. His smile dimmed, but he tried again.

"I told her you didn't have anything nice. I thought she'd help me pick something out, but she just *gave* me all this instead! Now you won't have to wear ugly things anymore! Her stuff is all soft and once I really started looking, I could see why it's better than the stuff we've been getting. You're going to feel so much better in these!"

When she still didn't react, he grew frustrated.

"Come on—I brought you something..." he whined. "Aren't you going to say anything?"

Nat stared down at the pile of clothes in silence, her eyes wide and dry. Finally she reached a hand out to touch one of the dresses.

"You're right," she said in a small voice. "They're much better. Thank you."

Caleb's brow pulled together. She didn't seem very happy to have them. And he *knew* she hated the things she had.

"She put some makeup in, too. She said not to use too much —just add some eyeliner and lip gloss to start. And she said you should use..." he dug around in the box. "...this product for your hair. She said put it on after you towel dry it and then just let it air dry."

Nat stared at the bottle he was holding out to her before taking it.

"Thank you," she repeated as quietly as she had before.

Caleb suddenly felt like growling.

"These are gifts, you know!" He flopped on the ground beside her, thoroughly disgruntled. "You told me we're supposed to be happy when someone gives us a gift."

Her eyes turned to his at last, and his breath caught as pain shot to his stomach.

"Sorry," she whispered, looking every bit like she had when he'd first seen her in the woods. "This was very kind. I'm just... not feeling very well. Do you think you could go run for a while? I want to finish my homework and lie down."

A second bolt of pain hit him. She wanted him to go away? She never wanted him to go away.

"Maybe...I could help with the homework."

Nat shook her head.

"It's algebra."

"Well, then I'll do the laundry," he suggested.

"I did it while you were gone."

Caleb looked over in surprise. Had he been gone that long? The light outside was fading so he guessed he had.

"Then I'll make dinner," he insisted, getting up.

"I'm not hun—"

"You're eating!" he snapped, not looking back. He resisted slamming the door behind him but still closed it with a loud click before marching down the hall.

He had eaten the Spam she brought him. *He* had pretended to like everything she brought him. But she couldn't muster the enthusiasm to be happy about the huge pile of super soft clothes he got her from the girl at school who everyone seemed to think dressed perfectly?

Caleb slammed a pan on the stove, ignoring when Nat's mother groaned at the sound, and started making dinner.

————

The last time he'd slept so horribly was during a particularly violent storm when even the trees couldn't shield him from the constant downpour. But he would have rather had that a thousand times than spend another night with Nat's back to him, flinching each time he touched her. In the end, he'd slept on the floor, the sick feeling in his gut waking him every few minutes.

Now he was sitting on the front step, breathing in the fresh air while he waited for her to get ready. She was taking longer than usual.

The door opened behind him and he turned to find her bundled up in her large coat, the hood over her head and her eyes down. He could see one of the new dresses falling a few inches beneath the hem to just below her knee, and she'd paired it with her ankle boots and one of the new pairs of socks. Weren't girls supposed to wear small shoes with dresses? He'd have to see if he could find her some shoes. Too bad Heather's feet were a lot bigger.

Nat kept her head down while they walked to the bus, which

didn't improve his mood, and by the time they made it to school he was glaring at everything.

"You don't need to go to my locker today," she said softly once they made it inside, and he turned his glare to her, not bothering to answer and even more furious when she didn't even look up as he stomped beside her.

He threw himself back on the row of metal beside her, crossing his arms and continuing to glare at her. She opened her locker and stood staring inside blankly, still not looking at him, before finally beginning to remove her coat.

A sudden heat rushed through him, burning in his stomach, and he stood paralyzed for just a moment before grabbing her and wrapping the coat back around her body tightly.

"What were you thinking," he said, his voice hoarse. "You can't wear this one to school."

Her eyes looked up at him uncertainly.

"It...looked like all the others," she whispered. "Is it that bad?"

Caleb felt like his eyes must be wider than hers at the moment. Was it bad?

"Caleb!"

The girls squealed as they approached with Heather, running up with far more familiarity than before. Caleb released Nat, trying to breathe steadily.

"Dude, you are so full of it!"

A couple of the guys who were in the locker room the previous day walked up with the girls.

"We heard everything about you and Heather. *Everything*."

"I told you—nothing happened!" Heather said, flustered as she opened her locker.

"Yeah, except he was in your bedroom with you...for like an hour..."

Caleb struggled to follow what they were saying while Nat stood in front of her open locker, slowly removing her coat.

"We were just going through my clothes," Heather said, turning red immediately. "I mean the clothes in my closet. Not the ones I was wearing."

The laughter only increased around them.

"Shane is going to be so jealous. You know he was hoping— holy shit!"

Caleb closed his eyes when Nat turned around at last. He felt her looking up at him, worried, but he didn't dare look back—he wasn't sure if he could resist shifting if he did.

Not that he needed to look. The image in his mind was all too clear.

She wore a soft blue cap-sleeved dress with a low scooped neck. Very low. So low, she evidently hadn't been able to find a bra she could wear with it. The fabric was thin...so, so thin it showed every outline. The urge to drop to his knees and suck her nipple between his lips had nearly overwhelmed him. He'd never seen them before. Her bras were so thick...he hadn't known. But now he knew, and he wanted to bang his head in the locker behind him until it hurt enough to distract him from the pain in his gut.

And the pain didn't end with her breasts. The dress hugged every curve, dipping into her thin waist before gently flowing over the soft, plump curves behind her. He knew how those felt, when he'd been pressed against her at night, but being able to see them as she moved...

Her hair looked different as well, flowing over her shoulders in glossy waves that looked so soft and framed her face so beautifully. A face with eyes that seemed impossibly larger somehow today and tender lips that glistened as if touched by the morning dew. He wanted to lick her everywhere.

And by the scent in the air, so did the other boys. He opened his eyes again and glared at them furiously, shoving them back when they didn't even notice, unable to take their eyes off Nat.

"Shit—uh—"

"Sorry—going to class now—bye!"

The boys took off while some of the girls released small sounds of outrage.

Caleb grabbed Nat's arm and pulled her away quickly toward her next class, trying to block her from male eyes as much as possible. *What had he been thinking!* If he survived the day, he was shredding every last piece of the new clothing.

Shane had been right. It was much better when they thought she was ugly.

———

By lunch, Caleb was miserable and thoroughly regretting his stupidity. He just wanted her back in a package that didn't torture him every second with wanting her and wanting to kill every guy suddenly looking at her.

Nat was waiting in line to buy lunch, and Caleb had let her go up without him for once. He'd been struggling with shifting all day, and his nerves were frayed. Besides, he seemed to have adequately terrified the boys who were all staying far away from her, so Nat was surrounded by Heather and her friends for the moment. Safe.

So he sat at the lunch table with his back to her, desperate to keep the image of her standing in line from eroding what little remained of his self-control. He couldn't resist listening in on her conversation, though, and only vaguely nodded along with whatever was being said at the table. His attention was focused on picking up the sounds across the loud room.

"Don't be mean, Megan," Heather was saying.

"I'm not! I'm just saying that when you get rid of your trash, you shouldn't be giving it to trailer trash or look what happens! Now you look like you chose slutty clothes. She doesn't know how to wear them with class."

Caleb went cold inside and the remaining sounds in the

cafeteria faded away while he listened. Someone just moved to the top of his list.

"I didn't have any bras that wouldn't show," Nat said, and Caleb's stomach clenched at the shame in her voice.

"Well then you shouldn't have worn it! Jeez. Why not just parade around school naked?"

Caleb waited for Nat to tell Megan that *she* never seemed to have a problem showing the outline of *her* nipples, but Nat said nothing more. He turned around at last and everything seemed to pour over him at once.

She was achingly beautiful…but she was hurting. Her arms were wrapped tightly around her body, covering her breasts, and her head hung low. Caleb wanted to rip the girl's head off, but guys weren't supposed to be rough with girls. But she could. Nat could slam her head on the wall—the girl was smaller and Nat was definitely stronger. Why wouldn't she defend herself?

He turned back around, continuing to listen as a few of the other girls joined in to criticize Nat a bit longer before switching subjects, shutting her out completely. By the time they headed back to the table, he no longer even pretended to answer when someone spoke to him. He didn't bother waiting for Nat to sit down but grabbed her arm and dragged her behind him to exit the cafeteria.

He'd had enough. They were going home.

7

Nat trembled while Caleb yanked her coat around her, zipping it up furiously before dragging her outside. The cold bit into the exposed skin on her legs as she rushed to keep up with his long strides.

She'd thought she was doing it right when she dressed this morning. Her bras had shown in every top and every dress she'd tried on, and she'd tried them all. At least this dress had been longer and was a pale blue that she didn't think would draw attention. But she hadn't been cold when she'd looked in the mirror this morning.

She was wheezing by the time they made it back to the trailer, but Caleb didn't let her stop until he'd dragged her back to the room and closed the door.

"Why didn't you tell them to fuck off! Why did you just *stand* there and let them talk to you that way!"

Nat stared up at him, her lungs hurting with each breath. He was listening?

She looked down, starting to remove her coat only for him to grab it.

"*Don't* do that," he growled.

She stood frozen in place, her big ugly coat now far too warm after the furious pace he'd set walking home. Wearing clothes he'd wanted her to wear. Not the cheap, ugly things she owned. The only things she'd been able to afford. The embarrassing things she had to wear. Embarrassing for her. Embarrassing for him to be around her.

Caleb had brought her makeup to fix her face. Hair products to fix her hair. And clothes from the girl he'd checked out so thoroughly in front of her to fix her body. But she'd tried. She'd tried so hard to do what he wanted her to do. And still it was wrong.

She collapsed on her knees, the air feeling heavy, and took the coat off, ignoring him as nausea threatened to choke her. The room had grown loud and her eyesight was dark at the edges. She knew this feeling—she'd fainted before. And she knew she needed to put her head down, but she couldn't bear to keep looking so weak in front of him.

"I'm sorry," she said, fighting back the sick feeling in her gut while she stared at the floor. "I am glad you're not like me, Caleb. I'm so glad for you. But I've tried defending myself before…and I…humiliate myself and cry. And that never stopped anything."

Tears were filling her eyes, but she focused on trying to hear herself speak over the rushing in her ears.

"This is the only way I know how to be okay. Inside," she whispered, staring at her hands in her lap. "And I know it must look really pathetic. Or…is really pathetic. But it's the only way I was able to figure out how to be. How to…be okay."

Her tears spilled over, and she thought she heard him speaking but she couldn't make out the words.

"Just listen, please. I can't really hear very well right now."

She flinched away when he touched her. She needed to get this out and be done.

"I'm sorry. I'm so sorry I'm not better. But I can't do the

things you want me to do. I can't be the person you want me to be. I don't know how to dress like they do. I don't know how I'm supposed to do my hair. Or my face. I really wanted to look better." Her face broke, and she pressed her palms hard on her eyes. "I swear I tried so hard this morning. I never wanted to embarrass you, and I am so, so sorry."

Then she drew a deep breath and opened her eyes again to look at him while he kneeled across from her, his eyes huge and horrified as he shook his head, his mouth forming words she couldn't hear.

"But I am tired of everyone around me looking down on me for being myself! For not being able to buy the right types of clothes. For not looking better. For not being better. For not being whatever you want me to be!"

His head shook furiously as he continued mouthing words, and her voice cracked.

"I changed my mind, Caleb. It wasn't a good idea for you to come here. Go back to your freedom. Or go live with Heather or someone who can dress the way you want and look the way you want and act the way you want! Maybe you can sleep in her closet since it's so much bigger than my small, ugly room!"

He had gone perfectly still, but she could barely see him through the tears and the narrow tunnel that remained of her vision.

"I have *tried,* and I have been doing the *best that I know how to do.* I don't have nice things, and I don't know what I'm supposed to say or do when people are mean, but I have done everything I can think of and I'm *sorry* it's not enough!"

The roaring in her ears was too loud now—she held onto the coat and sank to the floor, closing her eyes and curling her knees to her chest. The vibrations beneath her told her he'd shifted and was moving rapidly in the small space.

"I'm sorry I went into your space that day, Caleb...I'm really sorry."

She thought she heard yelping as a rush of air passed over her. The sharp sound of the window she always left open a crack being shoved open finally penetrated her ears. And then all was silent and still.

Nat couldn't move as the crushing grief spread through her body, and she lay in silence until sleep mercifully took her away.

———

The light had almost disappeared when Nat opened her eyes again. Cold silence surrounded her. She pushed herself to her feet and leaned over to shut the window. Caleb's clothing lay on the floor, and she stared at it, a sickness washing over her. She needed to get out of here for a while.

Heather's dress slipped to the floor, and she stepped out of it, reaching for a pair of sweatpants Caleb liked to wear instead. She pulled one of his sweatshirts over her head and left her room, stopping to check on her mother for a moment before she stepped out of the trailer.

The air had grown colder, but the sweats were warm enough. And she wanted to just be wrapped up in Caleb a little while longer. Just a little longer before she had to think…

She'd told him to leave. She had done this. But she wasn't ready to wait around the rest of the night, worried. Sick. Alone again. She wasn't ready to face it.

Her feet set out walking down the drive. Maybe she'd walk into town.

"Natty?"

Nat's stomach jolted a moment before she realized it was Preston.

"You shouldn't be walking around by yourself in the dark— it's not safe."

Yeah. From people like him.

"I've been doing it for years," she shrugged.

"Yeah, but I just heard some guy just got totally torn up by coyotes the other night a few miles away."

"A guy? Not a dog?"

"Yeah. One of his neighbors saw a pack of coyotes in his yard this morning, eating something. They fired their shotgun at them and they ran off, but the dude was in pieces all over the yard. Everybody's talking about hunting them down."

Nat's breath caught in her throat. Caleb was in the woods. Her stomach clenched until she realized he would have no reason to stay local if he wanted to live as a wolf. He would be fine. He had to be fine.

"Mind if I walk with you?" he asked. "I have to go to the store."

Nat hesitated, her gut still twisting with worry. Maybe she should just walk around the neighborhood instead. Maybe she should go back home in case Caleb came back. But...

The idea of waiting in the trailer, jumping in hope at every sound, was too painful. She was going to have a long night of that when she got back. Any delay would be better than that.

She turned to walk toward town without answering.

"I know you probably don't like me much—"

"You made fun of me ever since I've been here," she said flatly, not looking at him as he walked beside her.

"I know. I'm really sorry. I was a dick. I just...I didn't know how to talk to girls. Especially, you know...pretty girls."

Her steps halted, and she turned to face him, wrapping her arms around herself.

"Look, I don't know what you're up to, but I'm tired of being made fun of. So just get it out. Whatever you're waiting to say, just get it over with."

His eyes grew huge, and his mouth opened and closed multiple times without a sound.

"I...well, I guess...I guess I wanted to tell you that—that you looked real pretty today. Like really pretty. I mean, obviously you did, but, well, I just wanted to say it, I guess," he finished, looking pale.

Nat's brow furrowed so deeply it hurt.

"That makes no sense."

His eyes fell to the ground.

"Sorry. I'm not very good with words," he mumbled.

Nat stared at him harder.

"I meant it makes no sense to say I looked pretty. Everyone was making fun of me."

His eyes jerked up in surprise.

"Who! I didn't hear anyone making fun of you!"

"Just…everyone I saw. They'd just sort of…give a little laugh and turn away."

His eyebrows lifted.

"Ohhh…you mean the girls."

"Well, yeah. But guys were staring and sometimes made sounds."

Preston rubbed his brow, staring at her hesitantly.

"You know guys are kind of…dumb. Especially when they're thinking with their…you know."

Nat swallowed. Was he saying the boys were like the creep? That's what they were thinking? Her vision blurred slightly, and she looked down.

"Oh, shit, I'm sorry. I didn't mean anything bad. I mean, it's a compliment, really. They just all thought you looked really good."

Her lashes flew back up.

"Nobody said that. Nobody said I looked nice at all."

"Well, jeez, no. Not with your brother ready to kill anyone who looked at you!"

"He was just ashamed of me," she said quietly.

Preston snorted.

"I mean, no brother wants to think about his sister getting fucked—oh, shit—I mean, I don't have a sister, but I know a lot of guys try to make their sisters feel bad when guys want them. But he's just going to have to get used to it. You're super pretty!"

"You always called me Medusa," she whispered.

He groaned, covering his face.

"Why do you have to keep bringing up the things I did as a kid?"

"It was last year."

"Yeah, before high school! I'm not some immature middle schooler anymore!"

She couldn't seem to do anything except stare.

"You really hurt me." Her voice sounded so small to her ears. "For a long time. You and your friend. And the girl you walk with. You made fun of me every day. You threw things at me."

"God, that was *kid stuff.* Kids do shit like that all the time!"

Nat stared again. She shouldn't have said anything. It was pointless. And walking out here with him was probably stupid anyhow.

She turned to go but went rigid when he grabbed her arm.

"Oh, come on. You *have* to forgive me. It's not like I ever meant any of it!"

She heard the snarl before he did, and everything went still. Preston had his head cocked just a bit as he stood pleading with her. Just enough.

Nat didn't hesitate and grabbed his neck a split second before Caleb's fangs sank into her hand and his body took them all to the ground.

———

Caleb jerked away with a high pitched yelp, and Nat grabbed her hand, pressing down on the wound as she knelt on the hard pavement and looked over at him, her heart thundering in her chest.

He hadn't gone. She wanted to throw her arms around him and cry. Sing. Just…everything.

But he was jerking his head back and forth while he backed away, yelping and whining, and her eyes darted down to where Preston was lying on the ground.

Relief filled her. He seemed to be in shock but was otherwise unhurt, and her eyes flew back to Caleb, his whine growing longer, piercing the silence of the night.

"It's okay," she whispered, holding her hand out to him, the small trickle of blood moving in a slow line across her skin. "It didn't go too deep."

"HELP—" Nat turned and slammed her bloodied hand over Preston's mouth, blocking his yell.

"*Do not say anything!*" she hissed, and his eyes widened as he stared up at her. But he nodded. Releasing him carefully, she looked around to make sure no one had heard before turning back to Caleb.

His head was low, his whine a soft, constant sound, and she held her hand out once more.

"I'm sorry." Her eyes begged him to forgive her. "Don't go. Please don't go."

Except he shouldn't be on the sidewalk where someone might come out and see him. He was in the shadows, but if anyone turned on a nearby porch light, that could change quickly.

"Please go home," she whispered, too low for Preston to hear.

Caleb's whine grew, his head lowering even further.

"Please," she said thickly, tears springing to her eyes.

He stepped towards her, his whine never abating, until his muzzle just touched her fingertips and his tongue reached out to lick the blood from her hand. Every pained sound from his throat sent an ache to her heart, and her arm fell slowly. He stepped closer, licking her, until she could lean against him at last, his tongue still stroking her wounded skin.

"You're like the wolf whisperer," Preston breathed, starting to sit up but freezing when Caleb jerked his head toward him, snarling.

"Shhh…don't scare him anymore," Nat whispered, wrapping both arms around Caleb's neck and petting him softly. "And don't hurt him. He's just a stupid boy."

He turned his face into her, his whine returning.

"Will you…go home? I'm scared someone else will see you. Some coyotes killed someone, and there are too many hunters around here."

He grew heavy against her for a moment, his huge frame leaning on her small one, but she felt him nod. Her arms fell from his neck, and she started to stand, only to stop when he stepped over her body, forcing her to lean back and preventing her from moving. She lifted her head to look at him, and her breath caught in her throat.

Every bit of the wolf she'd seen the first time they met stood above her, his fangs bared and mere inches from Preston's face while a low, fierce growl rolled from his throat. His massive paws with their sharp claws were planted over her body protectively—possessively—and his message couldn't have been more clear.

Stay away.

Preston trembled, staring up at the enormous dark form.

"Wh—what do I do, Natty?" he whispered, jumping when Caleb snarled. Nat hesitated.

"Just…go on home. Or wherever you were going. You don't have to worry—he won't hurt you."

Caleb's vicious bark didn't agree, and Nat looked at the houses around them nervously. Preston began inching away.

"Preston, you won't tell anyone?" her voice had a touch of desperation in it.

He had crawled back far enough to risk standing on shaky legs, and he shook his head, keeping his eyes locked on Caleb.

"What would I say? You have a giant wolf?" he whispered, his eyes huge in his face. "Who would believe me?"

A nearby porch light came on, and Nat's heart raced. Caleb was still in the shadows, but if anyone came outside, it wouldn't take long to spot him. She pushed at him, trying to sit up, but he wouldn't budge, his eyes locked on Preston while the pale boy continued backing away.

"Better get it out of here, Natty. The guy in that house has a shotgun, and I dunno if he'd even care if we were standing close enough to get shot, too."

Caleb did react at that, grabbing Nat's wrist gently between his jaws and pulling her back toward the trailer.

"Geez. It's almost like it understands…"

Preston's whisper trailed behind her as Nat stumbled to her feet to follow Caleb.

"He's really smart—thanks, Preston!" she called out in a loud whisper. She walked quickly beside Caleb, trying to tug her hand from his mouth but giving up with a sigh when he ignored her. He didn't release her until she had opened the trailer door, and he pushed her through with a nudge of his head.

Her mother stirred as they walked in, but Caleb kept pushing her back to her room.

"Honey…? Did we get a dog?"

The slurred voice followed them down the hall, and Nat hoped she would just go back to sleep. She closed her bedroom door quickly as soon as they were in the room, locking it and leaning her head against the door.

Her heart pounded uncomfortably. She was wearing his clothes. And the things she'd said earlier…everything he'd overheard at school…the walking talking cringe fest that was her…

Nat closed her eyes. She didn't want to face him.

A sound behind her told her Caleb had shifted. She heard him pulling on what must have been jeans because a zipper sounded after a few moments. Then silence.

"Nat…" His voice was hoarse, and the sound sent a deep pang to her heart. "I never…*never* wanted you to change."

Her head turned to the side, looking at him from the corner of her eye.

"I can see how it looked that way…now," he whispered. "But all I wanted to do was—"

When he stopped talking, Nat turned slowly to face him, and the sight took her breath away.

His head was down while he stared at the floor, his dark, glossy locks falling forward on his forehead. The strong lines of his face were etched in masculine perfection above his bare, broad shoulders, strong arms, and well muscled chest. A soft line of dark hair trailed from his navel over the gentle ridges of his abs to the open button of his jeans, and she shivered as her mind conjured images of what she knew was below.

His eyes darted up to hers suddenly, hopeful but wary, and she dropped hers. Sometimes it wasn't so great that he was a wolf.

"I don't think it's really fair to keep kissing me, Caleb, and then just suddenly go out with someone else," she said, drawing a shaky breath as she tried to get her body under control. "It…it's like suddenly getting hit in the stomach when you didn't know someone was about to hit you."

A short whine sounded in his throat.

"But I didn't! I just wanted to ask her about clothes!"

Her eyes lifted to his reluctantly to see his own wide and pleading.

"You were checking her out at her locker. We all saw. And…it was pretty obvious you liked what you saw," she swallowed, trying to get past the pain in her gut.

"I was thinking of the things I could put on you! I just thought it would look good on you—that I would be able to see you better during the day—but…it was a really stupid idea," he muttered, looking back down.

Nat dropped her eyes as well, the sick feeling growing again.

"Sorry," she whispered.

He crossed the small space and pulled her firmly to his chest before she could take a breath, a hand in her hair pulling her head back to look up at his stern eyes.

"No, Nat! No no no! You were the most disturbingly, terrifying, horribly—" His voice was choked, and he growled in frustration at the growing hurt in her eyes—"*beautiful beautiful beautiful* girl in the whole world, which I already knew!"

His volume grew as he continued, the frustration of the day filling his voice.

"But I *didn't* know what your nipples looked like and then it was *all I could think about* all day, and I almost shifted every single time I looked at you, and every single guy was thinking horrible horrible horrible things—no, Nat, not that kind of horrible— horrible for *me*! Horrible because I don't want anyone else thinking about your nipples! Or what it would be like to have them in his mouth!"

"And I was in pain all day," he whined, leaning his head against her wide eyed face, "and I'm still in pain and I'm so frustrated that my body doesn't work the way other boys' bodies work and there is nothing I can *do* to make the pain go away!"

Nat's chest heaved, each breath dragging her breasts against his chest, and she shivered when the friction hardened her nipples once again. A deep groan left his throat, and his hands slid down to the hem of her shirt. His shirt.

"Can I see?" he whispered, his hands slipping underneath slowly. Her breath caught when his skin touched hers, his warm, soft hands flattening against her waist and slowly sliding up her ribcage.

Her lashes fluttered up to see his brow creased in a deep line.

"Doesn't this hurt too much?" she whispered.

His heavy lidded eyes met hers, and her heart jumped.

"Everything hurts," he whispered. "Being close to you is like playing with fire. But if I step away, it's cold. So fucking cold. And I'd rather burn than freeze to death. And when I thought you wanted me to go..."

His hands splayed around her ribs as a shudder went through him, and she raised a hand tentatively to his cheek, stroking softly. He shuddered again and nuzzled her palm.

"I don't ever want to hurt that way again. I can take anything except that."

He paused, his lashes falling to stare at the dried blood on the back of her hand.

"I'm so sorry," he whispered thickly, his eyes filling with guilt. Too much guilt.

A small sound escaped Nat's throat, and she reached down quickly and pulled his shirt over her head, dropping it to rest her hands on his shoulders.

Caleb froze, his eyes falling to her chest, blinking constantly, and Nat struggled to breathe while he stared at the hard pink tips moving up and down on his bare chest with every breath she took.

Her own body was on fire, heat pooling between her legs until she couldn't stand it and a small whimper escaped her.

The sound broke through his trance and he groaned, his arms wrapping around her and lifting her body as he bent his head to gently suck one of the hard, pink nubs into his warm, wet lips.

Nat gasped, her arms coming up to hold his head, and he moaned into her, pressing her into the door, a deep whine growing in his throat while desire pierced her body.

And then a zipper sounded just before the cold air surrounded her and she collapsed on her knees. His whine changed, the long, pained sound from his wolf form sounding more like a light howl. Her arms wrapped around her chest, and he licked her neck in long, slow strokes, the heat of his tongue soothing her as shivers of unquenched longing continued flowing through her body.

His tongue lapped at her shoulders, her hands, reaching between her arms and her body, and she groaned in frustration, trying to push him away as the edge teased at a nipple.

Caleb pressed in closer as the movement gave him greater access, the spread of his tongue covering her nipple completely.

"Caleb, would you stop!" she said, exasperated, but he ignored her and she whimpered, leaning her head back against the door while he continued licking her.

She reached up to pet him with a sigh.

"You know, you're impossible."

Then she leaned in to wrap her arms around him, preventing him from licking any further, and smiled at his whine. She held him close for a long time, stroking his fur, before finally pulling back.

She needed to go clean up her hand. The cut wasn't too deep, but she didn't want it getting infected.

A giggle escaped her when Caleb tried licking her once more, and she shoved his muzzle away, ignoring his light bark as she stood. She thought she saw a bright spot of pink on his stomach for a moment, but he bounded to his feet with her and she shrugged it away, reaching for his shirt again before going to clean up.

———

"Dammit, Caleb—you gave them to me—they're mine!"

Nat was still in her towel and needed to get dressed, but she was too busy playing tug of war with Caleb over one of the few remaining dresses Heather had given her. He'd already torn apart the majority of them before she could stop him.

He growled and shook his head back and forth viciously, ripping it from her fingers and tearing a cry from her when he dragged his claws and fangs through it. She grabbed the remaining clothes and ran from the room, slamming the bathroom door before he could reach her. Her heart pounded against the cold surface as she leaned against it in relief, listening to him whine and claw at the carpet on the other side.

A jolt of alarm went through her when he went silent, and she slammed her hand on the lock a moment before he tried opening the door.

"Nat..." he whined, shoving against the door. "I can't go through another day like yesterday."

"Caleb, if you break this door, I swear I'll...I'll...I will wear one of the torn dresses and let *everyone* see *everything*!"

"Not if I bury them first," he snarled, hitting the door again, harder.

"Then I'll sleep in my mom's room by myself from now on!" she cried in a panic. "I swear I will!"

He went quiet.

"You wouldn't," he said, but she heard the doubt in his voice.

"I would!" she nodded emphatically, even though he couldn't see her. Or know she was lying. "Caleb...let me try again. I can cover my nipples with tape. Let me try to look...I don't know. Normal," she finished morosely, turning to lean her forehead against the door.

She heard him exhale in a short burst before he whined again.

"I don't want everybody to see you, Nat..."

"How do you think I feel all the time! Girls drool over you constantly!"

"But guys are different," he whined.

"How would you know! That is the most chauvinistic... ridiculous..." her strangled tones couldn't seem to make it past her throat, and she took a deep breath.

"I'll cover up, too!" His voice was so bright and hopeful, she couldn't help laughing even as she groaned.

"Caleb…I've felt so bad for so long at school. Please…just give me a chance to try to fit in. I…" Her stomach clenched. A chance to fit in? The girls weren't going to think any better of her for wearing Heather's clothing. And evidently the guys were just thinking about sex. What was she even doing.

Her shoulders slumped, and she leaned against the door weakly for a long moment before opening it. She shoved the clothes into Caleb's arms and walked past him, trying not to think about his very gorgeous naked body.

"Nat." His voice was soft as he stopped her, holding the clothes to the side and lifting her chin. Her lashes stayed down, and he pressed his lips to hers for a moment. "I'm sorry."

"Forget it. It was stupid. I don't know anything about that stuff anyway."

"What are you talking about," he breathed against her lips, nibbling at them. "You just about tore the school apart yesterday. You can be whatever you want."

She gasped at the sudden feel of his skin when he pulled her close, dropping his face into her neck with a groan.

"I can suffer through it." The muffled sounds couldn't hide his petulance, and she pinched her lips together, trying very hard not to laugh. And trying not to think about only her towel being between them.

"You're a baby."

"I know," he muttered, but then raised his head with a hopeful look. "But aren't you supposed to take care of babies?"

"You're suppose to put them in time out when they're old enough to know better," she snapped but kissed him quickly before grabbing the clothes back. His mournful sigh trailed behind her as she went to finish getting ready.

A half hour later, she stood in front of him, worry filling her eyes.

"Is it okay? Does it look stupid?"

The scotch tape she'd tried hadn't stayed on her skin, so she just put one of her old, thin cardigans over the green spaghetti strap maxi dress. She'd done her hair and makeup the same as the previous day, and she *thought* it looked pretty. Even with the ankle boots. Actually, she kind of liked the look with the boots, even though she hadn't seen anyone at her school wearing their dresses that way.

She glanced up at Caleb, and he looked so miserable staring at her, all her worries evaporated. His eyes widened when she launched herself at him, throwing her arms around him tightly and closing her eyes, a happy smile stretching across her face.

"Thank you," she murmured, nuzzling him with a sigh.

His head dropped to hers, and he held her close, breathing her in for a moment before pulling her toward the door with a sigh.

"Come on. We're going to miss the bus, and it's getting too cold for you to walk so far. I shouldn't have dragged you home like I did yesterday." His eyes avoided hers, guilt in his voice again, and she squeezed his hand tightly before dropping it as they exited the trailer.

"Can't we just be a brother and sister who hold hands?" he asked.

Nat sputtered and covered her mouth as she looked up at his wistful expression, shaking her head.

"Well…can't we just…stop pretending then?"

Her brows lifted and her lips parted with a bit of a smile.

"Yes… But social services will make us both live with someone else because my mom is on probation. If she gets caught for faking everything, she won't be allowed to keep *either* of us."

When he didn't look convinced, she continued.

"And then even if miraculously they gave us to the same foster family, we would never be allowed to sleep in the same room. So would you rather pretend," she whispered as they drew close to the bus stop, "and still be able to sleep together or stop pretending and probably only see each other at school?"

He glared at her, not liking the choices.

"Well I don't see why we can't just be a really close brother and sister," he whispered back.

Her laughter bubbled over, and she put both fists to her mouth, her eyes bright with horrified amusement.

"Caleb...if we did that the way you're thinking, social services would *definitely* take one of us away."

He crossed his arms, his expression grumpy and spoiled, and she laughed behind her hands. Nobody had told him *no* for nine long years. He still had a hard time with not getting his own way.

Nat squeezed her eyes together tightly, trying to get rid of the feelings she feared she must be showing in them every time she looked at him. When she opened them again, he was staring at her. Not like a brother.

His eyes fell to her lips, and she turned quickly.

"Bus is here!"

She heard his frustrated exhale and bit her lip. God, she couldn't remember ever being this happy. Or feeling so completely beautiful. Or liked. Or...

Her heart skipped a beat, and she swallowed. She could feel Caleb looking at her while they sat on the bus, but she just stared out the window, feeling the warmth of his thigh pressed against hers, of his arm through the lighter jacket she'd worn. Her eyes closed, and she let the heat flow through her, the memory of his lips on hers, on her breast...

Caleb shifted and leaned over to whisper in her ear.

"Nat, if you don't stop whatever you're doing, I'm not going to be able to control myself." His voice was hoarse. Urgent. Her eyes flew to his to see his brow drawn in a severe line.

"Sorry," she whispered, a small smile at the corner of her mouth. "I'm just happy."

His brows raised in pained, frustrated delight, and he

groaned and dropped his head back against the seat, closing his eyes and holding his stomach.

"Talk to me, Nat. About something really boring."

So she did. And all throughout the day, they made sure to keep talking about boring, monotonous topics, trying to distract their minds. But Nat could barely keep her thoughts in check, even so.

It wasn't until the last period of the day, when she sat in class allowing her thoughts full reign while Caleb wasn't around, when she let the scene replay in her mind over and over of Caleb at lunch loudly calling out Megan for being an ugly, jealous c—well. She wouldn't repeat the word he'd used but she couldn't help feeling completely warmed by him championing her. Or delighted by his very public scorn of all the girls who had been mean to her. It wasn't until she was completely lost in so many beautiful thoughts that something tore her thoughts away from her daydreams.

In the end, it was such a small thing that did it. Two little words. Just a name. But when she heard it, when she realized whose body had been torn apart, everything came crashing down inside her. Because she knew. It couldn't be a mere coincidence. She knew.

Caleb—her beautiful, glorious wolf—was a murderer.

8

"Are you mad at me again already?" Caleb frowned down at her while they sat on the bus, and Nat shook her head fiercely, her eyes soft on his.

"No, Caleb. I'm so not mad at you."

His frown remained, and he crossed his arms.

"Then why don't you smell like before?"

A light whimper sounded in her throat. What could she say?

"Caleb…did you hear about…what happened? To that—that guy?"

His eyes grew guarded, and he uncrossed his arms and threaded his fingers together, staring down at his hands between his legs.

"What guy?" He rubbed the edge of his perfectly trimmed nails, and she watched him for only a moment before sagging back against the seat and turning to look out the window once more.

He was silent for a while before speaking in a quiet voice.

"Are you mad now?"

"No," she whispered, not looking at him. Mad at him for slaying her dragon? For caring so much? Never.

But she was scared. So very scared that he would get himself in trouble—get hurt—trying to protect her. And there was another fear. A fear she'd been trying so desperately not to think about. Not to believe.

Caleb had been on his own for a long time with no one to tell him *no*, and she adored how spoiled that had made him in so many ways. How completely cocky he could be. But this…

"Caleb," she continued whispering, trusting he could hear her even though she could barely hear herself. "When you attacked Preston, what were you going to do?"

The bus cranked to a stop, and kids around them got to their feet, walking down the aisle laughing and talking loudly. The smell of old vinyl and oil assaulted her nose as a chill wind swirled into the confined space until the door closed once again and the bus jerked forward.

And still Caleb hadn't answered.

Nat turned to face him at last. He sat staring at his thumbs, chewing on the inside of his lip a bit, but his eyes lifted to hers when she turned.

"He was mean to you." His tone was blunt. Unapologetic.

Nat grabbed her head, her eyes wide and her lips parting.

"You can't—you can't just go around—Caleb, you can't *do* that!" she rasped.

He cocked a brow at her.

"Yes, I can."

Her hands gripped her hair painfully, a high pitched wail of a breath coming from her lungs, and he grinned.

"You look really cute right now."

Her brows were ready to disappear into her hair as she wheezed, and she turned back toward the window, desperately trying to breathe normally. He was a beautiful, adorable, wonderful, completely perfect *psycho*. What was she supposed to do?

———

"Caleb, would you listen!"

He was lying on top of her, tugging down her neckline, and he whimpered until he freed her breasts.

"I'm listening," he whispered, his lips dropping to suck her gently into his mouth. She shoved at his shoulders, trying to think.

"Caleb…" she whined in defeat when he ignored her. "You can't go around killing people just because they're mean to me. You can't go around killing people *at all*."

"Why not?" he murmured against her skin, his brow furrowed in pain.

"Because it's *wrong*!"

His head lifted for a moment, and he frowned at her.

"What they did was wrong."

"Well, yes, but it doesn't deserve *death*."

A harsh, feral look entered his eyes.

"Yes it does."

But he dropped his mouth back to her breast once more, this time circling a pink tip with the tip of his tongue. A shiver went through her, and she slid her fingers between his mouth and her skin, covering her nipples. He looked up sadly at her for a moment before his eyes grew bright.

"No. There are laws and rules and when people do bad things, then—what are you doing?" Alarm sounded in her voice when her skirt slid up.

"I want to see everything." Interest lit his eyes as he leaned to the side to let his hand slide up her leg. She clamped her thighs together tightly, sitting up and shoving the skirt down between her legs, ignoring his mournful look.

"Caleb, you're spoiled! You are a big spoiled *puppy*!" She smacked his hand when he cupped her breast again and groaned when he leaned in to kiss her neck. He was impossible.

Although...

Her hand pulled at his hair until he lifted his face to hers, and she leaned forward to tease his lips with the tip of her tongue, sliding it deep inside his mouth and catching his hoarse cry just before he shifted.

Nat sputtered with laughter. Caleb stood whining on the bed, his jeans still covering his lower body awkwardly while his t-shirt stretched around his large furry chest. His whine grew more insistent, and he nipped at the fabric.

"Okay okay, wait! I'll get it," she chuckled, reaching down to unsnap his pants, trying not to pull his fur in the process. When he continued whining, trying to figure out how to get the clothes off, she sat back and crossed her arms.

"No, we need to have a talk. A *real* talk. So no more kissing—you have to take this seriously!"

He stood staring at her, his whine light but steady, but she refused to be swayed. Instead, she adjusted her clothing and pulled her bare feet up under her skirt, wrapping her arms around her knees while she waited. Eventually he shifted back, exhaling in a short grunt as he adjusted his own clothes before leaning back against the wall and crossing his arms.

"Fine."

He looked so adorably put out, she almost crawled over to him. Then she reminded herself that he was basically a serial killer—or a would-be serial killer...

"How many people have you killed?"

"Lately?"

He grinned when she sputtered.

"Just kidding. Just the one. For now."

Nat wanted to flop back on the bed in relief. But she tensed again almost immediately.

"Would you lie to me?"

Caleb hesitated, and her stomach sank. He exhaled in a short burst.

"I don't *want* to lie to you."

"Oh…well that is super reassuring, Caleb."

He started to grin again but bit the inside of his cheek when she glared at him.

"I'm not lying. I swear. My parents told me not to kill any humans, so I didn't. Besides, I didn't go around any until you, other than an occasional hiker I'd scare off. I'm not stupid. I know people would come looking around if bodies went missing in my woods."

Nat bit her lip.

"Your parents…wouldn't want you doing this then," she said softly. He hadn't talked about them, and she hadn't wanted to risk making him feel bad by asking him questions.

Caleb shrugged.

"Yeah, but they also said that if I ever had to break a rule, the most important rule was not to let anyone see me shift. So really, they would have wanted me to kill *you*."

Nat was surprised at the level of pain those words gave her, and Caleb frowned immediately.

"I wouldn't have ever done that though."

Her eyes fell. She knew that. Or she believed it, at least. But…it just felt somehow like his parents disapproved of her, even from beyond the grave.

"Hey," he breathed, reaching out to put his arms around her and pulling her onto his lap when she tried pushing him away. "What did I do?"

A sigh left her, and she leaned on his shoulder, letting him stroke her back.

"I just would have liked if your parents liked me, that's all."

His arms tightened around her fiercely.

"They would have *loved* you, Nat. Because…well, because *I* love you!"

The heat from his body suddenly began radiating off him in waves, and Nat was drowning in them, her eyes locked on the skin of his neck. She could feel his heart racing, and her own hammered against her chest unsteadily. Silence surrounded them but for their short breaths, and she swallowed, slowly tilting her head up to see him watching her with nervous eyes. And all the tension left her as a smile spread across her face and into her eyes.

"I love you, too." She pressed her lips together after she said it, feeling silly, but she'd meant it.

The nervousness faded from Caleb's eyes, replaced by a warm, soft expression, and he reached a hand up to stroke her cheek in gentle, slow strokes. His eyes fell to her lips, and he lowered his head. Nat's hand came up quickly to rest against his lips.

"Wait," she breathed. "Please don't kill anyone else. Please…"

Her hand drifted to stroke his cheek softly while frustration touched his eyes.

"I have to protect you."

"You can protect me without killing anyone! And—and there's this thing called accessory after the fact, or something. I heard one of my mom's old boyfriends talking about it. Basically, if you kill someone and I don't turn you in, which I would never, ever do, then we both go to jail. Or even get killed! They have the death penalty here."

His brow pulled together.

"I don't want you to get hurt."

"And I don't want you to!" Her eyes pleaded with him. "Please, Caleb. Find another way. Please don't kill."

His exhale was long and low, and he stared at her intently. Nat held her breath. Waiting.

Finally he groaned and dropped his forehead to hers, and she released her breath with a sigh of relief.

"Okay. But don't talk to Preston anymore. Because I'm not promising to let him keep his hands if he touches you again," he said testily.

Nat grinned up at him.

"Deal."

His eyes drifted back and forth from her eyes to her mouth before his lashes finally fell and he leaned down to press his lips to hers once more. And everything was exquisitely soft and perfect for just a few minutes before he had to shift again.

———

"Psst, Nat!"

Nat sat in detention, managing to do a bit of homework for once. Caleb was at practice, and she usually ended up watching him instead of getting anything done. And once they got home, he was a far more active distraction, particularly since they'd used the L word a week ago.

"Nat!"

She groaned inwardly. If she kept ignoring him, he might try talking to her when detention was over and Caleb would be there to meet her. And Preston might be a jerk, but she really didn't want him maimed. Or worse.

Her eyes lifted from her textbook at last, and she looked over to see him sitting at the desk beside her with his book propped in front of him in a way no student ever did unless they were hiding something. Nat's eyes darted to the teacher up at the front of the room. He was engrossed in whatever he was looking at on his phone, his feet up on his desk, so Nat turned back to Preston.

"Have you seen it again?" he asked in a low voice.

Nat flared her eyes at him briefly, glancing around pointedly at the handful of other kids scattered throughout the classroom.

No one seemed to be paying attention to them, but she didn't want to risk anything about Caleb being overheard.

"He ran off," she mouthed back, turning to her homework once again. Her eyes closed when she heard Preston scooting his desk closer to her, and she rubbed her temples.

"It's a boy? Cool. He'll be back though, right?" His arm nearly touched hers when he leaned in, and Nat lifted her eyes to the teacher again hopefully. No luck. He hadn't budged.

"Preston, I don't think we should talk about this here."

"No one can hear. And your brother's always around. I don't think he likes me."

No shit.

"How long has the wol—" he stopped at her insistent look. "The…dog been around?"

Caleb would love that.

"Not long. And he's gone now, so…"

Preston refused to take the hint.

"Can you charm other animals? How did you get it to like you?"

Nat could see there was no use trying to get out of the conversation. Maybe if she answered his questions, he'd scoot back before Caleb showed up.

"I can't charm anything. He's just nice."

Preston snorted.

"Nice to people who aren't mean," she frowned.

"I'm not mean, Natty! Not anymore…not to you."

The soft, pleading look in his eyes disturbed her more than his former insults ever had.

"Why are you even in here?" he asked.

"Mrs. Smith's homework policy," she muttered, trying not to look at his eyes. "I have like a ten day backlog I was supposed to serve from before."

"Holy shit," he grinned. "I thought you were a good student."

Another frown touched her lips.

"And what are you doing in here?" she asked before she thought better of it.

"I was giving myself a tattoo in science class." He lifted the hem of his shirt to show her an angry reddened patch of skin with black ink carving out a pattern that looked suspiciously like the beginnings of a wolf—on a surprisingly cut set of abs.

Heat rushed to her skin, and she turned back to her homework.

"Preston, you can't keep talking to me. My brother will kill you."

He shrugged, dropping his shirt.

"Meh. He can't be any worse than my old man. I can take pain."

Nat stilled.

"Your dad hits you?"

"He drinks a lot. And he's a total asshole. Put 'em together…" he shrugged again. "But I'm almost as tall as he is now. And I'm working out. Pretty soon, he won't be hitting me anymore."

Her chest constricted at the bravado in his voice, but his look of interest returned quickly.

"So where did he go? Does he just run around in the woods?"

"I don't know," she said with a breath of exasperation. "He just goes. And he's gone. So can we stop talking now?"

Hesitation entered his eyes. And hurt. *No.* She was not going to feel sorry for him! This was *Preston.* He had harassed her forever! But she chewed the inside of her lip.

"Have you ever told anyone? About your dad?" She should at least ask this.

"I'm not a wuss," he frowned. "I can handle it."

"But you shouldn't have to. Maybe if social services got involved, it would scare him and he'd stop."

Preston snorted again.

"My old man doesn't scare easy. And *I'm* gonna be the one to make him stop."

"What about your mom? Does she try to stop him?"

He waved his hand.

"She left a long time ago. Haven't heard from her in years."

"I'm sorry," she whispered, unable to stop her eyes from glistening.

"Whatever. I don't care," he said, surprising Nat by moving back to his spot and grabbing his textbook, pretending to read.

She stared at him a moment, unsure what to say, before turning back to face forward, her eyes drifting up absently toward the teacher.

Her airway closed in an instant as she met a pair of furious amber eyes watching her from the doorway.

———

"You promised." Caleb seethed as they walked out of the school, the crisp November air swirling around them. He hadn't said a word to her once detention had ended, instead staring at Preston in a cold fury. Not that Preston had noticed—he hadn't looked back once in Nat's direction since he'd pulled away.

"I tried! I swear I did!"

"What do you mean you tried? You said you wouldn't talk! You talked!"

"I just—I didn't want to hurt his feelings…"

"So you hurt mine instead?" he demanded, looking over at her with burning eyes.

"I was trying to get him to move away before you came back!"

His look of outrage pulled a groan from her.

"I just mean I didn't want to be talking to him, and I was trying to hurry up and get him to stop. Caleb…" she whimpered. "Don't be mad. I don't want to be talking to him."

"I can make him stop talking," he hissed, and she grabbed his arm, turning him to face her.

"You can't!"

"I can. And if you can break your promise, I can break mine!"

"That is not even close to the same thing," she hissed back at him, glaring up into his eyes. "I'm trying to be nice to someone who was mean to me, and *you're* trying to say you can kill him because you're mad he's talking to me!"

"You're twisting this around! I'm saying that if you can lie, I can lie!"

"I didn't lie! I was trying to do what I said!"

"Great. So when I try not to kill him and fail, you'll understand," he snapped, pulling away from her and taking long strides forward toward the form walking a good distance in front of them.

Nat scurried behind to grab his arm again, trying to hold him back.

"Caleb, this is crazy—and you can't act like this if you want to live in the human world!"

"I can if I can get away with it. And I can get away with it easy."

"Dammit!" she exploded, digging her heels in while she tried to slow him. "You are so pig headed! This isn't about protecting me. You're just mad that some other boy is being nice to me!"

Caleb stopped so suddenly she plowed into his back.

"So that's how you see him now? Not the asshole who threw things at you—"

"They were just snowb—"

"But someone nice to you," he continued, his eyes narrowing as he turned to face her.

"I see him," she said, a bit out of breath, "as a poor dumb kid who…may not have been as bad as I'd thought he was. And you can *stop* that look right now! You were in Heather's *room* with her for a long time all by yourself doing plenty of talking, so you don't get to be all upset at me for talking to a boy!"

"I never promised not to talk to Heather though."

"And I never threatened to kill her!"

"And I wouldn't try to stop you if you had!"

Nat smacked her hands over her eyes.

"What kind of insane thinking…" She took a deep breath, trying to get her strangled sounds to form words and let her hands fall back to her sides. "Caleb, are you seriously telling me you don't care about anyone else's life? At all?"

He crossed his arms and looked away, but his eyes held a measure of uncertainty.

"I just would understand, that's all," he muttered.

"So if I decided to just start killing everyone I didn't like, you'd think that was fine?"

"You could never do that."

"Duh. Of course I could never do that—I'm not a psychopath! And I don't think you are, either! Or you wouldn't have been so nice to me in the woods, and you wouldn't have tried to protect me ever since then."

She drew a shaky breath, more than a little relieved at the growing doubt in his eyes, although he avoided meeting her gaze.

"Caleb…I know you have had a lot of new rules—and you've been soooo great about them. But this one isn't just a rule. It's something you *feel*. And you must have felt it, too, because you never killed anyone before," she said, dropping her voice to a whisper.

He looked down at their feet, his arms still crossed.

"You think I'm bad now? For what I did?"

Her lips parted, and she reached her hands up to cup his face, hoping no one was looking.

"No, Caleb," she breathed. "I think you are a hero."

Her thumbs brushed his cheeks as his lashes lifted at last, his eyes vulnerable.

"I never killed anyone before. And I didn't feel bad about it."

"I don't feel bad about it either. He was a disgusting, horrible person."

Her hands slipped from his face reluctantly, but he grabbed her wrists, holding them in place.

"Somebody might see us," she said in a low voice, her eyes soft.

"Do you still love me?"

"Caleb," she breathed, looking at his worried eyes. "There's nothing you could do that could make me stop loving you...not ever. But I'd rather love you *not* killing off every boy who talks to me or everyone who does something bad to me."

He leaned his head into her palm, rubbing his cheek against her skin, his expression a bit sulky but with a grudging acceptance.

"I don't like him."

Nat sighed.

"I know. But maybe...trust me a little? I don't want to be super mean to anyone, and I do feel a bit sorry for him now, but that's all it is. I don't like Preston. I don't feel anything for anyone...except you."

His lids grew heavy, and his voice was husky when he spoke.

"I do trust you. I just don't like sharing you." He exhaled. "But I guess...I can suffer through it," he finished, almost pouting. Then he leaned in too quickly for her to move and kissed her before grinning and stepping back. Her hands flew to her cheeks, and she looked around.

"Caleb!" she whispered, staring ahead at where Preston had been...looking over his shoulder?

Caleb glanced up at the retreating form and shrugged.

"Did he see? Good. Maybe now he'll stay away."

"Or tell the whole school!"

"We can just say he's lying. Problem solved!" he grinned, grabbing her hand and starting to walk again.

She jerked her hand from his and held her fists to her chest while they walked.

"Unless you keep making it look bad in front of everyone!" she wailed.

"I'm just a guy who really loves his sister. What's so wrong with that?"

Nat groaned and put her hands over her face only to hear him laugh before grabbing her arm.

"You're going to fall if you don't watch where you're going."

She had already fallen, so very hard, and she was going to have to keep on her toes with Caleb if she wanted to keep them —and everyone else—safe.

PART II

CALEB SLAMMED his locker a bit too hard, and his new locker buddy jumped. A freshman kid, all limbs and no muscle yet. Caleb winked at him with a smile, and the boy smiled nervously back before Caleb stalked away, a glower returning to his face as he headed down the hall.

Senior year. Over three years of following this path and everyone still seemed to think he might want to stop and talk to them. *Get out of my way.* But he stopped and chatted, forcing himself to be friendly. Playing the stupid game.

"You still going out with that college girl? Christine, right?"

"Yep," Caleb answered.

"Ever gonna bring her to one of the games?"

"She doesn't want to hang out with high schoolers." Caleb caught a scent and lifted his eyes to scan the crowd, stopping abruptly when he found it. The other boy turned his head.

"Whoa, is the new kid really hitting on your sister? Guess he hasn't met you yet."

Caleb barely heard him, stalking forward and ignoring any further attempts to engage him in conversation.

Nat stood at her locker dressed in a knee length flowing pink dress cut a little too low on breasts that had filled out a good bit in the last few years. She'd paired it with the tan leather flats she wore with everything in the warmer months and no jewelry. Her long brown hair flowed down her back in waves to her waist, and only the faintest hint of makeup touched her face.

She was holding her books in one arm and twinkling up at a poofy haired guy in skinny jeans and glasses leaning against the lockers beside her. There was barely enough room between them for Caleb to slam his shoulder against the cold metal and smile down at the guy while Nat jumped back with a yelp.

"And who are you?" Caleb asked with narrowed eyes.

The kid didn't seem to catch on to the threat but just raised a brow.

"This is my friend Ethan," Nat said, glaring at Caleb and trying to move around him. He bumped her books with his elbow hard enough to dislodge them, and she nearly growled at him as she bent to pick them up.

His suppressed grin quickly turned to a menacing look when the boy bent with her. Or it *should* have been menacing. Ethan must be slow.

"This must be the brother you were telling me about."

Even the kid's voice grated on his nerves. Pompous little shit. Caleb glanced down at Nat to raise a brow, but she didn't lift her eyes, and he narrowed his when she instead smiled at Ethan for handing her a book.

"Why are you even bothering me?" she said. "We were just going to the music room so I can grab a bag for the food drive."

"Great! I'll walk you!"

"I don't need to be walked like a child!"

"Then I guess Ethan won't be needed here," he smiled smoothly, his arms crossed while he stared at the boy.

Ethan looked at Nat, and she rolled her eyes as they stood.

"I'll catch you tomorrow, Ethan. Sorry about this."

"Don't worry about it. I'm used to it. My sister is a bit of a bully, too."

Caleb frowned. He was not a bully. But his frown turned into a glare when the boy looked him up and down.

"At least she's off to college this year. Too bad it looks like your brother was held back."

Caleb almost admired his audacity. Even if he weren't a wolf, he'd hardly have to blow on the kid to make him fall over. But Ethan talked like he was every bit of Caleb's 6'3" of muscle—instead of 5'9" or so of skin and bones. Okay, maybe a bit of muscle, but seriously, did the guy have a death wish?

Nat shoved her books in his arms with a glare, distracting him. And saving him from having to think of a retort. Usually glaring and flexing was all that was required.

"If you're going to harass me, *you* can carry these!"

Caleb bit the inside of his cheek while she said goodbye to Ethan, feeling like he needed to say something to establish his dominance again. But he didn't like being accused of being a bully.

Nat turned back to him once more after Ethan walked away.

"There. Are you happy?"

She didn't lower her voice, and he raised his brow.

"I'm just being a good brother! Ready?" He inclined his head toward the music room, and Nat crossed her arms in a huff, walking beside him down the hall.

The lights were off when they arrived but the back door was open to the outside, presumably for students to come in freely to grab one of the school sponsored bags stacked in a pile on the floor. A closed, windowed door on the left led to a smaller room the music teacher used to store more valuable equipment, and Caleb picked the lock—a skill he'd learned rather quickly once Nat had told him he couldn't just go around killing people to solve his problems—and dragged her inside.

The books fell on the floor as he shoved the door closed and pulled her into his arms along the wall, crushing her lips under his.

"You're going to shift," she murmured, but her hands slid up under his shirt anyway, gliding over the lines of his muscles, and he gripped her harder, the pain in his stomach an almost constant ache. But this always made it so much sharper.

"I'm not going to shift," he muttered, lifting her dress and dragging down her panties, capturing her groan in his mouth. He dropped to his knees and pulled her skirt up, pressing her against the wall, his hands cupping her breasts while they held up her dress, to bury his tongue between her smooth, wet folds.

Her sharp intake of air stabbed into him, but he resisted the pain, pressing into her the way he knew she liked while she cradled his head in her hands, moaning.

"You're going to shift!"

His tongue searched until it found the hard nub, licking and flicking until she was moving her hips helplessly into him. The scent was overwhelming, the exquisite softness surrounding him, her cries…

He tore his clothes off a second before he shifted, trying desperately to push back between her legs as she fell to her knees with a whimper, pushing him away.

"Caleb…" she whined, wrapping her arms around his neck. She groaned into his fur, and he whined, trying to push her back.

"Shh…someone might hear you." She pet him, her hands sliding deep into his fur, and the urge he'd had for the past year to turn her around grew again. He nudged her, hard, but she gripped his fur.

"Will you stop!" she hissed. "You know I'm not doing that!"

His growl turned into a yelp when she yanked his fur.

"And you can stop growling at me!" Her scowl quickly turned into a whine again. "I'm so wet now…"

Caleb pushed her back into the wall hard, trying once more

to reach between her legs, his tongue just slipping between her thighs while she fought to keep him away.

"Caleb, I swear, I will actually start going out with other boys if you don't stop!"

His small yap echoed in the tiny room as he jerked back, frustration causing him to jerk his head back and forth while he backed away—and ran into something.

The sound of cymbals crashing down had Nat desperately reaching for them, and footsteps sounded out in the room.

"Someone in there? Natty...?"

Preston. Of course. No matter how hard Caleb had tried, he just wouldn't let go, always lurking around, watching. Nat had made Caleb invent fake girlfriends over the years, saying it would look too weird for him to never be dating anyone, but he hadn't thought Preston would buy it after the kiss he'd hoped he'd seen. But either he hadn't seen or he'd dismissed it as brotherly, because Preston hadn't gone away.

And now Caleb and Nat had a routine in public, one that had started to frustrate the fuck out of him: fight. It's not that it wasn't fun. It's that it was *too* fun. And the pain got worse every year.

"Stay over there," Nat whispered to him, cracking the door open to lean out.

Caleb stared at her hips, her small and gently rounded cheeks mesmerizing him while she talked to Preston. He didn't even think. He just needed to taste her again.

His muzzle lifted the hem of her skirt, and she froze when his tongue lapped up the inside of her leg. His center burned, the sensation driving away every thought with each slow lick that inched higher and higher along her inner thigh.

She was squirming slightly, the movement hiding and exposing her beautiful, soft lips. He'd tried to reach them for so long like this, and she always kept him just out of reach. He needed this. He hungered for this—he hungered for *her*.

His tongue spread as wide as he could make it, slowly lapping her from front to back, the barest hint of her hard nub gliding under the sensitive flat surface. Her voice sounded choked while she talked to Preston, and Caleb continued lapping in slow, hard strokes. He began letting his tongue curve inward, slipping between her lips at last, and he forced himself not to make a sound as the burning in his body blazed into a roaring fire.

His tongue slipped into her more deeply, and he pushed closer, feeling her jerk while she held herself still. Deeper. More.

And it slipped inside her. A fierce burst of air came from his lungs as he plunged his tongue as deeply as he could go. Her thighs shook around his head, her body flowing into his mouth, and he reached into her, wanting to be inside her. To be a part of her.

His hips began moving and a whine grew in his throat that he wouldn't release. She had to stay like this. She had to keep letting him do this.

He pulled back out and returned to the hard knot between her lips, pressing and gliding his tongue against it, over and over, as his hips continued moving helplessly. Her thighs were gripping his head like a vice, but she was so small compared to him. So soft. And he pressed harder.

The scent overwhelmed him as her body began to spasm, and he licked more furiously, holding her up with his muzzle when her knees gave out. It wasn't enough. He needed so much more. His center was on fire, hotter than he'd ever felt before. He needed *more*.

He yanked his head out from underneath her skirt and started to lift his front legs to wrap around her hips when she turned and shut the door.

"Get...your clothes...back...on..." she choked out between ragged breaths, her face as red as he'd ever seen it. When he tried to move close to her she hit his nose—hard—grabbing his fur when he yelped and started to back away.

"Do *not* run into *anything else!*"

She grabbed her underwear and pulled them on quickly, avoiding looking at him while he sat back, his center consuming him too deeply to risk moving toward her now. So he simply watched her, a soft whine coming from his throat. Not bothering to grab her books, she pulled the door open just enough to slip out, locking it before closing it behind her.

Caleb's eyes fell at last to see an impossibly long, thick, pink protrusion with thin curly veins extending from his center. He blinked down at it. It was huge. He'd never seen more than a pink tip peeking out before. The little pointed tip that looked so different from the head of his human cock, with its little opening at the edge pointing down instead of in the middle. And there was an enormous bulb at the base. The knot.

He had a cock. A working cock. This is what was supposed to go inside the female.

He looked up at the door, the fire at his center blinding him until all he could see was a set of milky white thighs and glistening, ruby lips.

He could put this in Nat.

———

"Nat, get in the car...."

Caleb forced himself to hang on to his temper, but ditching him to walk home with Preston?

"You're holding up traffic," she bit out, not even bothering to look at him. Preston eyed him a bit warily but stayed by Nat's side—where he'd gotten a little too comfortable over the years.

"I'm going to park in the middle of the road in a minute if you don't get in here," he snapped back.

He had bought the car two years before, and he drove it to school every day instead of walking so he could keep his hands on Nat. Which he couldn't do if she wasn't in it.

"I swear, Nat, if you make me late and Christine breaks up with me, I'm going to make sure *everyone* knows why."

Her head jerked towards him, her eyes stormy, but she reached for the door handle when he pulled to a stop.

"See you later, Preston," she muttered, plopping down in the seat and hugging her books to her chest.

"Seatbelt."

She glared at him again as he sat back, waiting, horns blaring behind them. But she yanked the belt across her body, shifting the books away from her just enough to secure it before hugging them to her once again and staring out the window mutinously.

Caleb pulled away from the curb at last, not wanting to look at her now. The shift was too close to the surface. He kept his eyes on the road, fighting back the urge while his stomach twisted in pain. Fighting back the images of tearing Nat's dress off and pushing her down on all fours to mount her…

His grip tightened on the steering wheel hard enough to risk breaking it, and he focused on breathing. Calm down. They'd be home soon enough. Where he could drag her back in the room and force her to accept him, force her to—

What the fuck was wrong with him! Caleb's heart raced, and he turned farther away from Nat, fear pulling at his brow. *This was Nat!* He knew what she'd been through. Jesus.

He ran a hand through his hair and saw Nat glance at him out of the corner of his eye. Tension gripped him, worried she might speak. Worried she might reach out. He needed to go for a run. A long, wild run. It had been quite a while since he'd done it, as the only thing he seemed to want to do anymore in wolf form was breathe in Nat…lick Nat…

He bit his fist hard enough to draw blood, furiously trying to get himself back under control. This should be easy by now. He'd made her cum before—it was always intoxicating. It always made him want more.

But this was the first time he'd realized he could *have* more. The first time he'd brought her to that point as a wolf.

Caleb parked quickly and threw the car door open, gulping in air as quietly as possible. His entire body went rigid when she stormed by him and her scent flew into his nostrils. He shouldn't follow her inside. He should just go. Just run to the woods.

His feet seemed to have a mind of their own, though, and he'd walked through the door almost before he knew it. Her mother was gone for the moment, probably getting a 'prescription' filled. Men didn't come around anymore now that Caleb was here. He stared down the hall where Nat had disappeared into their room. Just leave. Go for a run. She doesn't want to see you right now anyhow.

But he walked down the hall, a heavy heat settling on him as he approached the closed door. Standing and staring down at the handle, he swallowed before leaning his head against the rough wood.

"Nat?" His voice was quiet. Gentle.

That wasn't what he felt right now at all.

A deep line formed between his brow. It was his job to protect her. He was the only one she had.

"Nat, I'm going to go for run," he said more firmly. "And…I might sleep outside tonight. Don't wait up."

Breathing a bit more comfortably, he stepped back, proud of himself. He was just turning to go when she yanked the door open, her eyes blazing.

"Are you kidding me! You're going to do that and not even *apologize*? Just run away?"

His lips parted as he stared at her. She was so fucking beautiful like this. Sparks in her eyes, hair flowing wild down her back, cheeks flushed, breasts heaving…

Caleb stepped back, the pain clawing at his insides, and turned quickly for the door. He had to get out of there.

"Oh no you don't!" Nat grabbed his arm, and his body seized

up at her touch, the sharpness stealing his breath for a moment. "I had to stand there and talk—*talk*, Caleb! While you were… were…you never should have done that!" she exploded, moving around to face him.

Protect her. Caleb fought to hold onto that thought while every instinct he had was urging him to do something very different.

"Nat, I can't talk right now," he said hoarsely, pulling away. When she tried to pull him back with a sharp protest, he jerked out of her grasp and actually ran for the door.

Get out get out get out. He should never have followed her in. This wasn't safe. She wasn't safe.

He tore out of the house, heading toward the woods while she ran after him, her voice a little less angry and bit more concerned now.

He could have run. Making it to the line of the trees and tearing off his clothes to shift would have been a simple thing to do before she could catch up. But he just walked, letting her follow him, the pain growing with every step he took.

Go back, Nat. But he didn't say it out loud this time. His body was on fire, tightening in anticipation as he approached the trees. Just a little longer. Hang on a little longer.

And then he was past the line and tearing off his clothes.

"Don't you dare…shift without…telling me…what's going on!" she huffed, running in right behind him.

Caleb knew he should run. He should shift and run and not be close to her until he had this under control.

But his shirt fell from his hands on the forest floor and his fingers went to unsnap his jeans. He turned slowly, a heat in his eyes beyond anything he'd felt before.

"Nat…you shouldn't be here right now. It's not safe." His voice was the barest whisper as he kicked off his shoes and tugged his jeans down. After all this time, she still blushed and turned away when he got naked. Only this time when she turned away, he didn't want her to face him. He wanted her to stay just like that. Don't move, Nat...

A stillness came over him, the pain in his gut more severe than it had ever been. But he only stepped forward, heat radiating from his body so strongly it warmed the very air he stepped through. Until he stood directly behind her, his eyes heavy, falling down her body. He stepped forward the final step, and she gasped as his arms went around her.

"Nat..." he whispered, inhaling the sweet, musky scent that followed his touch, his body on fire now from the pain. "I tried to fight this...but I can't..."

His lips played with her neck while his hands came up to cup her breasts, and she grabbed his wrists.

"Caleb, you can't possibly think I'm going to let you touch me right now," she said, her voice sounding a bit strangled.

Holding back from the shift was like holding himself over a fire and letting it burn him. But he knew if he changed, it would be all over. Whatever remained of his sanity would disappear, and the wolf in him would take over completely.

"Nat," he breathed against her neck, his tongue feeling her and sending shivers through her body. "I need you to get on your hands and knees for me."

Her body went rigid, but he only pressed his hands into her breasts more fully, molding her body to his, scarcely aware of anything but the heat and the pain and the relief he knew he could find at last. Relief that only waited on her.

"I need you on the ground, spreading your legs for me," he breathed into her unsteadily, his lips caressing her skin. "Because I'm going to mount you. I'm going to push myself inside you... push my knot inside you until you can't get away. Until you're tied to me and there's nothing you can do to escape. And I'm going to hold you there while I fill you with every last bit of my cum—with everything I've wanted to give you for years," he whispered, a hand sliding down her body to press between her legs, driving the material of her skirt in between her thighs, feeling how wet she was, feeling her clench around him.

And he almost shifted. Almost fell over the edge to liberate himself at last in her body and take everything he had wanted for so long.

Until she spoke, dousing the fire that called to him with three simple, horrified words.

"That's *gross*, Caleb!"

———

Gross. She thought he was gross. His body. What he wanted. *Who he was.*

Caleb threw the football a little too hard, and his teammate doubled over, coughing and falling to his knees. The whistle blew, and he tore the helmet from his head, Nat's words from the previous week still going round and round in his mind.

He'd been sleeping outside since then, under the trailer where he could still keep an eye on things, although Nat thought he was out running in the woods. As if after watching over her every night for over three years he was suddenly going to just abandon her.

The hinges on the door to the locker room protested when he yanked the door open. Well, she could just think that. Why not. She didn't want him. He was repulsive to her. What did she care where he went?

Ethan glanced up when Caleb slammed his helmet on a bench, his cocky little smirk just the excuse Caleb needed.

"You have something to say?"

The smaller boy did not look like a football player, but Caleb had to admit he held his own on the field. Not that he would admit it *to* the little shit. He wanted him to stay *away*. Caleb's hands were already full dealing with Preston—he didn't need another fanboy of Nat's thinking he had any place in her life.

"Why don't you ask me when you're off your period."

Caleb raised a brow, stepping closer to where Ethan stood folding the shirt he'd been wearing carefully and putting it in his bag. He paused for a moment at Caleb's approach, looking him up and down in a quick glance, before returning to his task with a dismissive little laugh. Caleb shoved him back against the locker with a hand on his chest.

"You talk big for such a little guy."

Ethan raised a bored brow.

"If we're doing this, mind if I remove my glasses? They're just for aesthetics, but they were expensive frames, and I'd hate for them to get damaged while I'm teaching you a lesson."

Caleb snorted. Seriously, the kid had balls. Or mental issues. And if Caleb weren't spoiling for a fight, he might have laughed for real.

But he wanted to hit something, and the snooty priss with his snide remarks was a perfect candidate.

The locker room had filled around them, but the boys all remained silent, every eye on the two of them. Caleb felt a bit guilty. The kid was small. This wouldn't have been a fair fight even if Caleb *weren't* a wolf. Well, he'd just compensate. Maybe only fight with one hand or something and be really careful with his punches.

But he found himself at a bit of a loss once Ethan placed his glasses on his folded shirt and stood back up. Fuck. Was he supposed to just start hitting now? That seemed fairly unsportsmanlike. Nobody else had ever taken it this far. Caleb didn't actually know what to do in a human fight.

He was trying to figure out a way to get back out of the whole thing when Ethan's fist connected with his jaw. Hard.

He stumbled back in surprise. It hadn't really hurt, but if he were nothing more than human, he'd have been on the floor. His brow pulling together mirrored Ethan's a split second before Ethan hit him again, harder.

He saw that one coming, but he didn't try blocking it, curious to feel it again. To see if it really had been as strong as he'd thought.

It was, and Caleb rubbed his jaw for a moment, assessing the increasingly confused Ethan before finally throwing a punch himself. Not too hard but harder than he'd initially intended.

Ethan's head snapped back, hitting the locker behind him, and he blinked rapidly...an instant before launching himself at Caleb in a rage.

They tumbled to the ground, Ethan jabbing him over and over while Caleb tried to subdue him. But Ethan's fists were making contact painfully, and Caleb's own anger grew again until he forgot he was supposed to be pulling his punches. Forgot he was only trying to work off a little steam. He cared only about making the smaller male submit. To acknowledge his superior strength.

His hand slipped past the boy's defenses to grab his throat and slam him down on the ground while Ethan struggled fruitlessly to break his hold. Caleb lifted him by the neck only to slam him down again and again, the scent of blood assailing his nostrils and driving him on.

He barely noticed all the hands trying to pull him off. He wouldn't stop. Not until the boy yielded. Over and over he slammed his head against the hard floor, his hand crushing his throat, watching the boy's eyes. Waiting.

Until at last he saw it. The defiance evaporated and the lashes lowered. The kicks and desperate hits stopped. And Caleb stopped as well, his hand still locked on the boy's throat.

Blood splatters dotted the floor around Ethan's head, but he didn't appear to be suffering, and Caleb at last became aware of their teammates' worried exclamations.

"I'm fine," Ethan choked out when Caleb's grip relaxed. Ethan's eyes lifted to his again, this time with more caution.

Conversation went on around them, but their eyes stayed locked together.

Finally, Caleb stood and reached out a hand, pulling Ethan to his feet.

"Holy shit, dude, you're bleeding everywhere!"

Ethan reached a hand back with a frown, feeling the back of his head.

"Head wounds always bleed more. It's just a small cut."

Ethan raised his eyes to Caleb's once more, a question in them.

"Get dressed. We'll talk."

Giving him an order felt as natural as breathing, and Ethan nodded.

A few minutes later they were walking out of the boys' locker together with a few more cuts and bruises than they'd had walking in, eyeing each other thoughtfully.

"Are you what I think you are?" Caleb asked.

Ethan exhaled slowly.

"Well, that depends on how much you know. But…" Hesitation touched his eyes briefly before he sighed. "I think I might be your future brother-in-law."

———

Caleb grabbed Ethan's shirt with both fists, his eyes blazing.

"*You will stay away from Nat.*"

Ethan stared up at him with confused eyes, his lips parting for moment before giving a small laugh.

"No—no, I meant…I meant *my* sister. I mean, I can't be sure, but I think you might be her mate. He had a different name, but I'm guessing your parents might have changed your name to hide you from my dad. Lone wolves are too rare for this to be a coincidence, and there aren't any other packs in this area."

Caleb's anger disappeared, and a confused chaos of emotions

took its place. Shock and exhilaration at the confirmation he'd found another wolf. A gut wrenching longing to hear more about his parents. Utter confusion about a mate.

"You knew my parents?"

Ethan shook his head as Caleb released his shirt.

"Not me. I was too young. But I've heard the stories growing up. They...died about twelve or thirteen years ago? Car accident?" When Caleb's nod confirmed it, Ethan nodded. "Well that's it then. You're him. My dad moved us to this area to look for you after he finally tracked your parents down and found out about the accident. He moved my sister from school to school to try to detect you, but obviously...no luck."

Detect him?

"Was there some sort of...arranged marriage my parents didn't want or something?" Did they do that in packs?

Ethan laughed again, the sound more shocked than anything.

"It's so weird to meet a wolf who doesn't know...who hasn't had to think about it every day of their lives," he said, more to himself than to Caleb. But he shook his head. "When we're pups, we're taken to a type of annual conference to find our mate. The mate bond is a...physical bond. You just feel it. You *know*."

Caleb frowned, a deep line between his brow.

"Your parents met my dad there after you and Vick— Victoria, my sister—found each other. You were both around 2 or so. I guess she smacked you, and you shifted and pinned her. My dad says that was the first and last time anyone ever got the better of her. Your parents were supposed to stay in contact, but after they flew back home, they just disappeared. He hasn't been...happy about it."

Caleb could feel himself getting angry again. This was bullshit. He knew who his mate was, and she was probably waiting for him in the car right now, wondering what the hell he was doing. Not that she would ask. She'd just stare out the window and ignore him like she had every day since last week. Maybe he'd been ignoring her, too, but it was her fault.

He rubbed the back of his neck, suddenly desperate to get back to her.

"I have to go. Nat's probably waiting in the car, and it's hot out."

"I can't believe she's a wolf. She isn't anything like any female wolf I've ever seen. I'm guessing your parents never even took her to the conference...? Does she know her mate?"

Caleb glared at him.

"I told you—*stay away from Nat.*"

Again Ethan's eyes widened in shock, and he gave a little laugh.

"No—I'm not...I *have* a mate," he reassured him, and Caleb frowned.

"Then why are you always hanging around her?"

Ethan's eyes fell.

"She's just a nice person. I'm new." He shrugged but wouldn't meet Caleb's gaze, and Caleb narrowed his eyes suspiciously. But Nat was waiting so this would have to wait for another day.

"We'll talk about this later," he said, and Ethan studied the ground. Caleb barely caught his murmur as he turned to go.

"My dad isn't going to believe I actually did something right for once."

Caleb jerked to a halt and looked back.

"Ethan. Do not say a word about this. This is between you and me *only.*"

The smaller boy stared at him helplessly before answering.

"He's the alpha. I've never been able to hide things from him. Successfully," he finished lamely.

Caleb could have growled in frustration. He didn't want anyone intruding in his life. He didn't want anyone—and especially, *especially*, any other wolf—coming near his Nat.

And he sure as hell didn't want anyone trying to force some supposed mate on him when he already had one.

Turning without another word, he broke into a run towards the parking lot. Yes, he had his mate. Forever.

He just had to convince her to let him mate with her.

10

NAT SAT in the old car Caleb had worked so hard for over the summer a couple years ago. All so he could drive her. So she wouldn't have to walk in the cold snow anymore or the freezing wind. So he could have his hand on her knee below the view through the windows. So he could slip it up her skirt...

She shifted in the seat, trying to think of something else. Something that wouldn't make her feel as guilty as she'd been feeling for the past week.

She should not be feeling guilty. It was perfectly rational—perfectly normal—for her to *not want to have sex with an animal!* Why was she even worrying about this? Caleb was spoiled. He always got his way and, well, he would just have to learn there were some things he could *not* have!

But his face when she'd said that to him... She hadn't realized immediately. She'd been too busy being horrified at what she was hearing—horrified that she was getting *wet*—until she'd looked over her shoulder to glare at him.

He didn't cry often, and every other time she'd seen tears in his eyes, it had been for her. Because he was worried about *her* being hurt. But this time…this time she had cut him. And he'd just stared at her, his lips slightly apart, his brows lifted the smallest bit…and his eyes wet. Like she'd torn out his heart.

But before she could say anything, he'd shifted and run off. And by the time she saw him again, she'd gotten mad all over again remembering what he'd done. And *he* was the one to run away?

Nat kicked the hot dashboard while she waited, hanging one foot outside the open window, careful not to let it touch the burning metal. She would have loved to turn on the air conditioning, but it used up gas and they tried to make their summer pay last as long into the year as possible. Caleb needed time for sports and he insisted she be with him, so neither of them took jobs through the school year. But he always made sure to have the gas money to drive. For her.

She shifted in the seat again, the thoughts rushing back to torture her. How could he think she would be willing to do that? She was human! And she liked kissing him *as a human*. Touching him *as a human*. What was he even thinking?

A whimper left her throat as the guilt poured into her, and she covered her face with her hands, groaning and leaning back. And jumped with a small shriek when a hand lifted her ankle and the door flew open.

Caleb pulled her out and into his arms before she could say a word, crushing her to him and burying his face in her neck. She melted into him, clinging fiercely.

They stood that way a long while, their breathing a bit erratic. Long past the point where Nat remembered they were standing in the school parking lot, visible to everyone heading home after practice.

Let them talk. She was eighteen now. No one could break them apart. And there was no way she was putting any more distance between them after the week they'd had. Not talking. Not sleeping together. Not touching.

She clutched him harder, and his arms tightened around her.

"Caleb," she whispered, leaning on his shoulder and stroking the hair at the base of his neck. "What I said last week…I'm so sorry. I didn't mean it the way it sounded."

"Yes you did," he muttered into her.

She shook her head.

"No, I didn't." A deep sigh left her, and she let his glossy locks slip between her fingers. "I was panicking."

He stilled.

"Why? I wouldn't have forced you. I would never, ever do that." He pulled back to look down at her, his eyes serious. Firm. Intense.

She brushed his cheek softly, her eyes drinking him in.

"I know that. Although…you can be really insistent sometimes," she said hesitantly, "And you knew I didn't want you…licking me when…" Her cheeks flamed but she held his gaze. "When you're not like this. You're not the easiest to stop when you want something, you know."

Caleb's brow furrowed deeply.

"But it made you feel good."

A small sound escaped her as she stared up at him helplessly.

"It's not that simple."

"Why not?"

She groaned and hid her face in his neck, and he exhaled in frustration. Then she felt him glance around.

"Get in the car," he said in a hushed tone, pressing his lips to her head before muttering: "The last thing we need now is people nosing around."

Nat pulled back to look up at him with a frown. Caleb never cared if they were caught. Her eyes roamed his face, finally noticing the small cut on his lip.

"What happened?" she breathed, reaching up to feather her fingertips around the edges, her breath catching when he captured one between his lips, his eyes locked on hers.

Her lashes lifted slowly to stare back at him, heat washing over her as he slid his tongue underneath, sucking her softly.

She was leaning toward him with heavy eyes when he groaned and reached down to put an arm behind her knees, buckling them and easing her back into the car.

"Stay," he whispered with a light kiss before closing the door and hurrying around to the other side. By the time he'd gotten in, her brain was working a bit once more, and she held her hand up when he leaned forward.

"Wait! Tell me what happened!"

He looked like he might argue for a moment but just sighed and pulled her onto his lap instead, reaching over to roll up her window. Nat was so glad he'd thought to get a car with tinted glass.

The heat was oppressive without air flow, so he started the engine, turning the air conditioner on full blast before hugging her tightly while she curled up against him.

"Ethan's a wolf."

Nat stilled.

"What?"

"Ethan's a wolf."

She looked at him, his words forming the same sounds she'd heard before but they just didn't make sense.

He exhaled and leaned back against the seat.

"We got in a fight. And before you start yelling at me," he said with a light kiss on her lips. "He hit me first. Mostly."

Nat blinked at him, yelling the farthest thing from her mind.

"A *wolf?* Are you sure?"

He nodded.

"Evidently his family knew my parents."

Her lips parted in amazement.

"Wow. Little Ethan?"

A smile bloomed across Caleb's face.

"Oh, and he thinks *you're* a wolf."

"Wha—what?" she laughed. Then she thought about it. "Well, I guess that makes sense. He must think we're blood. But if he talks to anyone at all, it won't take long for him to find out I was here a few years before you."

She frowned.

"Caleb, when we met, you said your parents had rules. About not letting any humans know what you are. That they would have wanted you to kill me—"

"No, Nat. Never. I was just trying to defend what I'd done. They would never have wanted to hurt you." He stroked her cheek, and her eyes softened.

"So it's not really a rule? I mean, you don't think Ethan or his family would want me dead?"

Caleb looked away in thought, a line growing between his brow. When he looked back, the worry in his eyes wasn't reassuring.

"I'll talk to him. Tell him you don't know anything. Just…play dumb." Caleb swallowed, tucking a long strand of hair behind her ear. "Maybe it's a good thing he likes you after all."

Nat's brows lifted, and she bit back a smile.

"Caleb…he doesn't like *me*."

He frowned.

"Why is he always hanging out with you then?"

"Well," she chewed the inside of her cheek. "I can't be certain but…I'm pretty sure he's into Preston."

"What?" he laughed. "No. No, he has to be straight—he told me he has a mate. And mates have some big supernatural bond or something."

The smile left his face immediately, and he looked away.

"Well, then why did you think he liked me?"

"Because…the mate thing is stupid," he muttered, not meeting her eyes.

She tugged on his hair until he looked up, a confused grin on her face.

"Are you weirded out that he might be gay? Or maybe bi?"

"No, it's not that. It's…" He drew in a breath, hesitation in his eyes. Then he grew firm. "Nat, listen to me. It doesn't matter. Whatever weird rules they have—whatever they expect. It *doesn't matter*. I know who I am and what I want. And it will *always be you*. Forever."

She stared at him, her smile faltering. The sound of the air blowing through the vents surrounded them, chilling her skin.

"What are you saying?" she asked in a small voice, an old dread she'd thought long gone growing inside.

"I'm saying it *doesn't matter*. And…" he stared at her intently. "His sister was supposed to be my…mate."

———

"Your mate," she repeated, her eyes wide and dry on his.

"That's what Ethan called it. I guess it makes sense for wolves."

"Which I'm not…" she whispered.

"But you *are* my mate."

Nat stared at him. At his beautiful, perfect face so full of intensity. So completely determined to do exactly what he wanted always.

Or thought he wanted.

"But you said…there's a supernatural bond."

Caleb ran a frustrated hand through his dark hair, his brows together while he stared at her.

"I don't know. It's how Ethan described it. But I do know that it *doesn't matter*, Nat. Not to me. I don't care what I 'sense' about someone I don't know. Someone who *isn't you*. A girl who…" he paused, his eyes growing soft as he stroked her hair back. "Who went hungry just so she could bring food to a starving wolf. Who used her fragile, small body to try to keep him safe. Whose gentle hands," he brought her palm up to his lips, kissing it softly while he stared in her eyes, "fed him. Pet him. Made him feel not alone anymore…"

Tears burned in Nat's eyes, but she just watched him.

"A girl who brought me into the world again. Gave me a life. Family. Home. A girl so beautiful…and so strong. So tiny but so fucking brave. And so deeply kind," he whispered, cupping her cheek and rubbing away a tear, "and patient with a demanding, spoiled boy…who maybe is still a bit demanding sometimes."

"And spoiled," she whispered, and a smile touched his lips. But his eyes stayed serious on hers.

"How could anyone else ever mean anything close to what you have meant to me? I can't lose you, Nat. I can't. Not ever. I'd never feel whole without you. You're my family. *You*," he held her cheeks between both hands, staring into her eyes intently, "are my mate!"

Nat clung to his wrists and leaned her forehead against his, a shiver going through her. She wanted to believe him. Desperately. To believe that what they had was real for him. And that she wasn't just the lucky person who found him. That she hadn't stolen him from his own kind…

"And while we're on the subject of mates…" He pulled back, cocking his jaw a bit and raising a brow. "Why won't you mate with me?"

The spiral of self-recrimination she'd begun halted midstream.

"Are you seriously going to bring that up *now* after telling me you actually *have* a mate already?"

"Yes—because *you* are my mate, which you evidently completely ignored me saying, and I want to mate with *you*!" he glared at her, but his hands pulled her hips on his lap more firmly and his expression quickly switched to pleading. "Nat…I have something I can use now! Let me use it in you…"

He leaned into her neck, kissing her softly, and she made a

sound of frustration. She was a human! And she wanted to be with him as a human—not…

She wrapped her arms around him, holding him close against her neck as she stared into the car, her eyes filling with worry and doubt. If she wanted to be with him—to keep him from one of his own kind—she might need to be a little more open minded.

A groan escaped her, and Caleb pulled back immediately.

"You're thinking about it," he breathed, his eyes roaming her face. She glared at him.

"It is super shitty of you to bring it up now! Now when I'm all worried about this other girl…not even a girl. Someone like you. Someone who can be what you need—"

"*Nobody* else can be what I need," he broke in firmly. "And…if you say no…I'll keep bothering you about it the rest of our lives but it won't *change* anything, Nat! I'd rather be frustrated with you than whatever I would be with someone else."

Her eyes glistened, and she glared at him harder.

"And now you're just being *wonderful*! How is this fair? How can I keep saying no?"

His eyes were bright on hers, and his grip tightened.

"Are you saying yes?" he whispered.

"No!" She mock punched his chest, glaring one last moment before whimpering and falling forward on him to curl up in his lap. "I'm saying…you're spoiled…and every time you go after me for something…I can never keep saying no…so…"

Her whimper turned into a groan as she pressed her face into his neck, feeling him holding his breath.

"So I know I probably *will* say yes," she muttered, almost sulking.

"You will?" he asked hoarsely. "You mean it?"

"Maybe! Eventually! Just…don't go crazy, okay? Let me…get used to…it." She swallowed, torn between horror at what she was saying and a more horrible feeling between her legs.

"You like the idea…" The huskiness in his voice increased the pangs, and she smacked his chest again.

"I swear, Caleb, if you embarrass me about this, I will never say yes!"

"But why would you be embarrassed? Because you think I'm…gross?" he asked hesitantly, and she leaned up immediately to look at him, her eyes wide with concern.

"No! I told you—that was me panicking. You are perfect! So, so perfect! But…what if…what if I were the one turning into some other animal? Something you weren't used to being? Like…a camel!" she said enthusiastically, and he eyed her with skepticism.

"You're saying I'm like a camel to you?"

"No! You are *missing* the point! I'm just saying…imagine… I…wanted you…to have sex with me as…a camel. Or…a lion. Or any other animal besides a wolf!"

"But wolves are different."

"Caleb—"

"Okay okay! I'm thinking!" he cut her off quickly as her temper flared. But a smile lurked at the corner of his mouth. "If it were you, and you wanted me…"

He pondered the question for a few moments before answering, so cocksure she nearly smacked him again.

"I would mate with you no matter what form you were in. You could be a—a ball of slime! And I'd just hold you really carefully and—"

"That's disgusting!"

He grinned, leaning in to kiss her, his smile fading as his tongue slipped between her lips.

"I'll go slow and let you get used to it first. I promise," he whispered, his hand sliding up her thigh under her skirt. "I'll start with licking you. I can do so much more with my tongue that way, Nat. And I can feel it with you."

His voice grew husky when she trembled, and he pushed

aside her panties to slide a finger down her wet slit. She clenched around him when he pushed it inside her, his thumb rubbing her clit in slow circles.

"It doesn't hurt anymore as a wolf. Something changed. Like…I broke through some barrier. And when you came when I licked you before…" He buried his hand in her hair to hold her head steady when she whimpered, keeping her where he could kiss her between words. "I needed to be inside you. I needed it so much…"

"You're going to shift," she said with a crying groan, pressing against his hand helplessly.

"Yes," he whispered. "And I'm going to push my tongue deep inside you and lap your clit until you cum over and over. I'm going to mount you and rub my cock up and down right here," he stroked his thumb through her slick folds, "until you're as desperate to feel it inside you as I am."

Nat gasped into his mouth as he pressed hard deep inside of her—only for him to push her onto the seat beside him with a small cry, tearing his clothes off an instant before he shifted.

Nat whined along with him as his enormous form barely fit on the long bench seat. Feeling a little shaky, she moved to the side to give him room until he could shift back, but her breath caught as she saw the large, pink cock at his center. She stared wide eyed, and Caleb froze, staring back at her.

Neither of them moved for a long time.

"Will that even…fit?" she whispered at last, her eyes lifting to his, and she swallowed when he answered with a growl.

She looked around. The windows were dark but they weren't a replacement for solid walls around them. Her gaze narrowed, and she peered out more carefully at a shadowy form in a car across the lot.

"Caleb…isn't that Ethan's car? Are wolf eyes good enough to see through the tinted glass?"

Caleb leaned closer to her and looked out, his muzzle above her shoulder. She glanced at him when he shifted.

"Yes," he said grimly, his eyes fixed on the car. "Yes, they are."

———

"Stay here."

Nat watched while Caleb threw on his clothes once more and yanked open the door to climb out. She stared for just one moment when he slammed it before scrambling out after him.

"Nat!" he hissed across the roof of the car, pausing to lean across it and glower at her.

"What's the point of me hiding now?" she whispered back. "Besides, I have some questions, and I'd feel more comfortable asking while you're there…"

She fidgeted behind the car, not too sure of her chosen path. Ethan *seemed* nice, but Caleb said he'd thrown the first punch in their fight. He was a wolf, and what did she really know of their kind? Maybe Caleb was completely unique. But she wanted to know about this mate thing—without it getting filtered through Caleb.

"The point is that I don't want you anywhere near any other wolves! Just let me handle this."

Nat chewed her lip but walked around the car, her eyes never leaving his.

"No," she said with wide eyes, standing beside him.

He stared down at her, his arm on the top of the car, his jaw flexing, before taking a swift look around the parking lot. Her hands flew to his shoulders when he grabbed her around the waist and pulled her up to him, planting a firm kiss on her lips.

"You are the most frustrating, stubborn girl," he whispered, and Nat pressed her lips together, her eyes bright. Turning towards Ethan's car, Caleb raised his voice to a normal level. "Well? Are you going to make me come over there and get you?"

They watched as the door to a sporty looking BMW opened and a rather hesitant looking Ethan appeared. He walked over slowly, his eyes moving back and forth between the two of them, but he lowered his head once he got near, glancing up at Caleb in wary confusion.

"You planning on running to tell daddy this, too?" Caleb demanded, and Nat looked at him in surprise. She supposed she should have asked more about their conversation before, but Caleb could be so very distracting sometimes…

"I told you. He's the alpha."

"So, what—he has some type of magical lie detector?"

Ethan frowned.

"No. It's just…he's the *alpha*. You don't understand. You don't hide things from your alpha. I'd just get nervous, no matter how much I tried to hide it, and he'd either see it or catch the scent. Maybe both."

"Sounds like you're just daddy's boy to me."

"I'm not!" His face grew a bit red, and he faced Caleb more directly. "There are *rules* you have to follow!"

Caleb waved a hand dismissively, keeping an arm tightly around Nat's waist.

"Rules are for sheep. I thought you were a *wolf*."

"You only say that because you've been able to run free—you don't have a pack."

"I have one. And she can be a little bossy at times," he didn't look down when Nat made a face at him, "but I do what needs to be done."

Ethan snorted.

"A human is not a pack," he said snootily before blanching at Caleb's expression. "Look, *you're* the alpha in your…pack. You don't have to worry about anything!"

Caleb raised a brow and bit the inside of his cheek, finally looking down at Nat.

"What do you think?"

"I think you like to *think* you're the boss," she said, crossing her arms, still slightly peeved at his bossy comment. "*And* you're spoiled. And anytime I don't let you do absolutely everything you want, you say I'm bossy!"

He grinned down at her and turned back to Ethan, whose brow was growing more deeply furrowed as he watched them.

"See? I have to walk on eggshells." He tickled Nat's ribs as he said it, but stopped and pressed her tight against his side when she started to struggle to get away. His voice turned stern again. "But I still *make my own decisions*. So explain to me why you can't."

Ethan stared at him for just a moment.

"Because my dad would kill me." His voice was flat.

"And what do you think I'll do to you if you put her in danger," Caleb said softly, his eyes narrowing.

Ethan dropped his eyes again, confusion once more pulling his brow.

"Ethan," Nat began, squeezing Caleb when it felt like he was going to interrupt her. "Would your dad want to hurt me? Do… do you want to hurt me? What are these rules you have to follow?"

He lifted wary eyes to hers, shifting uncertainly to Caleb in question. Nat grimaced when he waited for Caleb's nod to begin talking.

"I don't want to hurt you. But my dad…if he knew Vick's mate was…*how are you even able to want her*?" he finally blurted out with a red face, turning back to Caleb in helpless frustration. "That isn't supposed to be possible!"

Nat swallowed. It wasn't? Did that mean…had she damaged him?

She glanced at Caleb to see him looking at Ethan darkly.

"Why not?"

"Because you have a *mate*! You're only supposed to be able to want *her*! Being close to someone else that way is supposed to make you sick!"

Nat's stomach sank as she looked back at Ethan. She was sorry she'd insisted on talking to him. Sorry she had ever talked to him at all.

All the years of pain Caleb had experienced with her....the thousands of times he'd shifted because it had hurt too badly as a human to be near her...

He didn't belong to her. He never had.

She didn't want to look at Caleb. She didn't want to see the same devastation in his eyes that was crushing her. But she forced back the nausea and turned toward him once again...to see him lifting a brow and smirking.

"Well. I guess this proves your rules are wrong."

11

ETHAN STARED at Caleb with tortured eyes before taking a small step back, his head shaking slowly, a shuttered expression falling on his face.

"It must just be because you haven't been around her in so long. But as soon as you see Vick again, it will change." His voice was flat. Resigned. And driving a knife into Nat's gut yet again.

Caleb snorted.

"You've already proven you don't know how this works. I know who I want. Who I *love*. And it is and always will be *Nat*."

He pulled her into his body more strongly.

"You know what? Tell daddy whatever you want. Because it won't make a difference. And if anyone tries to hurt her..." Nat swallowed at the menace in his tone and the darkness in his eyes. "They won't try again."

He looked down at her, a grin spreading across his face.

"I'm ready to go," he said as he swept her up into his arms to carry her around the car.

"Wait! I didn't get to ask anything!"

"Yes you did!"

"But he didn't answer! Caleb…" she whined, but he was already putting her inside the car.

"Didn't you hear? I'm the alpha. Shh. We're going home."

He snickered when she glared and tried to shove him away, pausing to kiss her softly for a moment and waiting until her lips softened under his before pulling back. His hand reached up to rub the worried line between her brows.

"You're giving *me* a headache with that line," he teased, but she couldn't bring herself to laugh. Fear was eating her up inside.

"What if—"

He kissed her firmly, halting her mid-sentence, before quickly pulling away and closing the door. Nat leaned back with a groan as she waited for him to get in the car with her, barely noticing that he stopped and spoke to Ethan for a moment.

And then he was climbing in beside her with a smile in his eyes, his hand slipping under her skirt. She didn't even try to stop him. She just clung to his wrist and turned to stare at the window as he drove.

"Hey," he said softly, squeezing her thigh as they pulled out of the lot. "Where are you going?"

Probably to some sort of wolf hell for stealing him.

"Just…thinking," she sighed.

"Yeah, bad thoughts. Don't listen to Ethan, Nat. Clearly he's bought into whatever his dad has told him but it's *not true*." His tone was stern, and she turned toward him, her eyes pleading.

"But what if it is?"

"It's not!"

"But what if it is!" she cried, getting louder as he glowered at her. "You don't know! What if you meet her and everything suddenly makes sense? And you realize you made a terrible mistake with me!"

"Nat—"

"No! You can say whatever you want, but you *don't know*!"

"I *do* know! I already met her!"

Nat blinked in shock.

"And you didn't tell me?"

"I didn't remember! Clearly she couldn't have meant that much to me. And she doesn't sound like the nicest person either, by the way. Evidently she hit me as soon as we met."

A frown touched her lips.

"When was this?"

"I don't know. When we were two or so," he mumbled, watching the road.

Nat stared at him. Blinked. Stared some more.

"SHE WAS A BABY!"

"That's a toddler! Not a baby!" he said, raising his voice and glancing over with a fierce expression.

"Caleb, that is the most ridiculous..." her voice was strangled, and he broke in.

"No—the most ridiculous is thinking I would ever—EVER, NAT—want anyone but you!"

She smacked her hands over her face with a small cry.

"Stop saying that! Stop saying everything nice and perfect and wonderful," she wailed behind her fingers. "I don't want to be even more heartbroken when you meet her again and find out you were *wrong*."

A deep sound of frustration welled up from inside him, and he gripped her thigh a little too hard beneath her skirt, pulling a squeak from her as she clamped down on his wrist. He eased his grip, soothing the skin softly, and she whimpered as her body responded.

"Come on," he said, tension heavy in his voice as he parked in the drive. "I want more privacy for this conversation."

"Caleb—no! What we talked about before—you can't do that now!"

"Why not!" he demanded, looking over at her with outrage in his eyes.

"Because you need to know if she's the one—"

"Nat, for the last time: I ALREADY KNOW."

"Well then *I* need to know!" she exploded, yanking her door open. She pulled out of his grasp when he reached for her, and he turned to shove his own door open, cursing under his breath as he got out. She saw him stop and rub his forehead when he saw her sitting on the front steps, staring off to the side with miserable eyes.

"Nat…" he sighed, sitting down beside her.

His head tilted while he stared at her, and she could see his expression softening from the corner of her eye.

"Nat," he whined. "Look at me…"

Her eyes went to his almost without thinking, and she frowned for a moment before lifting her brows helplessly when he spoke.

"Nat…I love you. Nothing can change that. Please…please trust me."

"I do trust you, Caleb," she whispered. "But I know you. You are so stubborn and so sure of yourself. And you haven't been around your own kind in so long! I just…I just don't see how you can possibly know this for sure."

He sighed and lifted a hand to tuck a long strand of hair behind her ear. He lingered on her cheek, his thumb stroking her softly.

"Then I guess…" he sighed again deeply. "I'm going to have to meet her again to prove it to you."

Fear clenched her stomach, freezing her in place, and he groaned before leaning forward to kiss her forehead.

"You are the most frustrating, stubborn girl…" he murmured against her skin. "Come on. Let's get something to eat and do our homework and definitely *not* take our clothes off so that I can slide myself deep inside you and tie you to me for thirty minutes…an hour… I wonder how long it will take my knot to shrink enough to let you get away again," he whispered into her neck, sending a shiver through her body and pangs between her thighs.

He groaned again, and she pushed him away quickly, her cheeks flushed.

"You're right. You need to meet her. Again. And…" she swallowed. "If it turns out Ethan is right, then…" She took a deep breath. "I will always love you. Like a sister."

His brows lifted, and he bit the inside of his cheek. Then a glint came into his eye.

"*When* it turns out that he's *wrong*, I'm going to love you like a brother who loves his sister a little too much…"

"That's sick, Caleb."

He just grinned, and she shook her head at him, trying not to laugh.

God, how could she bear it if Ethan was right?

"Come on. I'll make *you* dinner tonight," she said, standing and holding out her hand. He took it, his brows raised happily as he got to his feet beside her.

"What did I do to deserve that?"

"You're wonderful, Caleb," she said seriously, looking into his eyes, eyes growing soft again beneath her gaze. "And no matter what happens, I'll always, *always* think that."

He shook his head with a helpless sigh.

"Frustrating, stubborn girl…"

And then he pulled her inside, and they spent their evening laughing and working and playing and finally falling asleep side by side, while Caleb whispered all the things he was going to do to her once she changed her mind.

———

"Natty, what'd you get for number seven?" Preston whispered.

Nat mouthed the answer over her shoulder, glancing up at the teacher's back as she turned around to make sure she hadn't been caught. But he was droning on about the court system.

Civics might have been a bit more interesting if he didn't just read from his slides. At least he waited until the end of class to collect homework, so they had time to finish what they were supposed to have done the previous night.

"Are you going to the Homecoming dance this year?" he whispered again, and Ethan glanced over at him from his seat a row away. "Why not?" he continued when she shook her head.

"Did you have something to say to the class, Preston?" the teacher asked loudly, turning around.

"Uh, no, sorry. Keep at it, Mr. Jones. This is super exciting stuff!"

A few students snickered, but the teacher's expression didn't change.

"I'm glad to hear you like it, since you'll be joining me for detention this afternoon."

"Oh, come on—naw. I have work!"

"You should have thought of that before talking in my class. And don't think about skipping out again, or I'll have to call your father for an impromptu parent teacher conference."

Nat glanced back at Preston, seeing his growing anger, and held up her hand.

"It was my fault—I...had a question about the homework."

The teacher raised his brow.

"Well, then you'll benefit from some extra time after school as well. I'll be seeing you both at 3:30 sharp."

Nat's jaw dropped a bit. What a dick.

"Oh, come on, that's bullsh—"

"I'll be there!" she said loudly, trying to cover Preston's outburst.

"Shouldn't there be some sort of deferral offered when someone has to work?" Ethan asked evenly.

"I'll tell you what, Mr. Harland. Why don't you join them and write me an essay on the merits of an alternative system of governance! I will consider your feedback carefully. Anyone else wanting detention today?"

Nat waited for Ethan to point out he had practice—athletes were given special treatment when it came to things like this—but he said nothing.

Not daring to look around at Preston for fear of riling him up, she slumped on her desk with her head in her hand, keeping her eyes down so she wouldn't glare at the teacher. Seriously. Some of them acted like they never heard of students with shitty parents—students who might actually *need* their jobs.

The bell rang and the students shuffled out, the hum of conversation growing quickly in the hall.

"Natty, you shouldn't have done that."

They were headed to lunch together as usual. She and Caleb were in different lunch periods this year, a situation he was not happy about, so she'd been sitting with Preston, weirdly her only real friend at the school, a situation Caleb was *really* not happy about. She had a few sort-of girl friends, but she was so worried about people finding out about Caleb that she tended to keep everyone at arm's-length. Preston was just immune to her rebuffs.

And Preston had been remarkably persistent. Even after the little kiss Caleb had planted on her their freshman year, he just kept trying to talk to her. She couldn't shake him, so eventually she stopped trying. Besides, it turned out they had a lot more in common than she'd known, and underneath all his bravado and trying to look tough, he was a rather sensitive guy.

"Why? Caleb will be in practice—I would have just been sitting around waiting on him in the car anyhow. I'm sorry it didn't work though. Are you...going to be okay?" she asked hesitantly, looking up at him.

"You mean because of my dad? Fuck that. I ended that shit over the summer. Finally surpassed my old man," he said, flexing his now very filled out muscles.

Nat rolled her eyes but gave him the grin he was seeking.

"You should have tried out for football," Ethan said, sounding a bit bored.

Preston looked over as if surprised to find him walking with them, but Ethan had been joining them at lunch ever since she'd invited him early that semester when it became obvious—to her, at least—he wanted to know Preston.

"If I had a rich daddy who bought me anything I wanted, maybe I would have."

Ethan scowled.

"They have resources to help poor students. It wouldn't cost you anything."

Preston shook his head at him.

"Dude, you're so privileged, I can't even talk to you. I don't have time for sports because I have to work so I can do things like *eat*. And keep my piece of shit car working. Why are you even hanging out with us? Go talk to your own kind."

Ethan's face reddened when Preston turned back to Nat with a wave of his hand. She hesitated. She kind of agreed with Preston's general point, but she didn't want to make Ethan feel unwelcome. Plus, considering he was a wolf, it was probably better if Preston *didn't* get on his bad side.

"You know, Ethan stuck up for you in there."

If only Preston knew what Ethan was—that would certainly get his interest. He still asked about 'her wolf' on occasion, even though she'd told him that he'd run off years ago. And he'd had the tattoo on his stomach fully fleshed out by an actual expert. Nat wondered if that's what had first drawn Ethan's attention, since Preston had been showing off the rather fierce looking wolf to her after class one day. Either that or the six pack he hid underneath his standard I-don't-give-a-shit old t-shirts.

"Oh yeah," Preston said, eyeing Ethan again and scratching his head. "Well...thanks."

Ethan shrugged, not looking at him, and Preston rolled his

eyes as he turned back to Nat. *What?* he mouthed when he saw her expression.

After dropping their things off at their lockers, Preston took his packed lunch and secured their standard table while Nat and Ethan stood in line. Nat couldn't help but be a bit envious at Ethan's ability to simply order whatever he wanted. She was on the free lunch program, and beggars really weren't allowed to be choosers. But if she and Caleb got into college the way they were planning…

A sinking feeling pooled in the pit of her stomach. That was before. All the plans they'd made…

"What is your sister like?" she blurted out.

Ethan's eyes grew guarded.

"Well…I think…a lot like your brother."

The knot in her stomach grew. Generous, brave, loving, protective…and beautiful.

Her eyes fell, and she blinked rapidly, trying to chase away the stupid tears that were far too close to the surface lately.

"Does she…have you told her?" she asked quietly, lifting her eyes once more to see him cautiously examining her.

He shook his head.

"My dad is on a business trip right now and my sister is at college. I haven't told anyone."

Relief made her weak. Not yet. They wouldn't take him from her yet.

"How," he whispered, his eyes growing intense, "did it happen?"

"What do you mean?"

He stared at her in frustration.

"I mean is there something he did to make it possible? Some…medicine? Herbal supplements? Something he ate?"

His gaze was practically a glare, and Nat wrapped her arms around herself.

"Possible…you mean…" Her face filled with heat. What part

exactly wasn't supposed to be possible? Just how much had he heard them saying in the car? Because there were some things she couldn't even talk about with *Caleb*. There was no way she was going anywhere near them with Ethan.

"How did he ever kiss you?" he hissed, leaning close to her ear before drawing back to wait for her answer.

Nat's face was flaming, but confusion filled her. Kissing wasn't supposed to be possible?

"Well, it hurts him...but..." A sudden frown pulled at her mouth. "Ethan, how badly does it hurt?"

"It feels like you're being cooked from the inside out," he said, his eyes burning.

Nat blinked. Caleb couldn't hurt that much...could he? While she was feeling—while *he made her* feel—the most exquisite, perfect pleasure? Her stomach twisted as she stared at Ethan, countless memories running through her mind.

"And if..." she whispered, "you shift? What do you feel then?"

Ethan frowned.

"I don't know. We aren't supposed to in front of..." he inclined his head. *Humans*. "Why? Does it not hurt then?" he demanded.

Nat shook her head.

"I don't know...Caleb...might not have wanted me to know how much he was hurting."

But whatever he'd felt before, he'd finally, finally found a way past it. That's what he'd meant. After years of torturing himself to be close to her, his body had offered him a way out. And all she'd done was to push him away.

She swallowed. God, when had she become so selfish? With her perfect, beautiful wolf?

"But when he's...like you. He just takes the pain?" Ethan continued, frustrated confusion in his eyes.

Nat nodded dully. Every day. For almost four years. Kissing

her. Touching her. The pleasure was so intense she could barely breathe. Intense pleasure for her. And intense pain for him.

"It doesn't hurt at all with your mate?" she said in a small voice.

Ethan shook his head.

"And...you have a mate?" she asked hesitantly. She'd really thought he was into Preston.

Shrugging, he looked away.

"Yeah. They keep us apart mostly until we're done with school so the females don't get pregnant too soon. But we have chaperoned visits a couple times a year."

So much for her intuition. Maybe he was just lonely and wanted a friend.

They reached the food area and grew quiet while they checked out before heading back to Preston with Ethan's tray looking a bit more appetizing than her own. A couple of Preston's friends had joined him, including the one boy who used to throw rocks at her. She quickly nabbed the empty seat at the end of the table as far from him as possible, and Preston looked over at her with disappointment while Ethan hesitated, eyeing the only remaining seat.

"Natty, I saved you a seat beside me!"

"I like this spot," she murmured, not looking at him, and heard the other two boys snicker.

"When you gonna give it up, Preston? Those legs are locked."

"Shut *up*." Preston grabbed the other boy's shirt across the table while Ethan sat down with caution. The boy just kept snickering, and Nat couldn't help being disappointed that Preston wouldn't just go ahead and hit him already. He always grabbed him when he said things like that, but he never actually *did* anything. Caleb would have probably knocked him out. Not that anyone would say anything around him.

Caleb had been her protector for so long now, she'd almost

forgotten what it was like to be alone. Moments like these reminded her.

She trailed her fork through the instant mashed potatoes in slow circles, a heaviness inside her that wouldn't leave. What would happen if he was wrong? If he saw his mate and everything changed? Who was she without him?

Her fork stilled and her vision blurred. The answer was easy. She was what she'd always been.

Nothing.

————

"You could have gotten out of this, preppy. Your kind gets a free pass."

The three of them were sitting in detention alone, Mr. Jones having abandoned them for an argument he seemed to be having on his phone. They could hear his raised voice on occasion from far down the hall.

Ethan scratched whatever he was writing a bit harder.

"We're not as different as you think," he muttered, and Preston raised a brow at him.

"Oh yeah? You been on welfare, too?"

"Not everything is about money!" he snapped, looking over at him.

"Only rich people say that," Preston said calmly, leaning back with his arms behind his head, exposing a sliver of the wolf on the cut line of his abs beneath his shirt.

Ethan turned away again, his brow pulling together furiously as he dug the pencil into the paper harder until the lead snapped. Preston snorted, and Ethan turned back to glare at him.

"It doesn't matter how much money you have when your father chooses everything in your life!"

"So you do whatever daddy tells you or he'll take away your allowance? Cry me a fucking river."

"It's not about the money!" Ethan raised his voice, and Nat looked over at him with worried eyes. But Preston just laughed at him mockingly.

"So what's this—" he reached over and tugged Ethan's collar, causing him to jump. "And this—" He flicked the button on Ethan's designer jeans, leaning back again as Ethan blinked rapidly. "And that car you drive. And every single thing I've seen you wearing or using. You're like a walking CK ad."

"It's Armani," he whispered, staring at him wide eyed. Preston snorted again and put his arms behind his head once more, holding the back of his neck and exposing more of his stomach.

"Whatever, dude. The point is you clearly like daddy's money. So don't pretend you've got it tough."

Nat felt the blood drain from her face. Ethan was staring at him…and she knew that look.

"Ethan…?" she said tentatively, and Preston darted a glance at her before looking back to Ethan and frowning.

"Dude. You sick or something?"

Ethan's chest was expanding and contracting quickly, his eyes still locked on Preston.

Nat stood slowly, walking over and stepping between them, blocking Preston from his sight. He seemed to stare through her.

"Ethan," she whispered, carefully kneeling in front of him until his eyes turned to hers. "Think of something else."

"What's wrong with him?" Preston said, getting up to go squat down beside her.

"Preston, just—go watch the door!" she said, panic entering her voice as Ethan's eyes turned back to him and the look she knew so well began taking over completely.

"Fuck that. I want to watch the prep spaz out," he said fascinated.

"Would you go!" she cried, pushing at him, only to stop at Ethan's voice.

"I can't stop it," he whispered, his hands slowly unbuttoning his shirt.

"What the fuck?" Preston laughed.

Shit. Shit shit shit. What should she do? Nat's eyes flew around the room, spotting the closet. She ran over to see if it was unlocked and grabbed her hair when it wasn't. Shit.

Her eyes flew back to Ethan who was now standing, still undressing in a daze, his eyes locked on Preston who was laughing and pulling out his phone. She ran over and snatched it out of his hands.

"What the fuck, Natty? I seriously need to get this on video!"

"Will you stop?" she said desperately, her eyes darting to the door. She began trying to pull him toward it. "Go make sure the teacher doesn't come back!"

He let her pull him for a moment, grinning at her, but stopped short before they reached the door.

"Nah. Think I'll stay for the show. Is he on meds? Rich kids are always on something."

Ethan had nearly everything off now.

"Oh my god…give me my phone, Natty. Please. You can't do this to me."

The classroom door had a window. If anyone walked by…

She held onto Preston, yanking him hard toward the door with her.

"Ow! Geez. Shouldn't you be the one leaving? If your brother hears you've been looking at some naked guy, someone's head is going to roll."

"Preston, stand right here. Don't let anyone see in. And whatever you do, *don't scream!*"

"Scream?" he laughed before joking, "*I* have a bigger dick than *that*, Na—"

But his words cut off with a strangled sound as his eyes lifted over her shoulder, and she slammed her hand across his mouth a moment before the yell could make its way up his throat.

Preston grabbed her, frantically trying to pull her with him out the door, but she smacked him hard, jolting him out of his panic.

"Will you *stop?*" she hissed, pulling the door shut again and praying the teacher hadn't heard anything. The blood had completely drained from Preston's face, and he flattened his back against the wall, his grip a vice on her arm while he looked past her with horrified eyes.

Nat glanced over her shoulder and for a moment could only stare in awe.

Ethan was beautiful. He was smaller than Caleb, but his huge form still took up far more space than an ordinary wolf. His warm golden coat glinted in the sunlight streaming through the window, and she sighed for a moment, leaning her head on Preston's shoulder. It was just so amazing that they existed.

But the voice down the hall snapped her back to attention, and she dragged Preston to stand in front of the windowed portion. His body was taller and wider than hers, so if anyone did pass by, he had a better shot at hiding Ethan.

"Just stand here," she said in a soft voice, stroking his arm a bit to try to soothe him. He just kept clinging to her. Sighing, she turned back to Ethan, whose eyes were locked on Preston.

"Ethan, you have to turn back. Mr. Jones could come back any minute. Just…turn around. Think about…homework. Or… your dad! Think about your dad! What would he say if he found out you shifted?"

A whine sounded in the wolf's throat, and he took a step back, lowering his head.

"Okay, then, well…just *turn around and think!*" she said exasperated. Caleb got so fixated when he was like this as well. Maybe it was common not to think quite as clearly in wolf form. Or at least, quite as humanly.

Ethan whined again, his eyes turning back to Preston, and Nat looked up at him.

"Say something," she whispered. "Let him know it's okay."

"Okay?" he said hoarsely. "What the fuck. I mean...*what the fuck.*"

Ethan's whine grew more insistent, and he licked his muzzle, lowering his head further and starting to approach. Preston pressed himself against the door more strongly.

"Come on. You have a wolf tattoo! Are you seriously going to be a scaredy cat now?"

He glanced at her, and Nat was glad to see a bit of indignation enter his eyes. But they were all too wary when they returned to Ethan once more.

"Jesus," he whispered, swallowing. Ethan whined again, coming closer slowly, until he stood right in front of him. He kept his head low, his eyes on Preston's, and whimpered as he reached out to nuzzle the hand Preston had flattened against the wood behind him.

"Fuck," he said hoarsely when Ethan began licking him, and Nat leaned close to the door, trying to see down the hall. She couldn't hear Mr. Jones anymore.

Preston slowly let his hand relax, dropping it to his side while Ethan licked him more strongly and started to press into him.

"Ethan, I don't hear—" But her words were cut off when they all heard the footsteps rapidly approaching an instant before Mr. Jones pushed at the door, looking up in shocked annoyance when it didn't open fully. His eyes widened when he saw Preston and Nat's faces.

"What are you kids doing? Get back in your seats!"

He shoved harder, causing Nat to yelp when it hit her toes and pushing Preston over, pulling Nat with him into a heap of fur and bodies and tangled limbs.

And then they were all looking up, two pale faces in a bit of a panic...with one calm, naked boy between them.

12

NAT SAT between Preston and Ethan in a seat along the wall where Preston had dragged her when he sat down, using her as a shield.

Mr. Jones had called an emergency meeting with the principal, and they were waiting in the school office area while a couple of students discussed permission slips with the office staff.

"They…they were having some sort of…of…*orgy* in my classroom!" Mr. Jones's outrage drifted out into the office, and Nat tried to disappear behind her hand, sinking down into her seat as low as possible. "One boy was on top of the other boy—who was naked—NAKED—and the girl was on them both!"

"It—it's not what it sounds like." Preston's laughter was painfully strained, and Nat groaned into her hand. "We were just…pulling a prank!"

His voice brightened, and he elbowed Nat.

"Right, Natty?"

Nat peeked out between her fingers to see the two girls throwing side glances at them while the staff behind the desk instructed them not to take any notice of what was going on in the principal's office.

She closed her fingers again without responding.

"I don't see what the big deal is," Ethan said irritably.

Nat felt Preston lean around her.

"The big deal," he hissed, "is I like chicks! And guess what most chicks don't want in a guy they're dating? Another guy!"

"So you're afraid they'll think you're the bottom?" Ethan shot back.

Nat peeked out again to see Preston looking ready to explode.

"If I were gay, which I'm not, I would definitely be the top," he said in a choked whisper, putting a hand beside his mouth to hide it from the other students. "But I'm *afraid* they'll just think I'm *gay!*"

Ethan turned away to scowl at the ground.

"You're just chill about it because your girlfriend doesn't go here. Or maybe because you're a—" Preston seemed to remember himself suddenly because he stopped, growing pale again and turning to face forward in silence.

Nat looked back and forth between the two of them for a moment, biting the inside of her cheek. She was staying out of this one.

The muffled tones of a female voice must have calmed the teacher a bit because when he responded, his voice was too low to make out the words. Not that it mattered now...

After a few minutes, Mr. Jones left the office looking a bit disgruntled, throwing them a final angry glance before exiting the office area.

"Send them in," the principal called out, presumably to the staff who nodded at Nat and the boys. The girls at the counter stared at them with bright eyes, and Nat tried pulling her hair forward as much as possible to hide her face.

The principal watched them in silence for a long while, studying each in turn. Preston scratched his head when her gaze rested on him and tapped his foot furiously. Nat forced herself not to hide behind her hands, but she was sure she was cringing. Ethan just stared back at her calmly.

"Who wants to tell me what happened?"

Preston and Nat exchanged a look but neither spoke. Ethan sat in silence.

"Nobody? Do you all want to be suspended?"

Nat swallowed. She was trying to keep her grades up enough to get into the same college as Caleb. He'd already been recruited for a sports scholarship, but she knew he'd abandon it if she wasn't able to be there too. At least, he would have if he didn't have a mate…

"It's not what it—"

"It was just a pran—"

"I had an anxiety attack," Ethan said smoothly when they all began speaking at once. "I didn't know what I was doing. They were trying to stop me from walking out into the hall when Mr. Jones opened the door hard enough to make them fall on top of me."

Preston and Nat stared at him with wide eyes and parted lips before turning back with nods and sounds of agreement to the principal.

Her brow raised.

"Well, that at least makes sense. But I wouldn't have thought you were the sort to have anxiety attacks, Mr. Harland," she said, narrowing her eyes shrewdly.

Ethan frowned.

"Are you suggesting some people *are* that sort? Can you explain what kind of person you had in mind?"

Her eyes widened, and she blinked quickly.

"Oh, no, of course not! Mental health is—well—what I mean to say is…" She grew more flustered with each word. "My apologies. If you need to speak with a counselor at any time, just let your teachers know and they will excuse you from class! We take our students' health very seriously here—all types of health."

Preston and Nat exchanged another look, this time pressing their lips together and biting down on the urge to laugh. Thank goodness Ethan was clever because she and Preston were idiots. But so was the principal evidently.

She dismissed them soon after, repeating her apologies and actually thanking Nat and Preston for looking out for their fellow student. They hurried out of the office area before their faces could ruin what Ethan had accomplished.

"Holy shit, dude. No wonder your family's rich. You must have gotten your smarts from somewhere," Preston exclaimed in a loud whisper once they were finally out in the hall.

"Does everything have to be about money with you!" Ethan exploded, rounding on him angrily. But he whimpered slightly when Preston took a step back, pale once more.

"Sorry. Just meant…sorry," he mumbled, looking away.

Preston was looking down and didn't see Ethan staring at him in misery.

"Well, I have to get to my job. Catch you later, Natty," he mumbled again, not looking up, and headed quickly for the exit while Ethan watched him, a small whine welling up from his throat.

When Preston disappeared out of the doors, his eyes fell at last. Nat stared at him.

"Ethan…you said…you have a mate," she whispered, her eyes searching his face.

He rubbed the back of his neck, looking down.

"I do."

Her brow pulled together.

"Do you…love her?"

A frustrated exhale left his lungs.

"It's complicated to explain."

"Please try...*please.*" Desperation filled her tone, and he looked up at last, a measure of sympathy in his eyes.

"When she's around, I want her. But when she's not..." His eyes drifted back toward the doors, and his voice drifted into a whisper. "I want other things."

All the hope Nat had started to feel crumbled around her.

Caleb was so sure he wanted her. He *did* want her.

But as soon as his mate showed up, Nat would not be the one he wanted.

———

"What's wrong?"

Nat didn't say anything. She just pulled him into her arms as soon as the car door closed behind him.

Caleb scooped her out of the seat and onto his lap, crushing her to him.

"What is it?" he whispered, kissing her face softly and stroking her hair back from her neck.

"I just feel sick," she whispered.

"Because of me?"

"Not because of *you*. Just...because of the whole situation. I'm so scared, Caleb." Her voice was husky, and he wrapped his arms around her more tightly.

"I wish you would believe me," he said with a small whine, and she couldn't help smiling against him.

"You're always so sure you can do whatever you want...I love that so much."

"And have I ever been wrong?"

A deep sigh left her.

"You've never faced a situation where you weren't in charge."

"And you think I'm not in charge of my own mind?" he demanded, a hint of outrage in his tone.

"It's not your mind I'm worried about, Caleb," she

whispered, toying with the neckline of his v-neck t-shirt and trailing her finger across his skin. "Does it really feel like you're being cooked from the inside out when I touch you?"

He pulled back, outrage definitely in his eyes now.

"What the fuck has Ethan been saying?"

She tried curling back into him but he kept her away, looking into her face intently.

"Nat?" he demanded.

A groan escaped her.

"You won't tell me how bad it feels! And I know it's because you don't want *me* to feel bad."

"Nat, I told you years ago! It's like fire!"

"Yeah, but I thought it was like...you know...fire maybe like *I* feel!"

"It *is*," he said, his voice growing husky as he reached up to stroke her cheek. "There's just something else there at the same time that causes pain. And the more I want you, the more it hurts."

Her fingers kept tracing the skin at the base of his neck, and she bit her lip.

"But when you're a wolf..." she said looking up, a question in her eyes.

He exhaled, raising a brow.

"Then..." he whispered, his hand slipping up her jean clad thigh as he leaned in to kiss her neck, "it's a very different pain..."

A shiver went through her, and her lashes fluttered closed.

"I...I want to say yes, Caleb," she began nervously, rubbing her lips together when he went completely rigid. "But Ethan said that he only wants other things when his mate isn't around. So maybe you only want me now because she isn't here."

"Ethan and I need to have a talk," he bit out, pulling back to stare sternly at her. "Nat, Ethan isn't me." His voice was blunt. Final.

Then he exhaled again and leaned his head back on the seat, closing his eyes.

"You're mad at me?" she asked, her voice small.

"Yes, I'm mad at you. You make me insane sometimes. Because I *fucking love you*, Nat!"

He opened his eyes again to glare at her before sighing.

"Come on. We're going out," he said, setting her back down in her seat and starting the car.

"Out where?" she asked, fastening her seatbelt.

"Somewhere we don't have to hide or worry about anyone else coming around. We're not doing homework tonight. Or chores. We're staying out late, and we'll be tired tomorrow."

She grinned.

"You know, you've become a bit of a tyrant in your old age."

He kissed her palm as he drove, glancing over with wide, innocent eyes.

"I'm the alpha. It's my job."

She snorted. But she also leaned back and let him take them wherever he wanted.

They drove for about half an hour before she realized where he was headed: a forest area high up in the mountains where Caleb liked to roam sometimes as no hunters were allowed. They went more frequently in the summer, when they could spare the time in between working, but during the school year it just wasn't that practical.

It wasn't a place Nat would have wanted to get stuck in without him as the local wildlife also roamed the area, from coyotes to bears and all sorts of creepy crawly things. But with Caleb, it was heaven.

After almost an hour of driving, they pulled into a small area off the road that Caleb had scouted right after buying the car. No one had ever been here when they'd visited, and they could pull into the brush enough for the car to be mostly hidden.

He turned off the engine and turned to look at her, biting the inside of his cheek. She narrowed her eyes at him.

"What are you up to?"

Innocent eyes stared back at her, and he opened his door, stepping out and starting to pull off his clothes.

Nat eyed him suspiciously as she exited the vehicle, crossing her arms on the top and trying to keep from looking at him. It was always such torture seeing his gorgeous muscled body, aching to run her hands all over him, only to have him need to shift almost immediately if she did.

But he didn't shift after undressing, and she watched warily as he walked around to her. Her breath caught at the sight, her eyes helplessly running down his body.

"Nat…" He slid his arms around her waist, looking at her with heavy eyes. "Will you do something for me?"

She frowned up at him.

"I swear, Caleb, if you brought me all the way up here just to try to mount me, I will lock myself in the car until you're ready to leave!"

"You're so suspicious," he whispered, nibbling on her neck and breathing her in. "I swear I won't do that until you're ready. But I do want something from you…"

Her body was melting, the pain between her thighs growing sharper with every moment, and he shuddered.

"Take off your clothes for me," he said, his voice husky now. "I want to feel your naked thighs around me while I run. Your breasts pressed against my back. Your scent all over me…"

He groaned as her body responded to every word even as her alarm grew in equal measure. She would be pressed up against him as a wolf. Feeling him between her thighs as a wolf. She had ridden on his back many times but never like that…

"Will you do it?" he whispered, his hands sliding slowly under her shirt, lifting it to glide up her skin and unhook her bra. He paused when he reached the clasp, moving his mouth to hers, his tongue parting her lips to slip inside. "Nat, answer me…I can't stay like this for long," he choked out.

A small sound left her throat, but she nodded, and he groaned again, quickly undoing her bra and pulling it off with her shirt. Pain etched deep lines in his face, and his fingers rapidly unsnapped her jeans, yanking them down and dropping to his knees in front of her.

The breath left her lungs in a sharp gasp, and she buried her hands in his hair when he slid his tongue between her wet lips, his hands pulling off her shoes and jeans until she was as naked as he. He grabbed her hard from behind, pressing her into him and plunging his tongue in her as deeply as he could. Deeper and deeper until she gasped again. His hands fell away and he looked up at her, his tongue buried all the way inside her…while her hands were buried in his fur.

She stared down at him, trembling, and he slowly slid his tongue back out of her, gliding it along the sensitive nub until her fingers clenched him helplessly, only to slide it inside her once more.

"Caleb…I…" She swallowed, her thighs shaking, and he pushed on her until she fell back against the car, her hands still gripping his fur. And then all she could do was hold onto him as he licked and pressed into her, his eyes never leaving hers. Her thighs tightened around his head while she struggled to breathe, and he growled, pushing into her harder until she began convulsing all around him, gasping and pulling at him with a small cry.

And then she was slipping, sliding down the side of the car as his long tongue slid out of her. Wrapping her arms around him, she leaned her head against his weakly while he licked her neck, her face, in long, slow caresses.

"Caleb…" she whispered. "Are you…in pain?"

He whined, his tongue pressing harder against her, and a shudder went through her. She *wanted* to look. And…she was afraid to look. Afraid to touch… But this was *Caleb*. And this was the only way he could feel her.

She swallowed and sat back on her heels, small tremors running through her.

"Let me see," she said softly, running her hands along the underside of his coat.

He went completely still, his muzzle against her neck, and she swallowed again, scooting forward slightly. Wrapping one arm around his neck to hold herself steady, she slid the other farther down his stomach, feeling the fur give way to smooth, soft skin a moment before her fingertips touched something extremely warm and very, very hard.

Her chest shook with each breath while she slowly wrapped her hand around the smooth skin, and Caleb snarled into her neck. She clung to him more tightly, small sounds coming from her throat as she gently cupped the giant knot, and Caleb's growl became more fierce, his jaws snapping open to grab her throat.

A deep shudder went through her, and she tilted her neck, holding his head to her as she began stroking her hand up the impossibly long shaft, moaning each time his fangs pressed into her skin a little too hard. His snarl turned vicious and her grip tightened, moving back and forth, massaging down to the knot and back to the tip while holding his head to her and keeping her throat fully open to him.

She could feel his hips moving, his growl a constant rumble deep in his chest, and her body flowed anew as she stroked him, faster and faster, clinging to him harder each time he bit into her, until he was thrusting wildly into her hand, over and over, and hot liquid gushed over her arm while harsh, pained cries tore from his throat, piercing the dusk around them.

Nat didn't know why tears sprang to her eyes, but she turned her head to bury her face in his coat, feeling the warmth of his breath flowing over her and his fangs scraping gently across her skin as his jaws relaxed at last. He kept his muzzle against her neck, standing very still, panting heavily, while she continued holding the hot, hard length along her arm.

They stayed that way for a long time. Still. Silent. Until the swelling in the knot subsided and he shifted at last, kneeling in front of her while she still held him in her hand, both of them shaking.

When she started to pull her hand away, he held her to him.

"Stay," he whispered, his voice raw. "It doesn't hurt right now. And I want to feel you holding me while I can."

He cupped her cheeks, his eyes searching her face while her own glistened as she looked at him.

"Are you okay?" he asked, worry in his eyes.

She nodded, rubbing her cheek against his palm, and his eyes fell to her neck. His fingertips glided across her skin, touching the deep indentations his fangs had left, before he leaned down to touch them with his tongue. Her eyes closed and her head fell into his hand, exposing her throat to him once more, and he groaned.

"I need to do that inside you, Nat. So much. You don't know," he choked out, his lips and tongue sucking and tasting each spot on her skin. "Feeling your hand around me…"

A deep shudder went through him, and his lips trailed up her neck until they touched hers, brushing against her in the lightest kisses.

"It took everything in me not to yank you back to me and force myself inside you," he whispered, sending shivers through her once more. "It's overwhelming. Consuming. A pain so different…so fucking different."

"It…didn't feel good?" she asked in a small voice, and he pulled them both up on their knees to crush her to him, pressing her hand into him harder and gripping her hair as his lips moved against hers.

"Good…" his laugh was a harsh, pained sound. "It was so fucking good, Nat. So beyond good. Like every moment of pain

I've ever had was stuck inside me, trapped, and you let it all out...all over you..."

A deep shudder went through him, and he buried his face in her neck with a moaning cry.

"Fuck, it hurts again. No, stay. Stay...I need you touching me. But fuck, Nat... However much I wanted you before..."

He lifted his head once again and gripped her hair fiercely, pulling her head back to look down at her with burning eyes.

"You are *mine*. Forever. If I have to fight the entire fucking universe to keep you, I will. And I'll destroy anyone—*anyone*—who tries to take you away from me," he hissed, and Nat whimpered as his hand tightened in her hair.

His grip relaxed, and he kissed her softly.

"Ride me," he whispered. "I want to feel your naked body wrapped around me."

Her moans were soft beneath his lips, and she nodded, breathing him in for one last moment before he shifted again. His body was hard once more, but he only rubbed his head against her chest, trying to lift her. Standing on trembling legs, she slid her hands through his fur and climbed on his back, the feel of his silky black coat seductively smooth between her bare thighs.

A low growl sounded in his throat when she leaned forward, pressing her breasts against him and her face against his neck, and pulled her legs up to grip his body.

And then they were off. Tearing through the woods at a speed that set her heart racing, the cool evening air whistling by and soothing the burning flames that threatened to consume them.

———

"Forget to mention something yesterday?"

Caleb leaned against the locker beside Nat's, his eyes bright on hers, while she gathered her books for fourth period.

She parted her lips and stared at him, holding her locker half open.

"Uh...I got...distracted. I was going to talk to you about it..."

"Well," he said, looking away for a moment and rubbing the bridge of his nose. "The whole school is talking about it now."

Nat bit her lip.

"You're upset..."

He turned back to her, his eyes still bright.

"Why would I be upset? My *sister* gets caught naked with my two favorite guys in the world, on the floor, in a fucking manwich. Why should that upset me?"

"That is not what happened!" she hissed, leaning in close. "Ethan was the one naked!"

She groaned immediately at his look and closed her eyes.

"You *know* what that means," she glared at him.

"Yes," he hissed back, his eyes raging now. "That I'm going to break the promise I made our freshman year."

"Can you not be ridiculous!" she said, slamming her locker shut and turning to go, only to jerk to a halt when Caleb grabbed her arm. She rounded on him with a harsh whisper. "Would you think! I can't talk to you about this here!"

"Try," he ground out.

Her eyes closed again, and she counted to ten before reopening them.

"Caleb, Ethan had an anxiety attack. The kind *you* get sometimes with *me*. *He* got it from *Preston*. And the teacher came back to the room before Ethan was able to get back to normal again." Her eyes narrowed at the growing uncertainty in his. "And the fact that I have to explain *any* of that after last night makes me..."

Her voice trailed off in a strangled tone, but Caleb was biting his cheek now.

"You look really cute right now," he whispered, holding on

when she tried to yank her arm away. "I'm sorry...don't be mad."

She smacked his chest with her book when he tried to pull her close.

"Would you remember where we are!" she whispered, her eyes sweeping the hall quickly and noting the furtive looks.

"I don't care," he said, his voice growing husky as he rubbed her arm in small circles with his thumb. "I've been thinking about last night all morning. All night. I barely slept. I'm tired. And I'm so fucking hungry for you..." he finished in a whisper, starting to pull her close once more.

This time she hit his nose, bringing the book back to peek out over it when he began glaring at her again.

"Sorry," she said in a small voice, her eyes wide with apology. But her grip tightened on the hardcover when his eyes softened.

"You look really cute," he grinned.

Groaning, she raised the book to hide behind it completely.

"You can't look at me like that here." Her muffled whine didn't seem to have an effect as his grin had only widened by the time she peeked out again.

"Skip class with me."

"I can't," she said with real disappointment, lowering her book to her chest and inclining her head to go. Caleb fell into step beside her, his eyes still beseeching. "I have Mr. Jones's class right now. I'm not exactly on his good side, and you *do* want me to have the grades to get into the same school as you, right?"

"I still don't see why we have to go to college at all."

"So we don't have to live in a trailer the rest of our lives."

"I've kind of liked it so far," he murmured, his eyes running the length of her. His grin returned when she held her book up to cover her face once more. "You're going to trip."

Her eyes peeked up at him behind the book.

"You'd never let me."

His hand still held her upper arm, and he brushed her skin slowly.

"No," he whispered, his eyes soft. "I'll always protect you."

They stopped just outside the classroom, and Nat had to stop herself this time from being the one to pull him closer. But his head lifted and he narrowed his eyes as Preston walked by, avoiding his gaze.

Nat stopped him before he went through the door.

"What happened!" she breathed, staring at the dark bruise on his jaw and his black eye. "Did your dad do this?"

"Meh, just ignore it, Natty. He got too drunk to remember he couldn't win anymore. And Mr. Jones got him all riled up on the phone yesterday," he finished in a mutter, still trying to turn away from her.

Nat looked back at Caleb, worry in her eyes, to see him frowning at her hand on Preston's arm. She kicked him slightly and flared her eyes at him when he raised his eyes to hers.

What am I supposed to do? he mouthed in outrage.

She was still glaring at him when Ethan walked up and stopped beside him.

"Let me go, Natty," Preston whispered, keeping his head down and trying to pull away. "I know how to handle my old man."

Ethan frowned, staring at her hand on Preston as well, and she scowled at both of them.

"I know you do. But...you could stay with us." She ignored Caleb's horrified look and lifted her eyes to Preston. "You're eighteen. Your dad can't make you stay there."

"Natty, that's sweet but you've got, like, no room at all."

His eyes were a mix of appreciation and frustration as he looked down at her, still trying to pull away, but he jumped when Ethan suddenly walked around to face him and stared at the bruises with a darkness growing in his eyes.

They stood in silence while the hall around them cleared, the

last few students finding their way into their classrooms, and
Caleb stepped close enough to Nat for the heat from his body to
warm her back, his hand near the wall brushing her hip where it
couldn't be seen. She tried to ignore the heat it was building
in her.

"Stay with me," Ethan said quietly at last. "My dad's trip was
extended. He won't be back for weeks."

Preston blinked down at him.

"Dude. I can't stay with you. You're…I can't stay with you."

"You're worried about what everyone's saying?"

"No! I mean, *yes*, but…no! Because you're a…" he looked
around, eyeing Caleb warily for a moment before frowning more
intently. "Wait a minute. The black wolf…"

Preston looked at Nat, and she pressed her lips together, her
eyes going to Caleb who was glowering at Preston and Ethan, his
hand tightening on her hip.

"I think that's a great idea—stay with Ethan," Nat said
hurriedly, pushing Preston toward the door. *Sorry*, she mouthed at
Caleb as she followed Ethan and Preston into the room. *I'll see you
after lunch.*

They shared one last lingering look, Caleb's full of
frustration, before she slipped inside.

"It's *not* a great idea, Natty," Preston returned to the topic
with heat, thoroughly distracted once more. "At least with my
dad, I can defend myself!"

"*I would never hurt you*," Ethan said, staring at Preston with
burning eyes as they took their seats.

"Well I wouldn't be able to stop you if you changed your
mind," Preston muttered, looking away.

"I would *never* hurt you, and I will *never* change my mind. I
know what it's like."

Preston snorted, his eyes returning to Ethan once more.

"You? You're like a super hero," he scoffed. "What would you
know about it?"

"I'm small," he answered bluntly, "compared to my family. And my dad isn't the gentle sort."

Nat's gaze turned to Ethan while Preston frowned at him.

"He's hit you?"

"It's not exactly hitting."

Nat and Preston stared at him, but he kept his eyes locked on Preston's.

"Sorry, dude. That's fucking bullshit. You shouldn't have to take shit like that from anyone."

"Neither should you. Stay with me."

Preston's eyes grew wary again.

"Dude…even if you wouldn't do anything…it sounds like your dad might not be as cool."

"I told you. He's gone for a while."

"What about your mom?"

Ethan shook his head.

"She died right after I was born."

"Jesus…sorry, man. Shit. Maybe we do have more in common than I thought. Mine didn't die, though. She just bailed on me. Couldn't stand my dad, I guess. Maybe me. I dunno."

He scratched his head while Ethan watched him steadily.

"We have a big house. There's plenty of space. You'll be safe, I promise."

Nat looked at Preston, who still looked unconvinced.

"Are you kidding me right now? This is like winning a vacation at some super resort! You *have* to go and then tell me what it's like to have money," she whispered leaning into him. She knew Ethan could hear her, but she didn't think Preston knew he could.

He looked down at her, his eyes wavering, before nodding at Ethan hesitantly.

"Well, if you're okay letting me bum at your place, I guess it would be pretty dumb to say no…"

A smile lit Ethan's eyes, and he opened his mouth to answer when Mr. Jones suddenly stopped at Nat's desk.

"You three," he spat out, "are to be in here promptly this afternoon to serve your detention properly. I don't know how you weaseled out of a suspension, but this is *my* classroom, and I expect *respect*."

He didn't wait for an answer but turned back to stalk up to the front of the class to prepare his slides. Nat snuck a peek behind her to see Preston shrug.

"Doesn't matter. Can't go to my job looking like this anyway."

Ethan's eyes were almost tender on him, but Preston was too busy staring at Mr. Jones resentfully to notice. And Nat just turned back around in silence.

13

"It would give them all something else to talk about," Caleb whispered.

"Yeah—something worse!" Nat said, smacking his hands away in a panic while they stood outside the school. "I have to get to detention, and *you* have to get to practice! And *don't* give me that look."

His eyes were huge and sad, but she only glared at him and the smirk came right back to his face, turning into a pained look when his eyes roamed her body.

"Nat, we're eighteen now…what does it matter?"

"Legally we're full siblings since my mom got you all set up. I don't even know how much trouble she could get into for that now. Or what it might mean for college applications. We agreed to wait until after high school before trying to unravel it all!"

"Well I changed my mind," he said, a whine creeping into his voice. "I want to unravel everything now…"

She smacked his hands harder as they pulled at the ribbon lacing up her shirt.

"I'm going now!" she choked out, ignoring his laughing

groan. Her cheeks flamed as she hurried back inside the building, sure someone must have seen them this time. Maybe they really should come clean. This was getting impossible.

After all, how much worse could the gossip at school get? She couldn't go anywhere anymore without sudden silence greeting her the moment she walked into the room. Preston and Ethan had some of that from what she'd observed, but it seemed the girl always got the worst of public censure.

"I said *promptly*, Ms. Wilson," Mr. Jones seethed when she scurried into the classroom.

"Sorry," she huffed, a bit out of breath as she sat down.

Ethan and Preston were already in the room, but she assumed Mr. Jones had required them to sit far apart because they were each in opposite corners. Nat's usual desk was in the middle, and since he didn't have her move, her spot must be fine.

"I want an essay from each of you on the chapter I went over in class today. I hope you were paying attention because this is closed book and it *will* be graded."

Preston's muttered curses captured her own thoughts, but she suppressed her groan and pulled out her notebook, trying desperately to remember what chapter they were on.

The scratch of pens and pencils were the only sounds in the room for the next half an hour, when Mr. Jones stood, staring at his phone with his seemingly perpetual pissed off expression.

"You all better stay in your seats this time," he muttered, lifting the phone to his ear as he left the room. The door clicked behind him, shutting out the sharp tones of his voice launching into an argument.

"Oh my god," Preston exhaled loudly, leaning back with a groan. "Do either of you know what the fuck he talked about today?"

Nat looked at Ethan, relieved when he raised a brow and began giving them a summary. She and Preston scribbled madly, racing to finish before the teacher returned and breathing mutual sighs of relief when they did.

"Dude, I love you," Preston said with another loud exhale, flopping back and stretching out his legs while he closed his eyes. "God that guy sucks."

A small smile touched Ethan's mouth, but his eyes were serious as they drifted down Preston's body. He looked back at his desk without expression when Preston opened his eyes again and turned his head towards him.

"Aren't you missing practice?"

"It doesn't matter. I don't need to practice."

Preston snorted.

"That's true, isn't it? Are you like, actually superhuman?"

Ethan lifted his eyes to him once more, an almost innocent agreement in their depths. Preston snickered.

"Fuck. What I wouldn't give for that… Dude, can you bite me and make me like you?" he said, perking up suddenly and sitting up in his seat.

Ethan frowned.

"I don't have a disease. It's who I am."

Preston grimaced and leaned back once more.

"Meh. It was too good to be true anyhow," he muttered, looking away and scratching at his bruise.

Ethan's eyes filled with dismay.

"But…you *have* a wolf now. To protect you. If you want it." He looked a bit pale as he finished, but Preston just looked surprised.

"What—you mean like…having a dog?"

Nat barely refrained from visibly cringing, remembering how strongly Caleb had reacted to any such thought. She peeked at Ethan, watching the expressions struggling on his face.

"Yes," he whispered at last, his eyes pained. "Like a dog."

Preston grimaced.

"Sorry—that was bad to say, wasn't it? I'm not good with words."

Ethan shook his head, the pained look going away to be replaced with a serious one.

"No. It wasn't bad. I don't mind."

A hint of vulnerability touched Preston's eyes, but he quickly looked down at the paper on his desk, his brows pulling together.

Ethan looked as if he wanted to say something more, but his gaze flew toward the door and the blood drained from his face.

"Neither of you say *anything* about *anything* you aren't supposed to know," he whispered harshly, and Preston's head jerked toward him again in surprise. "Not even a whisper!"

Ethan's eyes were locked on the door, and Nat and Preston looked at each other before turning to stare at it as well. Was the teacher listening? No—she could hear the faint sounds of his voice from down the hall. She looked back at Preston, and he shrugged with a rather comical *I have no idea what the hell is going on* expression on his face. She almost laughed, but Ethan looked so traumatized she couldn't quite feel it.

So she just sat still, staring at the door with a growing sense of unease and feeling silly as the minutes passed without anything happening. She turned to look at Ethan again, but his expression was unchanged.

Turning back with a sigh, she toyed with her pencil, holding it at one end and shaking it lightly, trying to make it look like rubber. Her eyes were on the pencil when she vaguely realized the view behind it had changed, and her focus shifted...to see a pair of piercing, frosty blue eyes, staring out from the face of the most shockingly, exquisitely beautiful girl she had ever seen.

An ebony haired beauty with flawless, porcelain skin stared at Ethan through the windowed door, a seductive smirk on her full, glossy red lips. Thick, dark lashes blinked lazily as she ran the tip of her pink tongue under her upper lip, grinning with white perfect teeth when he didn't react.

Mr. Jones's irate voice could be heard approaching, and the girl's lush wavy locks swayed as she turned and arched a delicate brow, silencing him into helpless stutters. Her dulcet tones flowed through the closed door as she spoke.

"Holy shit, dude! Is that your girlfriend?" Preston choked out, staring at the door in wide eyed amazement. "You fucking *rock*!"

Ethan somehow managed to grow even more pale.

"She's not my girlfriend," he whispered, still staring at the door, and the sickness that had been growing in Nat's gut dropped the bottom out of her entire world with his final words. "She's my sister."

————

"Y-yes, of course."

Mr. Jones's muffled tones came through the door a moment before it opened, and any hope Nat had held inside deserted her completely as six feet of elegant, erotic femininity sauntered into the room, her long, shapely legs in their high heeled boots and tight fitting jeans gliding across the floor. A form fitting shirt revealed a gentle swell of small but beautifully shaped breasts, her hem at her midriff exposing a smooth, tight expanse of skin above her low cut jeans.

She had eyes for no one but Ethan, and her lips parted as she walked towards him. Her step faltered only once, her head turning slightly as she passed Nat's desk, but she ignored her and continued, straddling the seat in front of Ethan and leaning forward to cross her arms on his desk.

"Daddy told me you got in trouble, baby bro." Her lips puckered in a sympathetic pout when Ethan stared at her without expression. "He wanted me to check on you. Make sure you didn't. Need. My. Help." She punctuated each of her final words with a soft tap of her fingertip on his nose before trailing her finger down over his lips softly, grinning again when he didn't react.

"I'd love your help. Can you get me out of detention?"

Vick paused before releasing a small sound of amusement, her eyelids heavy.

"Now what kind of sister would I be if I shielded you from the consequences of your poor choices?"

"I don't know. Why don't you try it, and we'll see."

She made the same sound of amusement, but her eyes narrowed further. Then she grinned and stood for a moment before sliding onto his lap and putting her arms around his neck.

"Poor little runt." She ruffled his hair softly and rubbed her nose against his. "Life isn't easy for little guys, is it? And all you can use…" she breathed against him, "is your tongue. It would be a shame if someone ever cut it out."

"Uh, detention dismissed!" Mr. Jones said hastily, sounding flustered, and Vick glanced back at him with her lips parted in a knowing grin. But it froze on her face when her gaze drifted back and she caught sight of Nat staring at her.

Sliding off Ethan's lap in a fluid motion, she moved with catlike grace through the rows of seats until she stood in front of her, looking down with narrowed eyes.

Nat could barely hear anything in the room. Her face felt hot and cold at the same time, the sickness in her gut spreading throughout her body as she stared up at the cold blue eyes.

"And why," Vick said quietly, leaning down and into Nat's neck, "do you smell so weird to me…"

Nat swallowed while Vick touched the short, flowing sleeve of her thrift store dress, pinching it between her fingertips and wrinkling her nose in distaste. The exotic fingers feathered lightly across her neckline, her eyes narrowing further as she let the ribbon slip through her hands.

"Are you staying at the house?"

Vick frowned in annoyance when Ethan stepped beside her, frustrated confusion still in her eyes.

"Why would I stay in this horrid little town? I've done my sisterly duty and reminded you that I'm watching…out for you," she said, the smirk beginning to return to her lips as she turned to him.

"Then you won't mind if a friend of mine stays over."

"Ooh—the runt has a friend already," she said, turning to him completely and wrapping her arms around his neck. She stood about three inches taller than Ethan in her heels. "Is it a girl?" she asked with feigned excitement.

Ethan looked to the side, and Vick followed his gaze when he inclined his head. Her eyes swept Preston slowly from head to toe as he sat, still stretched out in the corner of the room, and his face was flaming by the time she finished.

"Oh little Ethan," she murmured turning back to her brother with heavy eyes. "To think all Daddy's dreams for a pack depend on you…"

Her smile slipped away, and a dead look entered her eyes.

"Don't torture yourself too much, baby brother," she whispered. "Or I'll start to think you like it."

"We both know that's not possible," he said evenly.

Her smile didn't touch her eyes, but she let her arms fall from his neck and stepped back, turning to glance down at Nat once more.

Mr. Jones cleared his throat for not the first time, but it finally drew Vick's attention. He paled at her glance but gestured toward the door.

"If you all wouldn't mind, I need to lock up," he said apologetically. Vick raised her brow as if contemplating, but finally sighed and reached down to grab Nat's arm.

"Let's chat," she smiled, pulling her up and towards the door, ignoring when Nat tried to grab her things.

Nat shot a worried glance behind her to see Ethan gathering

her papers, his own eyes cautious, and she tried to keep up with Vick's long strides. The dark haired girl didn't stop after she exited the classroom but pulled her down the hall toward the exit to the parking lot. The parking lot beside the football field.

Panic hit her. She wasn't ready for this. She wasn't ready to see them meet. To watch his eyes fall on the most perfect, beautiful match the universe could have possibly designed for him.

Tears sprang to her eyes. She wasn't ready. She *wouldn't* see this. Not yet.

When Vick refused to slow or release her arm, despite her attempts to stop walking, Nat abandoned any pretense of civility.

"Let me go!" she said sharply, trying to pry her fingers from her arm, her fear of the girl completely subsumed by the fear of what would happen when Caleb saw her.

A derisive sound was her only answer, and Nat stared at the rapidly approaching door before collapsing on the ground, the hard tile stinging her knees but making Vick pause at last.

The long, elegant legs in front of her were still for a moment before bending to crouch beside her, dry amusement in her eyes.

"Now that was very ungraceful. I only wanted to have a word with you out where I can breathe," she murmured, her eyes sweeping over Nat and dismissing her in a single take.

"You might have tried *asking*."

Vick's brow raised again with an incredulous little laugh.

"Does the lion ask the mouse for permission? Or the wolf the little lamb," she said with soft menace.

Nat narrowed her own eyes at her.

"If I recall, a mouse saved a lion once who was ensnared. I might be weaker than you, but I'm not entirely helpless."

"Well aren't you the cutest little thing," Vick breathed, her eyes bright. "I think I could just eat you up."

Nat's heart was racing, and she knew Vick could hear it. But she wouldn't back down. She could only kill her once, and she almost thought that would be better than whatever would be waiting for her if she walked out the door.

Nat heard Preston and Ethan's steps approaching, and a slow smile spread across Vick's face.

"The cavalry has arrived. I—" Her smile fled, and she stared with wide eyes at Nat, her chest expanding and contracting in rapid bursts. Her brow pulled together repeatedly, and a whimper sounded in her throat as her lips parted.

Nat felt a crushing weight on her chest as Vick's head turned slowly toward the door, and her own eyes followed, tears threatening to choke her. She could hear the footsteps now. She knew them by heart, every firm stride on the gravel outside breaking off a little piece of her.

Until the door flew open, and the same gorgeous, beautiful, *wonderful* face she had seen every day for almost four years stared into the hall, his brow pulled together in furious confusion.

A small cry came from Vick's throat, and she stood quickly as Caleb's eyes widened in shock.

"Fenri!" Pained, frustrated longing filled her voice, and she began walking forward, her hands gripped in tight fists at her sides. One step. Another. And with every step closer, Caleb flattened himself against the door behind him, his face a mask of horror.

Bile threatened to overwhelm Nat, and she covered her mouth with her hand, fighting desperately to hold on. To not lose it here. Not here. In front of her. In front of them.

She didn't want to see. To know. She couldn't...

But her wolf was not her wolf anymore. And between his legs was the unmistakable, rock hard proof.

———

Nat ran past Preston and Ethan, holding onto the contents of her stomach just long enough to make it to the restroom. The stalls were empty and she dashed into the first one she reached, retching painfully into the bowl until she had nothing left. Chills washed over her, and she sank to the floor, pulling her knees to her chest and leaning her head on her arms. Her eyes flew up in both hope and panic when she heard a knock.

"Natty? You okay?"

Preston. She leaned over the bowl once more, her stomach heaving again. Caleb never would have let her run off before. Ever. He'd have chased her down and made sure she was okay.

"I'm fine," she choked out once the convulsions passed, flushing and turning to walk to the sink on shaky legs. Leaning against the counter weakly, she stared into the mirror, her eyes huge and dark in her pale face.

The creak of the door sounded, and Preston's face came into view, his eyes darting around as he stepped inside.

"First time I've been in the girls' room. It's nicer in here…"

Nat turned back to the sink, cupping the water to splash it on her face before turning off the faucet and reaching for a paper towel. And then she just stood there, staring down at the wet brown paper in her hands.

Preston hesitated before patting her on the back awkwardly.

"She must have really shook you up, huh. What did she say?"

Nat shook her head and raised a finger to her lips, tugging on her ear.

They can hear? he mouthed, his eyes widening further when she nodded. *Wow.*

"Hey," he whispered. "Want to get out of here? I have a friend in town who's probably totally high right about now, but he has good video games. Wanna go play?"

Nat looked up in desperate relief, nodding vigorously, and his eyes lit up as he grinned. He started toward the door, stopping when she balked.

"I can't go out there again," she whispered. "Can we…go out the window?"

Her eyes lifted to his hesitantly, but he looked relieved.

"And avoid the crazy psycho bitch in the hall?" he whispered as quietly as possible. "Hell yeah!"

They quickly investigated the large rectangular window, forcing it open when the old dried paint prevented it from moving more than a few inches. And then they were climbing out of the single story building, the drop below a bit farther than Nat had realized. Preston went first and steadied her as she jumped down beside him.

"Life is always crazy around you," he whispered with a grin.

Only because of Caleb. She was pretty boring by herself.

They walked toward the road, away from the football field, and every moment she expected Caleb to show up. To come running after her. To tell her it wasn't what she thought. That somehow, miraculously, it could all be okay.

But he didn't show.

"Fuck, Natty. Are you actually sick?" Preston asked, hovering over her when she stopped to dry heave into the grass.

She shook her head once the convulsions had passed.

"I just need some water," she said hoarsely.

"Well come on. It's not too far from here—just a couple blocks away. Man, she must have really done a number on you..." He scratched his head as they continued walking. "Maybe I should have tried stopping her when she grabbed you. It was just all so weird. I didn't really know what to do."

"It's okay. I didn't either."

"They can't hear this far away, right?" He lowered his voice to a whisper but breathed a sigh of relief when she shook her head. "Holy fuck. I've been fucking spinning since yesterday. Wolves! I mean...werewolves, right? How is that even possible?"

"More things, Horatio..." she said, giving him a look when he stared at her blankly. "You didn't do our final project in English last year, did you. It's from Hamlet."

"Aw, jeez, you're quoting Hamlet now? I thought we were friends!"

That pulled a small smile from her, but it quickly vanished.

"What'd she say to you, though? Would they...do you think they'd actually, you know...kill us?" He swallowed at her nod. "Shit. Why you, though? You think she hates girls?"

Because she must have smelled her mate all over me. But she couldn't tell him that.

"I don't know."

She didn't know anything anymore. A vast sea of emptiness filled her. Emptied her. Until there was nothing left.

"Ethan said you'd be fine with her." His tone was doubtful. "That we should let you both talk."

A sharp pang in her gut took away her breath and surprised her with its sting. Did Ethan not really like her? Maybe he only liked Preston. She'd been so excited when a new kid showed up. And he'd been nice to her...but he must have just wanted to be close to Preston.

"Why do you even like me, Preston?" she whispered, the sidewalk blurring beneath her feet as they walked. "No one else does."

"What are you talking about? You're awesome! It's just, nobody knows you."

They knew enough.

"Am I too weird?"

"No! You're just...you know...different!"

He rubbed the back of his neck, looking flustered.

"Well...thank you. For being a friend, I mean."

"Uh, yeah, sure. Oh, hey, there's my friends place!" he said, a touch of panic in his voice.

Nat rubbed her brow. Hard. Maybe she was wrong. Was he her friend? Or had he just been hanging out with her because of what his friends said—that he wanted to have sex with her? Or was it because he'd seen a black wolf with her when they were younger and was curious? Maybe she shouldn't have come here with him, but the idea of going back home...of sitting in her room, *waiting*. She had never wished more for a mother who was awake. Present. Who might actually still care about her underneath all the pills.

But this was the life she had. The one she was born into and had been trying so hard to figure out. To manage. But she had let herself become so dependent on Caleb. For his smiles. For his attention. For his help in every single area of her life. For his love...

He was a wolf. His life would be beautiful no matter who he was with. Grand and exciting. That was simply who he was. Did she really want to hold him back? To keep dragging him down into the mud with her? Maybe it was better this way.

"Fuck, Natty, I'm sorry! You know I suck with words!"

She hadn't realized tears were streaming down her cheeks, and she quickly wiped them away.

"It's not you. Sorry."

He looked uncertain, but they had arrived at the house. He knocked on the door, cracking it open when no one responded.

"Dude? You home?"

A slow voice answered from inside above what sounded like an old action movie, and Preston pushed the door open fully, stepping in and waiting for Nat to follow him through before closing it behind her. It smelled terrible, and she lifted her hand to her nose, trying to block the skunk like odor.

"Hey, man, we're just going to play games in your room. Cool?" he said to the form on the couch, pulling Nat behind him when the boy nodded with heavy eyes and a smile, inhaling from the joint in his hand. Preston stopped in the kitchen, pouring each of them a glass of water from the sink, before heading down the short hall.

Nat couldn't stop herself from coughing by the time they made it back to his room, and Preston cracked the window.

"It'll air out in a minute. But look!" He turned on the flat screen tv at the end of the bed and grabbed a couple controllers, tossing one to her that she caught just in time before turning to put in a disc. "You ever play this before?"

Nat shook her head and sat beside him on the bed, leaning back against the wall since it had no headboard. But at least it was more than just a mattress on the floor.

Preston explained the game while it loaded, and Nat tried following along once it began. But the sick feeling in her gut was spreading throughout her body with each passing minute. Caleb could have found her. Easily. Her scent would leave a trail he could follow for hours.

She pressed a button and died again, and Preston made a sound of aggravation.

"Are you even trying? Okay, I'm going to go back and get you *again*, but this time try, okay?" he said irritably, turning to look at her. "Jesus. You look like shit."

"I'm sorry," she whispered, putting the controller down. "This was a bad idea. I should go home."

He paled and dropped his controller to pull her back down beside him as she stood.

"Wait, Natty! Shit. I'm sorry. I didn't think she could mess you up so badly." He tentatively wrapped his arms around her, putting her head on his shoulder and patting her back. "Here. Just…cry it out, or something."

She wanted to laugh. He was so painfully uncomfortable. But instead she burst into quiet tears, deep sobs shaking her body.

"Geez…did she threaten you?" he asked hoarsely, holding her closer and leaning back on the bed. He flinched slightly when she put her arms around him, but began rubbing her back softly.

She wished she could tell him. Could tell someone. Just…talk about it with someone. But she had to keep Caleb's secret for him. Her wolf—no. Not hers. But a wolf who had been her protector for so long and deserved her loyalty, no matter what happened now. She would never betray him.

The front door sounded from the other room, and her heart hammered against Preston as she lifted her head, looking toward the bedroom door.

"Shit. I hope his mom isn't home. She usually works late and then goes out."

Her breath was coming in short bursts when the bedroom door cracked open…and disappointment knocked the breath out of her as every bit of her hope pooled in a hard knot in her gut.

"Dude. Were you following us?"

Ethan's eyes were hesitant, but he came in and closed the door behind him.

"Not the way you think."

Preston frowned.

"Can you *track* us?"

Ethan nodded, but his eyes were on Nat. She turned her face back to Preston's chest, closing her eyes as she lay beside him. He rubbed her back, and she tried to stop shaking.

"Nat," Ethan began, sitting down on the side of the bed carefully.

"It's *Natalie*. Don't pretend we're friends, Ethan."

Preston's hand paused for a moment, but she kept her eyes closed and he slowly went back to stroking her back.

"I *am* your friend."

She turned to glare at him at that.

"You *actually* threw me to the wolves. And to one who…" Her eyes blurred, and she dropped her head again.

"I'm sorry. I just…I needed to see," he said, his voice dropping to a whisper. "You don't understand. My sister…she's always been the dominant one. Always in control of everyone except maybe my father. But you threw her. I just…I made sure she wasn't in a killing mood before I let you go with her," he said beseechingly.

"Jesus, dude." Preston's voice was a bit hoarse. "A killing mood? How much of a psycho is she?"

The bed shifted before Ethan answered.

"She lives by her own rules. And her main rule is to get whatever she wants."

"Fuck. And you let her just drag Natty off? Why'd you tell me it was okay?"

"Because it was! She wasn't going to hurt her. It was something else. Besides," he muttered. "There's nothing you can do when she wants something."

"Oh, that's bullshit, man. You're a wolf!"

"I can't fight her! She has always won—always!"

Preston snorted in disgust.

"Dude. You can always fight. Just because you can't win, doesn't mean you can't fight."

Nat looked up as his voice trailed off into a mutter and he looked away, lifting his hand to his jaw and rubbing his bruises lightly.

"Preston…tell me the truth. Did you really get your dad to stop over the summer?"

He avoided her eyes for a moment, but when she kept looking up at him, he sighed at last and leaned his head back against the wall, closing his eyes.

"I'm *really* close. I think. But my old man is a tough fucking bastard with a lot of fighting experience." His eyes opened again to narrow on Ethan. "But at least I don't roll over for him. He gets a few bruises, too, every time he tries to fuck with me now."

Nat frowned remembering his flinch and reached down for the hem of his t-shirt.

"Whoa, Nat—what are you doing?" He grabbed her hand as she started to pull it up, but Ethan's gasp told her he was too slow. She sat up to look as Preston groaned, putting a hand on his head as they both lifted his shirt.

"It's no big deal. My abs are strong. It's not like anything is broken."

Nat's eyes filled with tears as she stared at the purple bruising all over his stomach. What must he have gone through as a child to be so accepting of it now?

"Why don't you leave?" Ethan asked hoarsely.

"And go where? I'm eighteen, don't have a high school diploma yet. If I drop out of school now, the best I'll ever do is have a factory job. Besides. I *want* to beat him. I want to fight until I *win*. I'm not some abused kid. I'm just a guy who keeps… fucking losing," he muttered, forcing his shirt back down and out of their hands. "But I *still* fight," he added, staring at Ethan intently.

Ethan swallowed, his eyes pained as they stared at Preston.

"Why?

"Because I'm not a fucking pussy! Jesus. Because who wants to be a fucking slave? Just let someone else tell you what to do all the time? Beat you without it costing them anything? I'm gonna make it fucking *cost* him every single time!"

Ethan dropped his head, his eyes wet.

"What if it kills you," he asked quietly, not looking up.

"Then I die! I'd rather die fighting than live the way he wants me to live. Some things are *worth* dying for."

"But not your father, Preston," she whispered. "It's not worth dying to prove something to him."

"Fuck him. I need to prove something to *me*."

She looked at his angry face a bit helplessly. She didn't think she'd ever admired him more—or wanted more strongly for him to get the hell out of that house.

"And anyhow," he said, pulling Nat back to him and leaning back on the bed once more. "You don't let a little *girl* go off with a psycho that's too badass for even another *wolf* to handle!"

Nat flattened her lips, but he was *trying* to be supportive, so she didn't say anything about the little girl part.

"I'm sorry…I just…wanted to see her lose for once."

Nat stared at Preston's chest, her eyes bleak.

"But she didn't lose, Ethan. I did. I lost everything."

"I don't think so…" he whispered, and she felt the bed shift and Preston's body stiffen beneath her. Turning her head to follow their gaze behind her, her own body went rigid.

Caleb stood in the doorway with desperate anguish flooding his eyes.

14

"NAT?" Caleb could barely get her name past the lump in his throat. The sickness in his gut twisted and curled, and all he wanted to do was drag her into his arms and never let go.

But she had turned her back to him the moment she saw him, hiding her face against Preston. Lying on the bed with Preston. Clinging to him. Flanked by Ethan on the edge of the bed.

He stepped forward on shaky legs, a band tightening around his chest...ready to break him.

"Nat..." He reached the side of the bed and sank to his knees slowly, wanting so desperately to touch her. Needing so desperately to touch her...

Swallowing, he moved his hand to her back, his gut almost doubling him over when she flinched. He sat trembling, resting his hand beside her, feeling her heat.

"Talk to me," he whispered. "Please talk to me."

"What am I supposed to say, Caleb?" The tears in her voice tore his heart out, but she kept her face turned away, lying on Preston's chest.

"It's not…" *It's not what it looked like.* The line he'd heard too many boys say or too many girls complain they'd heard. But it *wasn't*. It wasn't at all. "Nat…"

Tears choked him.

He saw her draw a shuddering breath and swallow before speaking in a shaky voice.

"It's not your fault. I know that. But…but you *shouldn't have had me cross that line with you*," she said turning at last, her eyes wet with unshed tears. "I *trusted* you to know what you wanted, even though—"

"I *do* know, Nat!" he cried out, reaching for her and ignoring her flinch this time. He leaned over her, stroking her hair from her face as she stared up at him, struggling not to let her tears fall. "Nothing has changed!"

"Everything has changed, Caleb! I saw you!" she cried.

He looked down at her, his lips parted in agonized helplessness.

"It's not what you think, Nat! I *know* how it looks. I know…" he whispered, stroking her cheeks as his eyes filled with tears. "But I don't want her—I swear it!"

She shoved him away, sitting up angrily.

"How can you say that? I told you I *saw* you—"

"And it doesn't mean what you think, Nat!" he cried, pulling her into his arms and putting his forehead on hers. He closed his eyes, turning his head softly against her. "You were wrong before —what you said when we were younger. You were so sure it meant I wasn't attracted to you, and you were *wrong*."

He leaned back, his eyes burning.

"And you're wrong now!"

She pressed her fists against his chest, her eyes torn between uncertainty and deep, terrible hurt.

"How can you say that when you've been with her for…for… I don't even know how long!"

"Nat...no," he whispered, an almost relieved feeling of shock going through him. "I've been looking for you!"

He held her tighter around her waist when she went to shove him away again, holding her head against his.

"Listen, Nat...just listen. Please... I kind of...stumbled outside at first, back through the door, just...just fucking *sick* inside," he said hoarsely. *"I didn't touch her, Nat. I told her I wasn't the person she thought—I couldn't be that now. But she took a lot of fucking persuading before I could shake her."*

His voice lowered to a growl before turning hoarse again.

"But the scent was too strong. I couldn't...I couldn't *find* you," he choked out, the fear that had left in him filling his voice. The loneliness. "I looked around the school. I drove home... It just took so long for it to fade."

A shudder went through him, and her tears fell a bit more.

"Please believe me...I can't lose you. I can't." Terror clawed at him. He needed her. She was his entire world, and if she wasn't in it... "You're my home, Nat. My everything. And I fucking *hate* that this body doesn't work right for you."

His voice cracked, his own tears spilling over. But he pulled back to glare at her.

"But it does *not* mean I want *her*. It feels like...like..."

Fuck. How could he describe it? Her eyes were looking at him in desperate, agonized hope. He needed to get this right.

"The scent...the moment I caught it, it just...it unlocked everything—every fucking desire I could ever have. It's like it freed my body at last. And the closer I get to it, the more it unlocks."

He held on when she tried pulling away, leaning into her to hold her still. Hold her to him.

"It freed every fucking desire I had, Nat. Every single one. And *every desire is for you*. It didn't change who I wanted. It didn't change what I want to do to you. With you. And it didn't make me want her just because I could finally feel everything I've wanted to feel so badly with you," he finished in a whisper, his thumbs stroking her cheeks.

"But she's your mate," she said with a small sob.

"That's fucking bullshit. I don't believe any of that. *You're* my mate. And maybe there's some fucked up genetic thing that means her scent unlocks something in me, but that is *all it can do, Nat.* It *can't* change who I want. And it can never *never* change who I love…"

His lips brushed against her cheek, a familiar, welcome pain beginning to burn in his gut alongside the fear as he licked her tears away. Trailing his tongue lightly across her skin, he found her lips at last, kissing her softly with every word while her ragged breaths flowed over him. Through him.

"I told you. If I have to fight the entire fucking universe to keep you, I will. Even if I have to fight you as well," he whispered, fear threatening to choke him once more. "But I'd rather have you beside me…helping me…" His voice turned husky. "Please help me, Nat. You don't know how much I need you."

A shudder went through her as he stroked her neck with his knuckles, his lips soft on her upper lip, her lower, his tongue licking at her in slow strokes until she released a whimpering cry and ripped her lips from his to bury her face in his neck.

He crushed her to him at last, pulling her off the bed to straddle him while he knelt on the floor, shaking and kissing her everywhere he could—her temple, her hair, her neck—rocking them both back and forth and burying his face in her hair while he moaned her name and tried desperately not to shift.

He needed her so fucking much. He needed to be inside her. To be part of her.

His hands were reaching for his jeans when Preston's hoarse voice broke through his haze of desire.

"What the fuck is all this weird shit with your sisters?"

———

Caleb looked down at Nat lifting her head, apprehension growing in her eyes as Preston's words sank in. He just pressed her into him harder, pushing her hips into his while she straddled him and leaning down to kiss her cheek.

At least there was one good thing to come out of this whole fucking mess. Preston finally knew Nat belonged to *him*. The urge to shift still ate at him, but he ran the back of his hand softly across her skin, his eyes drinking her in. He wanted her to stay on his lap forever. Or maybe turn around on all fours…

The sharp pain in his gut reminded him he needed to control his thoughts for now. They'd be alone again soon enough…and she *had* to let him in. He needed to cleanse the sickening, cloying feel of the deranged she-beast off his skin.

The thought of her sent another feeling twisting through his gut. It was the same feeling he'd had when she had grabbed his cock, squeezing before he was able to break her hold and shove her away—that's when he knew for sure. When he understood the feelings coursing through his body, the insane heat, the intense, overwhelming desire.

His body desperately, feverishly wanted to fuck. Her scent set him on fire and *made* him want to fuck, and the sensation just got stronger the closer she was. But it didn't make him want to fuck *her*.

Because when she touched his cock, the feeling in his gut was something he had felt before. When the blood of the man who had hurt Nat had spurted into his mouth.

Disgust.

"Preston, you can't tell anyone—my mom could get in trouble. She got all the paperwork so it would look like Caleb was her son so he could stay with us."

Preston hesitated.

"Natty…are you a…wolf?"

A little laugh bubbled up from her throat, sending ripples of happiness through Caleb, and he leaned down to nuzzle her neck.

"No, I am just like you."

He frowned against her skin. He did *not* like that.

"So you two aren't…related…in any way?"

"No!"

"Yes," Caleb said, pulling back.

Nat's eyes flew to his, a question in their depths.

"We're *family*, Nat," Caleb said intently. His voice softened, and he reached up to brush her hair back from her face. "You're my family…"

Her slow smile warmed every part of him.

"So…he *is* the black wolf, right?" he said. "The one who attacked me that night?"

Caleb looked up with heated eyes.

"You hurt Nat."

"Fuck, man," Preston said, going pale. "I was a dumb kid."

"Use that excuse again," he said quietly, his eyes narrowing.

Nat reached up and covered his eyes with her hand. But her other arm held him tight around his neck, so he bent into her neck again, inhaling deeply. Trying to get the toxic aroma of his supposed mate out of his lungs. Out of his memory.

"Caleb was young, too. He wouldn't do anything like that now."

He grunted into her neck in disagreement. He would destroy anyone and anything that hurt her.

Don't worry—I'll kill her.

A low snarl rumbled in his throat at the memory. His attempts to get rid of Vick by telling her he had someone in his life had, for the first time, made him grateful that everyone thought Nat was his sister. He'd snapped at the threat, shoving Vick against the side of the school with his arm on her neck, but it had only seemed to excite her more.

"Ethan." His voice was low and menacing, and Nat tried to look at him but he clenched her more tightly, keeping his face in her neck. Keeping her close. "How much of a threat would your sister be to Nat if she knew?"

When Ethan didn't answer immediately, Caleb lifted his head to look at him, pulling Nat to his chest and kissing her forehead.

"She used to kill people," he said slowly. "But my dad put a stop to it because it of the attention it started bringing to the areas we lived in."

"And you let Natty go off alone with her and told her I was staying at your *house?*" Preston broke in, his brows raised, and Ethan frowned.

"I told you—I made sure she wasn't in a killing mood. And I told her about you because it was the best way to keep you safe. There's no way she'd risk killing someone who was linked to where we live—she's not afraid of much, but she's afraid of my dad. And he'd be angry. It would invite too many questions."

His frown deepened at Preston's wide eyed incredulity.

"I wouldn't put you in danger."

"Dude." He leaned forward and put his hand on Ethan's shoulder, ignoring or not noticing when he tensed. "You *are* danger. But your *sister*... Damn."

He let his hand fall as he leaned back, and Ethan looked down at the floor, a deep line between his brow.

"What is this about letting Nat go off alone with her."

Caleb was struggling to hold onto his temper, despite Nat's trying to soothe him.

Ethan eyed him warily.

"Vick came to the classroom. She must have caught your scent on Nat and wanted to talk to her."

Caleb looked down at the beautiful, warm brown eyes looking up at him from the most perfect, precious face leaning on his shoulder.

"What happened?" he asked huskily.

Her delicate hand stroked his neck, sending small shivers of need through him. He touched her cheek with his lips. No one would hurt her.

"Nothing much. She said she was trying to take me outside to talk where she could breathe. But…I didn't want to go…where you would see her," she whispered, looking up at him with glistening eyes.

"Nat…" His own vision blurred, and he leaned his forehead on hers. Fuck. It would have torn his heart out if her body had responded to another man. No matter the reason. It was bad enough walking in and seeing her lying in Preston's arms. And that had been pretty fucking bad.

"How do I get rid of your sister, Ethan?" he asked in a low voice, raising his eyes to the boy seated on the edge of the bed.

Ethan gave a small laugh.

"Don't you think I've been asking that question my whole life? She does whatever she wants and doesn't stop until she gets bored. But you're her mate—"

Caleb reached for his throat faster than Ethan could move, still holding Nat to him and ignoring her efforts to stop him.

"You will never say that again," he hissed, squeezing just enough to make his point while Ethan sat very still, watching him, and Preston leaned forward.

"I only meant she isn't going to get bored with you," he said quietly as Caleb released him. "And the effects of the m— Of the bond—"

"Of the *scent*," Caleb bit out.

Ethan nodded, his eyes a bit unsure.

"The scent. She's not going to let that go. She thinks you're hers. We've been looking for you for years, and she has hated the idea that she couldn't carry on the pack line. No other wolf is capable of mating with her."

"Why can't they just shift? She's a wolf. They're wolves. Shift and problem solved."

Ethan's brow pulled together, and he looked at Caleb intently.

"It doesn't work like that. Or at least…not for anyone I ever heard of. You're only supposed to be able to get hard for your mate, regardless of which form you're in."

Caleb frowned in confusion and looked down for a moment before turning to Nat, hope entering his eyes.

"If one is possible…maybe the other is, too," he breathed, the pain in his gut returning with a vengeance when she swallowed.

He kissed her hard on the mouth and pulled back quickly, turning to Ethan once more but keeping Nat locked to his chest. She curled into him again, shaking a bit this time, and he struggled to keep his thoughts from drifting where they very much wanted to go.

"There has to be a way. You know her. How do I get rid of her?"

Ethan's brows lifted and a small whine left his throat. But his eyes began searching around him as if thinking. His gaze returned to Caleb's after a few moments.

"Actually, you might be able to answer that. She's like you. All our ma— All our scent…pairs?" He rushed on at Caleb's glare. "Their personalities are a lot like ours."

"I am not like her," Caleb spat out. But his brow twitched. Was he? Ethan had said he was a bully, but he was just dominant! He was a wolf! But…so was she.

Caleb rubbed his brow and looked down at Nat.

"Am I?" he whispered.

Her eyes were soft on his as she leaned up and cupped his face in her hands. Shaking her head slowly, she stroked his cheeks with her thumbs.

"You're kind, Caleb. Protective. You gave up everything to be boxed in, trapped, in something even most humans could barely stomach. You work so hard to take care of us…" She peppered each of her statements with small kisses, and Caleb watched her beneath heavy lids, his breath caught in his throat.

"I didn't see any of those things in her. I don't think she takes care of anyone but herself. She might be bold like you, but she uses it differently."

Nat frowned.

"But she is quite bold. And I know what you're like when you want something. So if she is like you, Caleb..." Worry filled her eyes, and he felt it with her.

Because the only thing that had ever stopped him from doing exactly what he wanted was Nat.

———

Caleb stroked Nat's hair, navigating the car slowly through town while she rested her head on his thigh. She'd curled into him the moment they'd pulled away from the curb, sending his heart to his throat.

His.

He bit back the growl lurking inside him. *Nothing* would take her from him. But his hand shook, and he glanced down, fear still holding him in its grip.

Long, beautiful brown lashes lay against a pale, delicate face, the faintest trace of tears still present. His knuckles grazed the silky strands, capturing the last of the moisture, and he cupped her cheek, rubbing softly with his thumb as he looked back at the road. His heart caught when she pressed her lips into his palm.

Desire ate at his stomach. He needed to get home. To take their clothes off and curl up with her. Into her. To tie them together. He *needed* to be tied to her. To *show* her how much he wanted her—and *only* her.

Pain filled his gut, and he took a ragged breath.

Just a little longer.

"Caleb..."

Her whisper fluttered inside his chest.

"What are we going to do?"

Visions of exactly what he was planning filled his mind, the pain piercing him until he feared he wouldn't last the drive. His grip tightened on the steering wheel, tension making his body rigid, and Nat lifted her head.

He pushed her back down, forcing himself to be calm once more.

"Stay, Nat," he said, his voice husky. "I need you close. Today was…" A shudder went through him. "I don't ever want to feel that again. Any of it."

"But you will, Caleb." Her voice was small. "She'll be back. And you'll feel the same for her."

"Not *for* her, Nat," he growled. "But as for what I'm going to do about it, maybe I'll get a nose plug."

Her delicate snort almost made him smile through the fury of revulsion and fear thoughts of the she-beast brought. Revulsion that anything other than Nat could affect his body. And fear that she would leave him because of it.

"Do you really think it's just scent?" A touch of hope laced her tone, and it pulled at his heart.

"Yes. I do," he said firmly. "I don't know if a nose plug is enough to stop it, though," he muttered. Wolf senses were strong. "I don't really know how it might work. But I know—" he looked down at her, his brows fierce— "that I *don't* want her and I would *never* want her. Even if you left me."

Nat's eyes were soft and wide, and she turned over on her back, looking up at him.

"Leave you? Caleb, without you…" She swallowed, a sheen growing in her eyes. "I thought about it a lot today. When I thought you were with her. You came into my life and made me forget that I'm nothing."

Her hand reached up to flatten over his mouth when he

opened it in outrage, so he only glared down at her, glancing up occasionally to watch where he was driving.

"I'm not beautiful. Or smart. Or talented. Or evidently very likable. I never know what to say with people. But with you…"

She stroked his lips slowly, her eyes tender.

"It's never mattered. I never had to be anything more than I was. If I failed a test or wasn't good at sports or art or anything… it never mattered. I didn't need to be good at those things. I was enough being just me."

He bit her fingers, and she snatched them back.

"You are beautiful and smart and talented and likable and everything, Nat!"

A small twinkle shone through her tears.

"So you won't mind if I sing you to sleep?"

"As long as you're beside me, you can do whatever you want," he said, his voice husky again.

It won him an eye roll and a grin, but he meant it.

"But you're right about one thing," he whispered. "Just you. That's enough. Because it's everything. You're my world."

"And you're mine."

Heat filled him, impossible heat.

"Nat…let me be inside you."

Familiar alarm filled her eyes. Uncertainty.

"Are you…really sure, Caleb? That you know what you want? What if we do this and…and you change your mind…and you want a wolf like you…"

He frowned. Okay, that *did* sound gross. Shit. That was how he seemed to her? Could he really ask her to be with him that way? A whine tickled the back of his throat.

Nat's eyes fell.

"See…you can't really be sure."

Momentarily confused, he stared down at her with a line between his brow before grunting in frustration.

"No, Nat, no...that is the last thing..." Fuck. "I just realized for the first time...how gross that sounded."

His mutter seemed petulant even to his own ears, and silence filled the car for an instant before she burst out laughing.

"Well at least you finally understand!" she grinned, leaning up and wrapping her arms around him to nuzzle his neck.

He held her close, his eyes feeling a bit raw.

"Is that how I seem to you then?" he whispered, and she pulled back quickly, all traces of her laughter vanishing.

"No. No, Caleb. I mean, I'm glad you understand how it *could* seem but...but I've had years to get used to who you are. And you're...you! Some insanely gorgeous wonderful creature who... sometimes...looks...different." She swallowed, and he lifted a brow.

Groaning, she hid her face in his neck, and he held on tight, the band inside his chest relaxing as she snuggled in close.

"I can't pretend it isn't scary. Or maybe not scary but..." A shiver went through her. "Okay, yeah, scary. But I *know* it's you. And if that's the only way you can want me—"

"I *always* want you," he said fiercely, clenching her to him. "Just because my body doesn't work doesn't mean I don't *feel* it inside!"

Leaning into him, her fingertips toyed with the skin at the base of his neck.

"I know," she whispered. "And...and it must mean something that you can be with me as a wolf when your kind isn't supposed to be able to do that at all with anyone who isn't your—"

"Don't say it," he growled and felt her smile.

"It must mean something..."

"It means *you* are my mate, Nat. You are the one I love. The one I *choose*. Nobody else could ever take your place. I'm tied to you forever...and...I'd like to be tied to you...physically, too," he finished, his voice husky once more.

Trembling, she turned into him more deeply, her arms tight around his chest.

"So much happened today... I need to think...but..." She swallowed, and if his hearing had been any less than what it was, he might not have caught her final whispered words. "I want that, too."

His breath caught, a tumult of feeling coursing through him, the blood rushing through his body, and for one incredible moment, for one exquisite moment of hope, Caleb didn't feel pain. He felt *hard*.

And then he turned onto their street, and the scent became unmistakable—along with the sight of the car parked in their drive.

Vick was waiting for them.

15

"NAT, I want you to drive back into town and go sit in the diner until I come and get you."

Nat looked up, startled when Caleb pulled over to the side of the road and removed her arms from his neck, pushing her away. His eyes were locked in front of him, narrowed and deadly, and she followed his gaze to see a very expensive looking car parked in their drive.

"Is that her?" she whispered.

"I'll get her out of there," he said, opening his door. "But I don't want you anywhere near here."

"Wait—is she *inside*?" she asked horrified. Shoving open her door without waiting for a response, she heard Caleb mutter a curse and rush forward to stop her before she could get far.

"Nat, get back in the car," he hissed.

"I know you want to protect me, but I am not leaving while she is with my *mom*, Caleb!"

"Nat, I can hear *everything from here,* and your mom is okay." The look he gave her told her to watch her words. "And I'm going to make sure she stays that way." *Trust me*, he mouthed, his eyes pleading with her.

I do, she mouthed back. *You'll keep me safe.*

He looked ready to throttle her when she crossed her arms, but she wasn't budging. It wasn't just her mom—there was no way she was disappearing again to let that girl try anything more with Caleb. That stunning, perfect wolf girl who didn't know how to take no for an answer. Because whether Caleb wanted to admit it or not, Vick scared him. His own body scared him. And Nat wasn't leaving him to face that alone again.

But right now, she wanted to make sure her mom was safe.

"You are the worst sister in the world," he ground out, keeping pace with her when she stalked ahead. But his face grew pale as they neared the trailer, and Nat glanced up at him worriedly.

The screen door opened when they were still a few feet away on the ground below, a long elegant arm throwing it to the side.

"Oh my god, Fenri, how have you survived!" Scrunching her nose in an exquisitely beautiful look of disgust, Vick's lithe form stepped through the doorway, inhaling deeply. Long black locks reflected the last rays of the sun as she shook her head in a small shudder. Then her blue eyes narrowed on them, her gaze sliding down Caleb's body. "But it looks like you're happy to see me..."

Nat couldn't help glancing down as well, her stomach plummeting instantly at the sight. *It's not his fault.* But it still hurt.

"My name is Caleb." The venom in his voice gave Nat some comfort, but Vick's eyes only brightened more. "What are you doing here."

"Well you ran off before we could finish our conversation, Fenri." A slow smile accompanied his name, but Caleb only clenched his jaw. "I never expected you to be such a frightened rabbit."

"And I never expected you to be so pathetically desperate."

Her own jaw clenched at that, her eyes growing dark—and

shifting to Nat. A thin smile touched her lips when Caleb pushed Nat behind him.

"Aw, have you been playing protective big brother? But how will you save her from the big bad wolf if you can't face her yourself?" she said with deceptive softness, her eyes returning to Caleb.

In a swift movement that took Nat's breath away at the sheer grace and beauty, Vick vaulted over the wooden rail to land directly in front of them. Caleb's hand shot out immediately, holding her back while holding Nat behind him with his other arm, and Vick grinned, reaching between his legs.

Nat's hand darted around his body before Vick's could make contact, covering Caleb's rigid length and drawing a harsh gasp from him.

"*Don't you touch him.*" Fury made her voice tremble while she cupped as much of Caleb as she could, and Vick's eyes widened.

"Little *sister*…" she breathed, her tone exaggerated shock.

"Nat…" Caleb's hoarse voice barely choked out her name, trying to push her farther behind him while still holding Vick away.

Vick's eyes seemed unnaturally bright as she clasped her fingers over Nat's, squeezing, and Caleb pulsed beneath them.

"Enough!" he growled, shoving Vick back into the trailer's small wood platform. He moved Nat's hand quickly, stepping back and keeping her behind him.

"Yes, that is enough," Vick hissed, yanking her shirt over her head and exposing small but perfectly firm bare breasts. Her fingers began unclasping her jeans, and her gaze returned to Nat, a gleam in her eyes. "I did say I could just eat you up, didn't I…"

"Nat, get inside," Caleb said hoarsely, yanking off his own clothes, and Vick grinned, her eyes drinking in every bit of exposed flesh.

"Someone could see you both," Nat said, a sickness growing in her gut as she backed away, making her way up the steps toward the door on trembling legs. Caleb's body already went crazy for Vick in his human form. She didn't want to face what would happen when they were wolves...

"Won't we be the talk of the town then," Vick grinned. "But do stay, little mouse. It's getting late, and I'm feeling hungry."

"Get inside, Nat!"

The last of their clothes fell to the ground, and pain nearly took Nat to the ground as well at the sight. She couldn't move. She could only stare, her chest so tight she could barely breathe.

Caleb naked had always been almost more than she could bear. But Caleb naked and hard...

He was perfect. Every part of him in absolute perfect proportion, from his chiseled, well muscled body to the huge, rock hard length jutting up from his center, pressed tight against his stomach.

And Vick's tall, elegant body, firm and dripping with heat, was his perfect match.

Nat swallowed back her tears as they stood apart, neither shifting, Vick's eyes heavy with desire as they roamed over Caleb. No. No no no! Caleb wasn't hers. He was Nat's! Nat was the one who found him! Nat was the one who had been beside him, year after year, working with him, playing with him! Sleeping with him...

He was *Nat's* wolf.

Caleb didn't have time to stop her before she jumped over the railing between them, less elegantly than Vick had but she didn't care. Caleb said he didn't want Vick. And Nat believed him. This was not his fault, and she *would* fight for him—no matter the cost. Because Caleb was worth it.

"I'll stay. But *you* need to get the fuck out of here."

A small, incredulous laugh sounded...an instant before a blur of black leapt for her throat with a snarl, white fangs gleaming in the fading light.

And a roar followed immediately as Vick's wolf was thrown

into the wooden platform, a sharp snapping sound and a yelp mingling with the fury of a strong set of jaws, viciously shaking her body.

"Caleb! Stop! Stop—you'll kill her!"

Nat's arms wrapped around the thick fur of his neck, pulling desperately as blood spurted over her.

"Caleb—let go! Let her go! Please—we won't be able to explain this!"

Vick's claws lashed out in a mad scramble to free herself, and Nat fell back, gasping at the gash it left in her skin. Caleb's head jerked toward her, his jaws releasing Vick long enough for her to race furiously toward the woods.

With a fierce growl, he took off in pursuit, and Nat pushed herself to her feet, holding her injured arm and running after them, her heart pounding wildly. They were too fast—much too fast for her! But...

Nat blanched. Vick was injured, running in an almost limping gait. Caleb caught her just before she reached the line of trees. No no no!

Tears clogged Nat's throat as she raced to them, desperate to make it in time. Caleb was already shaking her again, and the fading yelps shot terror through her, propelling her the final few yards to throw her arms around Caleb once again.

"Stop! Stop, Caleb! Please! Oh, please stop—they'll take you from me...please, please stop..." she choked out, burying her face in his neck.

Caleb stilled at last but he didn't release the smaller wolf. Deep, low snarls came from his throat while he held her down, his fangs buried deep in her fur, blood pooling around them.

"Caleb..." Nat's whisper floated over the soft sounds of the wind blowing through the trees. Vick had gone quiet. "It's okay now. You can let her go."

Slowly, so very slowly, Caleb relaxed his jaw, his growl a steady stream of sound. Vick didn't move, and a chill shot through Nat's body. *Please let her be alive...oh please.* Caleb stood very still, a menacing sound continuing to come from his throat, keeping his muzzle close to the bloodied fur once his jaws released her.

Relief made Nat weak when Vick darted away the instant she was free. This time she moved more slowly, however—and headed back toward the trailer.

Nat kept her arms around Caleb, his snarls never abating, until the sound of a car pulling away reached them and she collapsed into him in relief. Trembling, she pet him softly.

"Shh...we're okay now."

But he didn't stop snarling.

"Caleb? Are you okay?"

The rumble from his chest grew, the sound as menacing as when Vick had been near. Nat relaxed her arms around his neck, sitting back on her heels and looking around worriedly to see if she'd missed some other danger.

"I don't see anything—what is—"

Her voice caught in her throat when she turned back toward him.

He had planted his front paws on either side of her, his claws digging into the earth. And inches from her face were huge, bared fangs, snarling in feral savagery.

At her.

———

"Ca—Caleb?" Nat's voice caught, the blood draining from her face. "It's me. Nat—"

She choked on her name when he lowered his head with a surging snarl.

"What's wrong?" she begged, tears in her voice.

His head dropped further, the sound in his throat fading to a harsh whisper, until his muzzle reached her knees. She jumped at the feel of his cold nose on her leg, the skin exposed where her dress had bunched around her thighs as she knelt on the ground.

"Caleb, you can change back now," she whispered, only to jump again when he nudged between her knees. When she didn't move, he did it again. Hard.

"Caleb, stop!" Her voice was sharper now, a different type of panic beginning to creep in. When he shoved his muzzle between her thighs with a growl, she tried shoving him away, only to gasp and fall on her back when he pushed her down with his paws.

Keeping one paw on her chest, the pressure almost too much for her to breathe, he shoved his muzzle between her legs once more, this time forcing them to part enough for him to reach her center.

Twisting her hips, she kneed him hard on the side of his head, pushing and pulling at his paw and trying desperately to suck in the air. The sound he made in response was like nothing she'd ever heard. Nothing from Caleb.

A deep, guttural cry of rage, wild and savage.

The pressure on her chest eased for just an instant, just enough for her to twist over on her stomach and try to scramble away.

She realized her mistake too late.

Claws and fangs raked her back, cutting through the thin fabric of her dress and into her skin in shallow slices that had her gasping and pushing herself into the ground. Vicious snarls snapped at her ear each time she tried to move away, and she covered her head with her hands, sobs shaking her body.

But when his legs yanked her up on all fours and she felt the hard, hot length feverishly sliding between her legs, she began struggling again, fighting and sobbing at each bite that nipped her just enough to draw blood until he clenched her neck between his jaws, holding her still and thrusting wildly between her thighs, coming ever closer to finding the entrance.

"Caleb," she screamed. "You're just like the bad man!"

The evening stopped around them. Nat heard nothing, not even the wind she could feel blowing over them.

Caleb held perfectly still, his fangs in her flesh, his front legs hard around her waist, holding her in place. The hot length pressing against her stomach terrified her, and she struggled to keep herself from collapsing into tears once more, her body trembling uncontrollably. Waiting.

Heat flowed over her in waves from deep beneath his fur until the fur disappeared and she could feel his skin against hers, sliding off.

She turned to see him collapse unconscious beside her, his face pale as death.

"Caleb? Caleb! Wake up!" Her hands were on his face, her injuries forgotten as she felt for a pulse, a heartbeat, her own heart hammering when she felt the weak throb. And whatever panic she'd felt before was nothing to the terror filling her now.

Shoving herself to her feet and holding the tattered remains of her dress around her, she raced back toward the trailer, her boots flying over the rough ground. Falling to her knees, trembling hands searched through Caleb's clothing until she found his phone, quickly scanning his contacts for the number she needed.

She was already racing back as it rang on the other end.

"Yo."

"Preston?" she said, gulping in air as she ran. "Where's Ethan!"

"In the other room dealing with some shit for his dad. He said not to disturb him, but I saw it was your brother—er—well, Caleb—and thought it might be important."

"It is—please, please get him!" she rasped, dropping to her knees next to Caleb and struggling to catch her breath. "And if you're at his house, his sister might be on her way there. She's injured—I don't know how badly, but I can't imagine she is in a good mood. I don't know if it's safe for you to be there."

"Fuck." Preston said hoarsely, and she heard a door in the background. "Dude, you heard?"

"I heard." Tension laced his tone. "We need to get out of here."

"Ow—I can walk myself," Preston muttered, but Ethan didn't respond, and the sound of an engine roared to life soon after.

"Okay—you're on speakerphone, Natty."

Nat took a shaky breath, fighting back the tears and feeling Caleb for a pulse again. She gasped.

"Ethan, Caleb's burning up! He and your sister got in a fight, and after he changed back, he just…he's unconscious," she said hoarsely, not sure what to say about the rest of it. "What do I do!"

"Check his eyes," Ethan said. "What color are they?"

Nat carefully lifted a lid and released a small cry.

"They're black! All the way to the edge," she said, her voice cracking.

"Nat, that's a *good* thing—because that's something I know how to treat. I don't suppose you have any wolfsbane over there, do you?"

"Dude, is that even a real thing?"

"It's a plant—a lot of plants, actually, and most very poisonous. But it will counteract the effects of the mate—uh—scent bond."

"I don't even know what that is, Ethan. Can I find it in the woods? Where do I go?" Panic was clawing at her. Caleb was so still, his fever almost painful to the touch.

"Just give us a few minutes. I'm taking a back route so Vick doesn't spot us if she's headed this way, but I have some in the car. You're at your place?"

Relief made her weak, and she collapsed on the ground beside Caleb, stretching out beside him and holding him close.

"Yes. Thank you, Ethan," she whispered. "And please hurry."

They hung up, and she curled closer to Caleb, the heat from his body keeping her bare skin warm in the crisp evening air. She supposed she should try to cover up before they got there, but she would have to leave Caleb lying there.

Tears stung her eyes.

He was going to be okay. Whatever had happened...he'd changed back. He was going to be okay!

But a sickness filled her as she lay there, her body torn and bloodied.

Because her wolf might never be the same again.

———

The evening light had almost disappeared by the time Ethan and Preston arrived.

"We're over here," she said softly, her voice catching as she stared at Caleb lying so pale beside her. Lifting her upper body, she covered his lower half with some of her torn skirt, trying to give him some privacy.

It didn't take long before she heard footsteps running toward them.

"Jesus, Natty—she attacked you, too?"

Preston crouched down, his hands running over her a bit, checking for damage. She let him, unable to do much more than watch Caleb through blurry eyes.

Ethan gave them a quick glance before kneeling and pulling out what looked like an old fashioned metal lighter with a flip top. Holding one hand on his nose and turning away, he put the lighter near Caleb's face and pressed down on the edge. And immediately dropped it as Caleb sucked in air and the two of them turned, coughing and hacking into the grass while Nat looked on in desperate relief, reaching out to stroke Caleb's back gently.

His fever had disappeared completely, and another wave of

relief hit her until she could barely hold herself upright. She planted a hand on the ground to hold herself up while she kept a palm flat against Caleb's back, needing to feel him.

The coughs subsided at last, and Ethan took a deep breath, picking the lighter up once more to put it in his pocket. But he paused, looking at Nat, and held it out to her instead.

"Actually, you might want to hold on to this. I replaced the fuel cell with a Wolfsbane mixture. It won't hurt you so long as you don't try ingesting it, but the scent can pretty much incapacitate us. It will get weaker each time it's opened though, so only use it when you really need to."

Nat nodded, reaching out to take it, and Ethan's eyes fell to her arm.

"Vick did that?"

Nat looked down at the long jagged line cutting an ugly red streak through her pale skin. It wasn't too deep, but it would leave a scar. She nodded again, clutching the lighter and grateful that he'd asked about a cut that actually was from his sister. The rest of them…

Her eyes turned back to see Caleb still lying on the ground, his body twisted away from her, his hands buried in the grass and his head hung low.

"Caleb?" she whispered. "Are you okay?"

Tension rippled the muscles of his back, and her chest constricted as she watched, the sick feeling in her gut growing with each passing second.

"Caleb…?" Her voice wavered, and he flinched as if she'd struck him. His chest expanded and contracted in shallow breaths, and a tremor worked its way up his spine until his entire body shook with it.

"Caleb?" This time the tears wouldn't stay out of her voice, and his head jerked to the side, enough for her to see his face in the shadows.

He was crying.

A keening sound came from her throat as she threw her arms around him, ignoring the jolt that went through his body.

"Nat, stop! You have to get away from me!" he choked out, shaking in her arms hard enough to shake them both.

"You would push me away—now!" she cried, hiding her face in his back and clutching him as tightly as she could.

"I'm not safe," he said hoarsely, his hands digging into the earth. "Ethan, keep her away from me!"

"Don't you dare, Ethan!" she turned her head fiercely toward the boy who sat watching them so quietly.

"What happened?" he whispered, his eyes running over the cuts in Nat's exposed skin.

"I attacked her. I tried to kill your sister and then I attacked Nat. I...I can't be trusted." Horror filled his voice, and Nat clenched him even tighter.

"You weren't trying to kill me. You just...weren't yourself."

"Don't make excuses for me!" he cried out to the ground, his body unyielding stone in her arms.

"Caleb," she whispered, pressing her lips to the back of his neck and holding him harder when he flinched, his shoulders shaking. A tremor touched her voice as she continued. "You can't do that and then desert me—you just *can't*. It was scary, and I *need you*."

Her face broke in silent tears, and she leaned her forehead against him, trying not to let him hear.

Turning his head to the side, he looked over his shoulder, his cheeks wet.

"Nat..." His eyes fell to the bloodied arm that clenched him so tightly, and his own arms buckled. Falling to the earth, he reached for her hand, holding it to his forehead as he wept. Then a growl sounded in his throat, and he pushed himself up to turn toward her, swallowing at the sight of her lying on the ground, looking up at him through teary eyes.

His own eyes were raw as he reached for her, his hand

shaking. Tears broke through again when his knuckles touched her skin, tracing the small lines of blood up her arm to her neck where his fangs had pierced her.

Nat slid her hand to cover his.

"You stopped. You heard me, and you stopped."

His eyes shifted to hers, burning and tormented.

"But I didn't want to." His gaze fell once more to the myriad of scratches marring her body, and his voice grew choked. "I didn't mean to tear your skin…"

Leaning down, his breath shuddered over her body as he touched his lips to her shoulder, his tongue slipping out to glide across a cut until he reached her neck and the bloody indentations left by his fangs.

"But…" His voice grew husky. "I wanted to mark you. I wanted to claim you, Nat. Forever. It's all I could see…"

She shivered and wounded tenderness filled his eyes, his hands slipping beneath her slowly to lift her into his lap. He rocked her gently back and forth while she hid her face in his neck, curling into him and letting everything else drift away.

The sounds of the night echoed around them, and leaves rustled in the trees. But no more words were spoken for a long while.

"Ethan…" Nat roused herself at last before the comfort of Caleb's arms could lull her into sleep. "You knew what to do. Does that mean this has happened before?"

"Not exactly this but… When we're around our m—when we're young, the adults use wolfsbane if we lose control. Otherwise a lot of couples would start mating too soon. Sometimes a wolf will react really strongly to being stopped. It's rare for them to lose consciousness, but it's happened before."

"So this happened because Caleb stopped himself from being with your sister?" she whispered, an ache in her chest.

"No." Caleb said flatly. "The moment I shifted, that all stopped."

"What do you mean?" Ethan's question echoed Nat's thoughts, and she leaned up to look at Caleb's face, swallowing when she saw the darkness in his eyes.

"I mean as soon as I shifted, her scent stopped making me hard."

Ethan's brow pulled together in a deep line.

"It didn't affect you anymore?"

"Oh," Caleb said quietly, his eyes narrowing. "It affected me. But instead of making me want to fuck—" he glanced at Nat, his eyes growing raw again for just a moment before turning back to Ethan, acid in his voice—"it made me want to feel her bones cracking between my jaws and her blood spilling into my mouth."

Ethan sat back on his heels, fierce confusion in his eyes.

"Then why were you…" Nat couldn't finish, and Caleb's eyes returned to hers, two deep pools of remorse.

"That wasn't about her, Nat," he said huskily. "I didn't feel that way until after she was gone."

"But you weren't yourself, Caleb," she whispered up at him. "Something was wrong."

Touching the tattered remains of her dress, his red rimmed eyes following his fingertips as they skimmed her wounds, he took a shaky breath.

"I felt…free. And I wanted everything I wanted. I knew I could have it. No one could stop me from having what I wanted."

He swallowed, and his eyes shone with tears.

"It was still me, Nat."

"It was your wolf," Ethan frowned. "It's just normally you'd be going after your…scent match. And she wouldn't be resisting."

"So I caused this?" Nat asked in a small voice.

"NO." Fury shone in Caleb's eyes, but for once Ethan wasn't deterred.

"How?" he demanded, leaning forward. "How do you do it, Caleb. How do you break the mate bond? *I need to know*."

"Dude, calm down." Preston put a hand on Ethan's chest, eyeing Caleb nervously.

Ethan looked down, intense frustration in his eyes, but he let Preston push him back. His gaze stayed on the hand touching his chest, watching it move with every breath he took.

"The better question is why have you just accepted it," Caleb snapped. "Stop giving in, and start fighting for what you want."

"You think I haven't been fighting?" Ethan kept his eyes on Preston's hand, his voice strained. "I've researched everything I could get my hands on, tried using wolfsbane in a hundred different ways, exhausted my body, my mind, everything before being around her, but every single time I'm with my mate it's all there. And it only gets stronger when I shift."

Caleb's exhale was rough with annoyance.

"Well, what are you fighting it for?"

Ethan lifted his head at last, glaring at him.

"You are perfectly well aware of that answer."

"That's not what I meant. My point is…" Hesitating, his eyes fell to Nat, and he reached for her cheek, stroking gently. His voice grew husky. "If you want to beat whatever is in our blood, maybe you need something stronger to replace it."

Ethan looked down for a moment, his expression helpless, before lifting his eyes slowly to Preston.

"Uh, you okay now, dude?"

Ethan swallowed, nodding, and Preston let his hand fall away with a somewhat wary look.

"So this was…normal? It just…happens sometimes?" Nat asked.

Ethan's gaze returned to her, hesitation in his eyes, and Caleb tightened his arms around her with a shudder.

"I don't think anything about this is normal," Ethan answered carefully. "But I know some wolf pairs go a bit crazy when they can't mate. I always thought it was because they were being separated from their scent match. I heard—"

Stopping mid-sentence, Ethan pressed his lips together and looked down. Caleb narrowed his eyes.

"Spit it out. What?"

Ethan didn't lift his head, and a long moment passed in silence before he spoke again.

"I heard about one mating that…didn't end well. It was one of the more aggressive couples and they'd had a lot of trouble stopping them from getting together. I guess the two of them snuck out to meet each other and the male was too rough."

Lifting eyes heavy with apology, he spoke his final words softly.

"She didn't survive."

16

"ARE YOU KIDS HAVING A SLEEPOVER?" Nat's mother's sleepy voice greeted them from the couch when they walked inside.

"Yeah, Mom," Nat said, trying to stay hidden behind Caleb and get back to their room before her mother roused herself too much. "Can Ethan and Preston use your room?"

"Sure...the sheets are clean...I haven't slept back there in a while," she murmured, her eyes heavy.

Nat wished she had more to offer, but at least it was better than sending them off to face Vick or Preston's dad. Even Caleb had wanted them to stay, which had surprised her until she realized what he was thinking.

There was safety in numbers. For her.

"Towels are in here," she said after they made it down the hall, indicating the small linen closet just inside the restroom. Ethan looked as if he were having trouble breathing, and she hurried into her mother's room to open the window. "Sorry..."

Caleb shot Ethan a sharp look, daring him to complain.

"It's fine," Ethan choked, and Preston pat him on the back heavily.

"Dude, you think this is bad—you would die at my place. My old man is a total slob. At least Natty's place is clean."

But Ethan ran forward to lean his head out of the window, drawing in deep breaths, and didn't respond.

"You can use the shower first, Preston, and I'll get you something of Caleb's to wear."

"He can wait until you've had a chance to use it—you're torn up, Nat," Caleb said, his sharp tone fading into a husky whisper.

"Take your time, Natty—don't worry about us. Besides, I want to look through these old VHS tapes," he said, eyeing the stack beside the TV with interest. "We can play one, right?"

Nat nodded and rubbed her eyes, and Caleb slid his hand behind her knees and had her in his arms before she could take another breath.

"Do whatever," he said gruffly, carrying her back through the doorway and into the tiny bathroom. The room felt uncommonly silent as the lock clicked behind them.

Nat lifted her eyes to Caleb's, her arms around his neck, to see him staring down at the ground with unseeing eyes.

"Caleb…it wasn't your fault," she whispered.

He didn't answer but set her gently on her feet and stepped to the shower to turn it on. Turning back to Nat, he slowly pulled the shirt he'd put on her outside over her head, revealing the torn dress beneath. His eyes grew red, but he said nothing as he slid it off her shoulders to fall in a heap at her feet.

Shivering, she stepped into his arms, wrapping her own around him while he unclasped her bra. His fingertips were soft on her skin as they glided the straps down, and she let it fall to the floor as well, her naked chest pressed against his.

The steam rose around them, but neither moved.

"Nat…" The huskiness in his voice sent another shiver through her, and she pressed closer. His fingers traced around each cut on her back, careful not to touch the injured skin.

He tensed when her hands moved between them to undo his jeans.

"Aren't you getting in the shower with me?"

His stomach clenched against her knuckles, but he nodded, his forehead leaning into her. The hard metal button slipped through the dense cotton, and Nat held her breath as she slowly began lowering them...and her fingers grazed the thick, soft flesh inside.

The hope she hadn't even realized she'd been holding onto deserted her, and a sickness filled her gut. He wasn't cured. Whatever had happened while he was a wolf with Vick...it hadn't undone anything. Or at least, it hadn't made him able to feel what Nat felt. And she felt it so strongly she ached with it. Nothing that had happened had taken away from that. Caleb was Caleb. And she wanted him. Always.

"I'm sorry," he choked out, and her eyes flew to his. "I never thought I could do anything like that. Ever."

Oh. What had happened. Her eyes fell again, and she slid his jeans down until they dropped to his feet. He kicked them away and stepped with her into the small tub, droplets spraying around them and leaving her skin chilled in more places than it warmed.

Wrapping his arms around her, Caleb moved them beneath the water more fully. And held her.

Nat knew she needed to clean herself quickly—the hot water wouldn't last long. But she couldn't bring herself to move.

Caleb reached for the soap and lathered his hands before slowly stroking her body, and Nat closed her eyes, letting his touch soothe her. And excite. As much as she tried, she couldn't stop her body from responding, and every pang at her core cut her heart.

Caleb's lips touched her shoulder, his strong hands gliding smoothly over her skin, and Nat hid her face in his neck when he slipped a finger slowly between her soft folds, stopping when she tensed.

"Did I…make you afraid of me?" he asked hoarsely.

Nat shook her head.

"It's not that. I just…" She swallowed, trembling slightly as his finger remained frozen between her lips. "It's hard to be the only one able to feel this," she whispered at last.

"You think I don't feel this?" he asked, his voice thick as he slid his finger into her more deeply, pressing his lips to her forehead at her soft gasp. "I always feel it, Nat. Always. I will always want you, no matter what this body does. It's there inside me."

They both trembled when he began slipping in and out slowly, and her hands clutched his wrist, fighting not to grind into him.

"Let me make you feel good, Nat," he whispered. Her small groan was all the encouragement he needed, and he cupped her head to his neck with one hand, his finger now moving in steady circles at her center.

Her lips parted against his neck, breathing him in with small gasps as the pressure grew. His grip on her hair tightened at her every sound, his finger moving faster, until her fingers dug into his wrist and she cried out into him, her body shuddering over and over while he held her up, his touch never stopping until she leaned against him, spent.

Warm water scattered across her skin, the sting of the heat on her torn flesh morphing into a soothing numbness. She blinked soft, tired eyes when Caleb began washing her hair, only to lift them in confusion when he began washing his own.

"What are you doing?"

"I was lying in the dirt."

She frowned at his explanation.

"You aren't going to shift tonight?"

They'd saved a lot of money over the years from Caleb not needing to do anything but shift to get cleaned.

He hesitated.

"Nat..." His eyes were soft as they looked down at her. Tender. And absolute. "I'll never shift again."

———

"It won't work, Caleb."

He lifted his head to kiss her before letting it fall back to the pillow, and she leaned on her elbow, frowning down at him.

He'd tended to all her cuts very carefully, rubbing ointment into them and lingering a bit too long on the bite marks on her neck, while kissing her unharmed skin softly. Now she was shiny, sticky, and growing frustrated with her stubborn, loving wolf.

"Shh. Go to sleep."

Her brow furrowed more deeply when he tried pressing her head back to his chest, and he sighed, looking up at her with raw eyes.

"Nat, you were right. Something was different. I didn't feel... human. I didn't have thoughts going through my head. Everything was just...I don't know. Instinct maybe. And even what you said..." His voice faded. "Even then, I barely heard you. Instead I almost..."

This time he did pull her back down, and she let him, stroking him softly as he clung to her.

"Caleb, it had to be because of her. It doesn't mean you have to stop being you!"

"That's not how it felt," he whispered. "When I got away at the school, I could feel the effects fading. But after she left when I was a wolf...nothing was fading. I just felt...*free*. Like whatever had been holding me back before was gone."

Nat was silent for a moment.

"Have I been holding you back?" she asked in a small voice.

"No! No, that is...fuck, no, Nat. Never. You were what I wanted to go *to*—not escape! No, it was more like...like...it was like being a wild animal," he said in disgust.

Worry pulled her brow into a painful line, and she stared at her hand smoothing the soft cotton of his shirt over his chest. Cotton he never would have had between them before in the night.

"So...she made you feel free?"

She was lifted above him in an instant to stare down at his annoyed face.

"Yes, free to kill her! Free to be a rabid dog! Free to take you and—"

The annoyance left as quickly as it had come, and he laid her back on his chest, his breath a bit shaky.

Her hands stroked him softly.

"I *know* you're scared right now," she said, her voice full of worry. "So am I. Your body went through...crazy things today. But...please don't let it make you deny such an important part of who you are, Caleb! You're a wolf...my wolf..." Her last words were just a breath of a sound, but he froze, his heart pounding hard against her cheek.

"Say that again," he growled, sending a shiver through her.

Pushing herself up slowly, she stared down into his burning eyes.

"You're my wolf," she said quietly. "And I don't want you to be anything other than what you are."

Caleb's grip tightened, the moment between them perfect stillness. Until he shoved her aside to roll off the mattress quickly, pushing her back with a growl when she reached for him in worry.

"Don't touch me!"

His harsh whisper stung, and Nat pulled her hand back, for the first time in a long while not knowing how she should be with him.

"I'm sorry, Caleb," she whispered, stopping when his growl became more fierce and he pushed to his feet and put his hands against the wall, tension in every line of his body.

When he began rocking back and forth slightly, as if he were about to take off, she crawled out of the bed to stand beside him.

"I know you're afraid to shift, but you wouldn't hur—" Her words stuck in her throat as the line of his spine suddenly grew very sharp. Very sharp and...was it moving?

Nat took a quick step back, struggling to calm her heart. The shift was always so fast. There had never been time to see anything other than his human or wolf form. But this...

Something was moving beneath his skin, as if furiously trying to get out. His head was bowed low as he leaned against the wall, his eyes clenched fiercely, while the line of his spine bowed and curved in ripple after ripple. Until his fingers broke through the drywall.

"I need to sleep outside tonight," he said through gritted teeth. "I don't feel...right."

His words cut and she knew they shouldn't. Not after what she'd just seen. But...she needed him to hold her. To remind her he was Caleb. That what had happened earlier was because of Vick. Not because he was different. Not because he'd changed. Not her wolf...

"Will you shift outside?" she whispered.

"I told you," he bit out, his eyes still shut tightly, "I'm not shifting again."

"That doesn't sound very comfortable. I can just go sleep on the floor beside my mom and you can stay in here."

He turned to glare at her at that, but his expression turned to helpless remorse the moment he saw her eyes glistening.

"Nat...I love you. But I don't know what's going on inside me right now, and I'm so scared I'll hurt you again," he ended hoarsely.

She nodded, blinking back her tears.

He leaned his head against his arm, a sheen in his own eyes now.

"I'm sorry...don't cry. I won't go far."

She just nodded again. There was nothing else she could do.

He gave her one last lingering look full of helpless frustration before snatching a blanket from the closet and opening the bedroom door.

Nat watched him walk down the hall, never looking back, until the front door closed behind him.

Turning back, the room felt so cold and empty. So much worse than the nights they'd fought and he'd slept outside angry. Because he wasn't angry this time. He was pulling away from her for something much deeper.

And it scared her.

———

"Dude! That is *not* cool!"

Nat blinked bleary eyes and pushed herself up, torn from the hour or so of sleep she'd finally fallen into just before dawn. Ethan's disgruntled reply drifted through the thin walls.

"I was asleep. I can't control it then."

"Then you shouldn't have curled up next to me last night!"

"I was trying to keep you warm!"

"Yeah, and that was fine when you were a *dog*."

Nat heard a faint growl and got to her feet with a groan. Time to go remind them their voices—and growls—could carry out to her mother, who tended to be more lucid in the mornings.

"Did you just growl at me?"

Nat opened her door just in time to see Caleb stepping inside looking as exhausted as she felt.

"Were you camping outside, hun?"

Caleb turned his head at her mother's voice, a shuttered look quickly replacing the longing in his eyes.

"Just trying a new training technique for football," he said, nodding at her murmured response before walking down the hall toward Nat, his expression guarded. He hesitated once he reached her but simply turned to rap on the door to her mother's room.

"Fuck. Get your clothes on!" Preston hissed from the other side.

"It's us," Caleb said dryly. "And you are making enough noise to wake the dead."

At the muffled cursing, his eyes met Nat's, humor sparking within them for a moment before flickering out when they fell to her cuts.

"How are you feeling?"

"Bad. Really bad, Caleb," she whispered, the pain in her chest growing each moment she stared up into his gorgeous face and felt the distance he wanted to keep between them.

"I'm sorry," he said, his voice thick with shame.

"Not from the cuts!" She stepped forward only to have him step back. "What are you going to do? Stop touching me forever?"

"I don't know. I don't know!" he whispered, his eyes tortured. "I have to keep you safe!"

"Well you're not doing that by being away from me! You're not!" The tears she'd been holding back all night clogged her throat, and she wrapped her arms around her body. "You weren't trying to hurt me. You said it yourself. If I'd just cooperated—"

"No, Nat!" Fury lit his eyes. "Don't you even think it. I was out of control. And you heard what Ethan said about that couple. *She* cooperated and ended up dead. A *wolf* ended up dead, Nat," he hissed before his eyes broke, and he reached up to run the back of his knuckles across her cheek. "And you're fragile…"

He jumped a bit when she smacked his hand away, temper in her own eyes now.

"I don't know about them, but I know *you. And you wouldn't hurt me.*" When his eyes fell to the cuts once more, she exhaled in a short huff. "Yes, you scraped me up, and scared me, but I've been thinking about it all night. Whatever happened that you said made you feel free—"

"I was fucking rabid!"

"—you still stopped! So even at your worst, *you love me*. I *know* that's real, and *I'm not afraid of you*!"

"*I'm* afraid of me!" he exploded.

"Kids…? Are you fighting?"

"We're fine, Mom!" Nat called, her burning eyes never leaving Caleb as he tore his hands through his hair. "Caleb's just being stubborn."

He shot a glare at her before collapsing back against the door with a groan and covering his face.

"Stop looking at me that way. I'm trying not to hold you."

She was about to reach for him when the door flew open and he stumbled backwards.

Preston stormed by them, his face red, while Ethan stalked toward the bedroom door, pulling a shirt over his head and glowering.

"Where are you going?" Nat called after Preston in worry.

"Home. My dad should be at work by now."

"But it's Saturday!"

He stopped short.

"Shit."

"You kids are kind of rowdy this morning." Nat watched as her mother shuffled toward the kitchen. "Do you want some breakfast? Sweetie, why don't you help me make the boys some breakfast."

Nat cringed. Her mom had kind of missed the advances in gender equality the last few decades.

"Go shower," Caleb sighed, his eyes roaming over her with a mixture of warmth and remorse. "I'll go help her."

"Preston's our guest—he should go first."

"Forget about it, Natty. My dad's probably dead to the world right now. I'll take a shower there."

"You shouldn't be alone," Ethan said testily, watching Preston down the hall.

"And *you* shouldn't *crowd* me," Preston snapped back at him, his cheeks still flaming. "If I want to go home, I'll go home!"

The screen door slammed behind him.

"He doesn't know what he wants," Ethan muttered, pushing away from the doorway to follow after Preston. "We'll be back."

Caleb bit the inside of his cheek and raised a brow at Nat.

She started to smile but frowned at him again quickly.

"And *you* should stop trying to get away from *me*! We need a different solution, Caleb."

"You think I wasn't up all night trying to think of some other way to keep you safe?"

"Well I was up all night, too, and *I* have an idea. And I'll tell you all about it after we're cleaned up."

––––––––

"You and your mom should go to your grandma's."

Nat grimaced at Caleb across the small space of her bedroom where the four of them had taken refuge once Ethan and Preston returned. She'd sat on one corner of the mattress and Ethan on the other, only to have Caleb and Preston take positions across the room as far from them as possible. With the window cracked to keep the air flowing and without Caleb to warm her, she was freezing and frustrated.

"Like she'd even let us stay there."

"She would if you agreed to go to church with her."

"You know my mom would never do that!"

"And you know she will if I ask her."

Nat grimaced again before frowning in thought. That was true enough. And it would keep her mom safe while they waited to see what Ethan's sister might do next.

"Okay, that's actually a good idea for my *mom*. But you can just stop trying to get away from me, Caleb, because I won't allow it! And besides, I told you I have an idea." She took a deep breath. "We can just tie you to a tree and you can practice shifting!"

Silence filled the room.

"*That's* your idea?"

"It's a good idea," she frowned. "You're afraid to shift and you're afraid of hurting me. This way, you can practice. Maybe it's like how you used to have a really hard time not shifting, but over time, you were able to last longer and longer."

"Nat, I'm not shifting anywhere near you! Ever!"

She groaned and turned to Ethan.

"Ethan, could you do it with him? Make sure he's okay and untie him afterwards?"

"Whoa, Natty." Preston leaned up from where he'd been studying the carpet, avoiding looking at Ethan. "I've seen him in attack mode. He hurt you back then, and we all saw what he did to you last night! You can't ask Ethan to be around that."

Ethan stared at him, his chest moving a bit faster than usual.

"He's right, Nat," Caleb said. "Besides, Ethan is too small. He'd never be able to handle me if I went out of control."

Ethan turned toward him immediately, the warmth that had been growing in his eyes evaporating with his frown.

"I know how to tie a knot a wolf can't escape."

"Have you even seen him as a wolf, Ethan?" Preston leaned forward more, his gaze intent on the smaller boy who was growing rapidly more annoyed. "He's huge. Way bigger than you."

"Have you ever heard the saying *brains versus brawn*?" he said, irritation coloring his voice.

"Yeah, and his brawn will smash your brains out," Preston snapped.

"He'll be tied up and if he gets out of control, I can just use wolfsbane. It pulls us back to human form. It won't be a problem," he gritted out, turning his gaze back toward Caleb.

Preston snorted.

"Fine. Get killed. What do I care," he finished in a mutter, leaning back once more to glare at the carpet.

Nat swallowed, feeling a bit guilty, but Ethan knew about these things. He'd helped Caleb the previous night. He knew what to do!

Her eyes lifted to see Caleb's filled with doubt.

"Ethan has lived his life around wolves. He *is* a wolf. And he knew exactly what to do last night. Please let him help you, Caleb."

Caleb rubbed his brow and looked at Ethan hesitantly.

"You're sure those things could stop me?"

"After my mom died, my dad was out of control. And he's even bigger than you. And meaner. I was just a baby, but my sister brought him back using wolfsbane. If it worked on him, and it worked on you last night, there's no reason to think it won't work again. And like I said—" he glanced back at Preston peevishly—"I know how to tie a knot."

Preston didn't look up.

Caleb looked back at Nat, indecision still in his eyes.

"I want you out of town. Out of the state. Go with your mom."

"Forget it, Caleb."

"Then I'm not doing it!"

Nat smacked a pillow over her face, groaning her frustration into it.

"You should both go somewhere safe while we're doing this," Ethan frowned.

"Why the hell should I go somewhere?"

"Because my sister is unpredictable and I won't be there to protect you."

"Yeah, because you're gonna get yourself killed!"

When Ethan reddened and looked closer to exploding than she'd have imagined he could, Nat intervened.

"What if Preston and I drive my mom to my grandma's? She lives out of state, so it will take us a few hours. That will give you plenty of time and we can meet you back here!"

When Caleb and Ethan exchanged glances, Preston crossed his arms.

"Yeah, I'm not going *anywhere*—"

"You can take my car," Ethan interrupted. "You said you liked it."

"Your Beamer. You'll just let me drive it."

"Bimmer. Beamer refers to the motorcycle."

Preston stared at him.

"Thank you, Ethan," Nat broke in quickly before Preston found the sarcastic response she knew he was searching for. "We'll be really careful with it. And…and you both…you'll both be really careful too, right?"

She wasn't worried. Not really. Ethan knew what he was doing and Caleb was just being too cautious! So she wasn't worried.

But when the two boys looked at each other again before nodding, the knot tightened in her gut.

Everything would be fine. She would just go to her grandma's house and back again and then everything would be fine. Caleb would shift and if he was still out of control, Ethan would shift him back with wolfsbane and they could try again some other time. And they would just keep trying until Caleb could control himself again.

Because anything else was just not acceptable.

17

"Has he texted yet?"

"Not yet." Nat didn't even get annoyed after answering the question the same way for what must have been the hundredth time. She was as worried as Preston, checking both of their phones every few seconds while he drove and her mother slept in the back seat.

"You shouldn't have asked him to do it, Natty. Ethan's too cocky and your brother—or...whatever—is just going to get extra pissed."

"Ethan's smart, Preston. You know that."

"That's even worse! Smart people are too sure they're right!"

"But how could he be wrong! You really think he doesn't know how to tie a knot a wolf can't escape?"

"I think your brother would chew his own leg off to get at whatever is pissing him off! That's what I think!"

Nat made a small sound and looked out the window, worry flooding her eyes. Was he right? Caleb was very single minded in general and especially so as a wolf. But as an out of control wolf? She swallowed at the memory.

Perhaps she had been selfish. Maybe she was wrong to ask Ethan to risk himself. But...

But she would do it again in a heartbeat. Caleb meant more to her than anything in the world. And Ethan *had* thrown her to the wolves with his sister, after all! She was glad to see Preston had thawed towards him, but Preston didn't care about Caleb the way she did. Or...at all. Not that she could blame him, but still.

Exhaling, she leaned her head back against the seat and closed her eyes. Just a few more hours of this. That was all. A few more hours and hopefully Caleb would be back to normal. And if he still hadn't been able to control himself, at least they'd have some answers and could figure out where to go from there.

Because there was no way she was letting him go. Not ever. Not when she knew how much he loved her and wanted to protect her—even from himself. Would she have left him if he had some medical condition that stole his mental faculties? Of course not! She'd be right by his side, looking for the best medical treatment possible and trying to stay safe in the meantime. This was no different.

Caleb had given up his life of freedom for her. He'd given up being a wolf time and time again. For her. And he was ready to do it once more. To reject this part of himself that...that was *him!* And not just when he was in wolf form. She saw it all the time! Caleb was a wolf. A strong, proud, fiercely loyal, pushy, loving *wolf.*

And she loved him. All of him. When he was tender and when he was furious. When his touch made her melt and...and when it terrified her!

Thoughts of the previous night tore through her mind. She'd been so afraid. So stuck with horrible memories of the men who had touched her before. Men she'd nearly forgotten during her years with Caleb. His touch had washed everything away.

But when she'd felt him probing at her, she'd remembered.

How their disgusting bodies had felt pushing into her. The fear. The pain.

For a moment, she'd forgotten this was Caleb. This was her wolf. And whatever madness came over him, she *knew* him. She believed in him—even if he didn't believe in himself!

Her eyes opened and she stared at the dashboard, her brows pulling together in a furious line.

That's right. She did believe in him. She shouldn't have left. She should be with him in this and if he went crazy, she should *be* there to help him.

"Preston, turn around."

He darted a glance at her, stark worry in his eyes.

"What's wrong?"

"Nothing. I just realized I shouldn't have left. No matter what Caleb said."

Preston didn't probe further, taking the nearest exit to get back on the highway and head back home.

"What about your mom?"

Nat turned to look in the back seat, chewing her lip.

"She's not going to like it but...we can have her committed. I'll say she's suicidal. That will keep her safe for a couple days. We can stop at the hospital before we head to the mountains."

"The mountains?"

She nodded. They hadn't told her where they were going, but she didn't think they would want to be anywhere near her place just in case Vick showed up. And since neither of them were responding to their texts, chances are they were out of range.

So she had a very good idea of where they'd gone.

"Don't worry. I'm pretty sure I know where they are, and there's no cell signal up there. And if Caleb is out of control when we get there, well..."

She drew a deep breath.

"I think it's time for me to handle him alone."

———

The visit to the hospital took longer than expected, even though Preston had helped her with the paperwork, feverishly filling in everything he knew before pacing while he waited for her to finish. The light was fading when at last they made their way up the winding mountain road.

"Nothing on your phone?"

She shook her head, feeling as pale as he looked. It had been hours since they'd heard anything. If things had gone as planned, they should have heard by now.

"That's our car."

"No shit," Preston muttered, but she heard the tension in his voice.

Her heart raced as he parked beside it, her eyes searching the area frantically. She didn't see anything.

"Maybe you should wait here," she whispered, starting to open the door.

His brief snort was the only answer before he shoved his own door open and stepped out.

Silence surrounded them. Too much silence. No crickets. No birds. No animal cries. Just the wind blowing through the trees.

"Preston, I really think you should wait in the car," she whispered again. The blood pounded in her ears, every beat of her heart sending vibrations through her body that she could feel on her skin.

Where were they?

A dense, dark line of trees waited for them, their gnarled branches twisted together and reaching for the sky. Heavy brush at the base created a wall, barring entrance, but for a small expanse she knew well.

She glanced at Preston, but he showed so sign of backing down. Okay. She'd just have to stay in front of him.

Taking a deep breath, she stepped toward the dark passage.

Leaves crackled underfoot with every step, the crunch of the brittle fragments declaring their presence to the expanse around them. Holding out a hand, she stopped Preston once they passed beneath the trees, her heart pounding wildly. Silence.

Struggling to adjust to the faint light inside, she peered down the path, looking for some sign of Ethan and Caleb. Of where they'd gone.

She looked up at Preston, at his worried young face, and tried one more time.

"Please go back," she whispered. "He won't hurt me. But... he would hurt you."

"And Ethan," he said, swallowing and staring into the forest. "I'll go when Ethan goes."

A chill stole over her, an icy grip tightening in her chest. But she turned back to the darkness. And stepped forward.

Crunch.

Pause. Listen. Silence.

Crunch.

Stop. Silence.

Deeper and deeper into the woods. The light behind them faded to nothing, and the twilight sent only the faintest shimmers through the trees above. All was dark. All was quiet.

They nearly stumbled over the body in front of them.

"Ethan?" Preston's frantic voice cut through the night as they dropped to their knees, both of them reaching for the boy lying so still on the ground.

Something wet covered Nat's hands the moment she touched his body, and she froze.

"Ethan?" Preston's voice was more choked now, his hands running over him, and Nat nearly collapsed in relief when a small whisper responded.

"What are you doing here? We said we'd call..."

"Are you fucking kidding me right now?" Preston said

furiously, beginning to lift Ethan in his arms. "I fucking *told* you, dude."

"Are you seriously saying I told you so right now," came the slightly annoyed response. But he didn't try to stop Preston from lifting him.

"What happened, Ethan? Where's Caleb?" she whispered, her worried eyes sweeping the area around them. She couldn't keep them safe if she didn't know the direction he might come from.

"He shifted before I could tie him up. He didn't mean to. I wasn't expecting it…" His voice faded, and Preston's voice was rough when he answered.

"You're so fucking smart you're stupid sometimes. Are you going to fucking die on me? Because I don't want to carry you all the way to the car if you're just going to fucking die."

His voice cracked and he cleared it quickly, looking at Nat in worry. She nodded.

"I'll walk back with you."

Relief flickered in his eyes, and he lifted Ethan more securely in his arms, turning back toward the car.

A low snarl wrapped its way around the trees, coming from everywhere. Nowhere.

"Caleb?" Nat's voice was tentative as she looked around. Silence.

Her hand gripped Preston's arm, ready to pull him away if Caleb attacked, and the snarl came again. Deeper. Harsher.

Nat swallowed and dropped her hand. Silence.

"Caleb…where are you? Please…let me see you… I…have something…something I want…to give you," she finished, her throat scratchy.

The wind blew around them while Preston stood, frozen with worry, his arms gripping Ethan tightly.

And an enormous dark beast with glistening fangs locked in a fierce, wild growl stepped between the trees.

"Caleb…" Nat's heart ached with relief and fear. Fear for Preston. For Ethan.

But not for her. Because she knew Caleb. And he would never hurt her.

"Preston, take Ethan to a hospital. I'll stay here."

"Fuck. Are you sure Natty?"

"The wolfsbane. I dropped it," Ethan whispered, stopping when Caleb's growl bit out in a harsh bark, his snarl growing more wild.

"It's okay. I don't need it. Go on. I'll be safe with Caleb."

Tension held her body taut, worried they would argue further. And Caleb could move so quickly when he wanted to.

Preston looked at her in indecision before glancing down at Ethan and looking back up. This time with a nod.

"Wait—we can't leave her here—he's gone rabid," Ethan tried lifting his head, but Preston subdued him, striding back toward the car with hurried steps.

"Shut up, dude! She knows him better than you and you're bleeding all over me. And you're not light, so just be quiet."

His voice was already fading behind her as Nat stared at Caleb. Caleb. His eyes with a madness in them she'd never seen.

Caleb.

And she began taking off her clothes.

———

The wind whistled through the trees in soft whispers that swirled around her, chilling her bare skin as piece by piece her clothing fell at her feet.

"Caleb," she whispered, the sound floating through the air between them. "I'm not afraid of you. I'm not afraid to be with you. Not anymore."

A dark, deep chaos raged within the eyes that watched her— twin hollows of madness held in check by some thin thread that couldn't hold. Crouching low, his body jerked with each soft pat of her clothes hitting the forest floor.

"You have always fought for me. You fight everything for me. Even yourself. But I don't want you fighting yourself, Caleb. Fenri…"

His claws dug into the dirt in front of him.

"You're mine. *All of you.* You're *mine. My* wolf," she said, her voice growing husky. Tremors racked her body. From the icy mountain air. From standing on a knife's edge, hoping she wouldn't slip…

He jerked back with a snarl when the last of her clothing fell to the ground, and she took a shaky breath.

"I trust you to take care of me. As I will always take care of you."

Closing her eyes, she took one last deep breath…and slowly turned her back to him to fall to her knees and lean forward on all fours.

Blood pounded in her ears. The air vibrated against her skin with every beat of her heart. And she waited. Struggling not to shake. From the cold. From the fear she was trying so desperately to hide. That he was lost to her.

Sharp crackles of leaves sounded behind her, and she looked over her shoulder to see him in a type of madness, creeping forward only to rush back with a vicious shake of his head. The muscles of his enormous body tensing repeatedly, locked in some internal war.

"Caleb, it's okay—Caleb!" Shoving herself to her feet, she swiped at the ground to grab her jacket and race after him when he thundered off deep into the woods. "Caleb, stop!"

Broken bits of branches and scattered leaves bit into her bare feet, and she struggled to get her arms into the soft hoodie while she ran, unwilling to slow for even a moment, to risk losing him.

"Caleb, please come back! Please don't leave!" Tears choked her, and she wiped her eyes furiously with her sleeve.

She needed to see. He was already so far away, and it was so dark!

She stopped calling for him, needing to hear which way he'd gone, needing to know which way to go, running, stumbling, desperately trying not to cry, trying not to cloud her vision.

She was his mate. She *was*. He *chose* her! He was still her wolf!

The harsh chill of the air tortured her lungs, but she hurtled ahead, leaping over fallen branches, ignoring when the forest floor cut into her flesh. Deep into the woods, twisting and turning to follow the only open passages she could find that she thought he might have used.

Until she could no longer hear anything but her own labored breaths and the wind whistling past her ears. Until the pain in her side bowed her over. And still she stumbled ahead. Crying freely now. Calling again, knowing his own ears would hear her long after hers had failed.

Because she wasn't a wolf. No matter how much she wanted to be. Wanted to be what he needed. She was too fragile compared to him. And slow. And she couldn't hear him. Couldn't see any further signs of where he'd been. It was too dark.

She had lost him.

Fresh tears sprang to her eyes, and her head shook back and forth. No. He would come back. He just needed to run this off. And he would be back.

A deep sound of pain came from her throat, and she fell onto her knees, her arms wrapped around her body, rocking back and forth.

Except his eyes...they hadn't been like they were before. They were too wild. And this was the forest. The home he'd abandoned for her. To live as a human, denying the wolf inside him over and over. For her.

And what had she done? Let him. Denied him as well. Too afraid. Wanting only the human part of him. Afraid to want the wolf.

But she wanted him now. So deeply and it tore at her until she screamed it into the night. On and on, screaming and sobbing, until her throat grew raw.

Nat knelt on the hard, cold ground, her chest shaking with each breath, staring numbly at her bare thighs. Listening. Hoping for any hint of a sound. Any whisper of hope.

But all was silent.

She waited. He would come back. He wouldn't want her to get hurt. He would come back...

But the minutes crept by and the night grew darker. Colder.

Nat lifted her head at last, looking around. She'd run without thinking of anything but catching up to Caleb.

And she had no idea where she was.

Wiping her tears away, she stood on trembling legs, pinpricks running up and down her skin as the blood flowed freely once more. She couldn't feel her toes, but perhaps that would be a mercy walking over the rough terrain. Wrapping her jacket around her more tightly, she turned back the way she'd come, the faint light of the moon glistening through the trees above.

Maybe Caleb would run back home. Maybe he just needed time.

A sharp pain stabbed her stomach, and she struggled to breathe.

Just walk. One foot in front of the other.

She plodded along, trying to guess at her direction each time she came to open pathways. Minutes passed by. Maybe hours. She didn't know. She had no watch. No phone. Just a thin jacket and a growing sense of unease.

When the path she was on opened to a large, rocky creek, she knew she'd taken a wrong turn. But she was thirsty, so she scanned the area before quenching her thirst and starting to turn back.

A howl sounded in the distance, the mad shriek piercing the

night, high and shrill. On and on it went until another call answered it, the screaming yelps filling the mountainside.

That wasn't Caleb. And it wasn't nearly far enough away.

Nat turned back toward the creek, looking around frantically. Where could she go? Should she follow the creek? It should spill out eventually into a river, and maybe she could swim out far enough where no animal would chase her. How long could she last in the cold water?

When the shrieks suddenly went silent behind her, she didn't hesitate, splashing into the shallow, frigid water to head downstream, hoping the water might mask her scent.

She stumbled along as quickly as she dared, afraid to end up bursting into another animal's territory in her mad dash from the banshee creatures behind her. Coyotes. She knew their call. They weren't large, but they would tear her apart if hungry enough.

The water grew deeper, and what little feeling she'd had remaining in her feet and lower legs disappeared completely. Worried she might twist her ankle on the uneven creek bed below, she slowed her pace, treading with extra care. Her teeth chattered, and she tightened her arms around her body, trying to hold in whatever warmth she could, while the sound of the rushing water filled her ears, masking further sounds from the forest. She glanced back over her shoulder. And her heart flew to her throat.

A pack of coyotes had emerged, bounding along the edge of the creek, their eyes bright and alert. On her.

She didn't run. She could never hope to outpace them. There was only one thing she could do.

Scream.

18

CALEB'S CLAWS tore up the ground, his female's cries for him to return singing in his ears, beckoning him back with images of soft, milky white thighs in the moonlight and the ruby red lips spread for him so willingly.

Snarls ripped from his throat, a pain unlike any he'd known tearing at him with every bit of earth that took him farther and farther from her. From her anguished cries that grew more faint with each passing moment. Again and again his heavy paws came to a halt, trying to turn, but he forced them forward. *Away.* He had no thoughts save one: *stay away.*

Away from the delicate figure that had offered herself to him at last.

Away from the red gashes marring her pale, beautiful skin.

He could not think beyond the red madness that had overtaken him, red from the blood he'd spilled that night. From the signs of all the pain he had inflicted on his female's body.

From her soft red lips...

His body halted once more, and he snapped at the air,

fighting not to release the howl so desperate for escape. Fighting to keep going. To keep her safe. From him.

Her tortured calls for him ceased at last, and he stilled, panting, gripping the ground fiercely. Listening. Yearning with everything in him for one more sound. One more sight.

His head turned back, an ache building within until he fell to the ground to fight the intense longing, clinging with all his might not to go back. Not to race back and take everything he'd wanted for so long.

A low whine crept from his throat as he crawled back toward her helplessly, inch by inch creeping across the forest floor, the deep ache inside him numbing his raging desperation to flee.

His female. *His.* He would not hurt her like before.

Shame washed over him, and he paused, gripping the ground once more, every muscle in his body tense, preparing to force himself away yet again.

And in the distance, a coyote howled.

Blinding terror shot him to his feet, spurring his body into a savage run. Alone. He'd left her alone. Panic and fury fueled his flight, fury at anything that would dare touch her. Fury at whatever it was within him that had dared force him away. He had run so far—too far! Back back back he raced, dark images assailing his fractured thoughts.

When her scream pierced his soul, leaving nothing behind but a white hot madness. And silence.

Blood filled his vision, the demon within him unleashed, pounding the ground beneath him in a terrible mania, lost to his terror. She had moved too far from where he'd left her, and he'd been too far away to realize. To protect. To shield her from the lesser creatures that roamed the hills, so small to him he'd forgotten, his mind a dark chaos consumed with protecting her from the only threat he could see: himself.

The sounds of water flowing mingled with sharp yapping

barks the moment before he burst from the trees in a blaze of shadows and fur.

His mate. His achingly beautiful, delicate mate, stood on the far bank, her hair tumbling over her shoulders, her pale face locked on the three grey coyotes that surrounded her, darting forward, nipping at her bare legs while she dodged their teeth, swinging a thick dark branch swiftly at their jaws.

At his cry of rage, her eyes flew to him, widening with desperate relief, and the branch faltered. Just enough to leave an opening, and a blur of gray flashed towards her throat.

Caleb caught it in his jaws, toppling his mate to the earth and covering her body with his own as he shook the smaller canine viciously before throwing it a distance away, hearing a pained yelp as it hit a tree. The coyotes scattered immediately, racing back into the night, their high pitched barks fading in the distance until nothing remained but the sound of the water flowing behind him, the wind in the trees, and his mate, breathing softly beneath his body.

His gaze fell, blazing, to the perfect creature staring up at him with soft, glistening eyes. Leaning back on her elbows, her lithe form extended beneath him, pale skin glowing softly in the moonlight. The cotton of her gray jacket had fallen open, exposing two milky white breasts with rosy red nipples tightened in hard peaks. His eyes wandered lower, following the gentle line of her abdomen to the baby soft skin she kept so smooth at the juncture of her thighs, thighs parted to reveal the deep, pink lips with the sweet scent that drove him mad.

Whatever madness had made him run was gone now. He knew only his female was beneath him. And the thick pink shaft, fully extended with bulging veins that throbbed painfully against his stomach, needed to be inside her.

———

Lowering his muzzle, Caleb gently nuzzled his mate's neck, breathing her in, a deep warmth spreading through his body when she returned the gesture. His tongue reached out to feel her, taste her, and a small growl escaped him when he felt the chill of her skin.

Lapping in long, slow licks, he began warming her, letting the heat of his body shelter her while his tongue trailed from her shoulder to the tips of her fingers before gliding down her body, the thick shaft beneath him tightening with each touch, each taste.

He warmed her until her skin glowed in a soft pink blush all over, until her breath caught with each new stroke. Until at last he allowed the lure of her scent to draw him where he longed most to be.

His tongue flattened against her smooth, full lips, a blinding heat rushing through him at the feel of the delicate petals that teased him with every lick. Pressing deeper, he slipped inside, massaging the hard nub again and again, and his heavy fringe of lashes lifted to watch her face.

She still held herself up on her elbows, her lips apart while she watched him, her face flushed and her thighs trembling. Holding her gaze, he pressed harder, stroking, teasing, faster and faster, watching her breasts rise and fall in short, rapid breaths. Until a moaning gasp caught her, the small cry shooting through him with a fire that gathered every last particle of desire in his body, every thought, every feeling, and sent it to the rod pulsing violently against his stomach.

He'd reached his limit.

Tearing his muzzle away, he nudged her side, forcing himself to be gentle, her scent nearly overwhelming him. She didn't hesitate, rolling over and pushing herself onto all fours.

Heat blinded him, and his cock twitched violently. Tightening his front legs on her waist, he positioned her against his hips, unable to stop himself from thrusting against her even while he struggled to go slow. To be careful this time. The thought growing dimmer and dimmer with each pass that brushed the tip of his hardened shaft against her soft lips.

Until it found the warm, wet entrance at last, and he stilled, panting, the thick head enormous against the small opening.

A tremor coursed through her, the vibrations gripping him with sensation, and he pressed his muzzle on her neck, feeling her. And slowly pushed forward, parting her body and sinking into the impossibly tight passage.

His cock pulsated furiously, stretching, filling, the shallow breaths of his mate growing faster as her body clenched around him. Sliding in deeper and deeper, her panting matching his own as he desperately fought to go slow. To not hurt her.

He stopped, shaking with restraint, when the bulb at the base of his cock pressed against her entrance. He needed to be inside. He needed to be tied to her. Forever.

His legs tightened, his jaw opening at last, and she turned her head, letting her hair fall across her shoulder, exposing her neck to him fully. Holding her gently, carefully, the warmth of his breath flowed over her, his scent the woodsy scent of the forest, wild and free. Free to choose. Free to love her. His mate.

And his hips shot forward, forcing the thick knot past the narrow opening and embedding himself deep inside. Her sharp cry mingled with the scent of her arousal, and he was lost.

His hips thrust violently, shoving himself deep within the smooth, velvet passage over and over, the burning at his center driving him to a madness that could only find release deep within her body. Pained cries came from her throat even as her desire swirled around him, and he buried himself fully again and again, feeling her shatter beneath him, her violent spasms sending him over the edge he had waited so long to find. His seed shot deep within her womb, gushing into her, filling her completely while the thick knot trapped it inside, tying her to him.

Forever.

Convulsions rocked him as he held her hips tight against his own, the last of his cum spurting inside. Small sobs shook her, and he released her neck with a whine, licking the gashes he'd made before. Comforting. Soothing. Nuzzling her cheek even while her body continued contracting around him with every twitch of his knot inside her.

She turned her face to his, rubbing against him, her breath hitching with tears, and he licked them from her skin, warmth flowing through his body while his knot shrank within. Locked together. United. Bound.

This was his mate.

Everything was warm. Perfect. He had everything he wanted now. Everything except...

He longed to touch her. To feel her breasts. To kiss her shoulder. Her lips.

With one final lick along her back, his fur fell away. And he knelt over her, naked, his body burning, needing to hold her. To feel her.

"Caleb?" she whispered, a soft tremor in her voice as she turned to look up at him.

And fire hit him. His center was on fire. Terrible, beautiful fire. A softness around him that burned, tearing the breath from his lungs, a white hot blinding flame he couldn't escape. Couldn't control.

His eyes met hers with a gasp as his body acted on its own, thrusting into her once more, plowing into her fully again and again while he continued gasping desperately for air, his eyes locked on hers, drinking in every shocked, helpless sound of desire torn from her lips. Driving into her until the fire that had tortured him for so long—every last painful, tormenting flame—gathered into one and erupted within her and he cried out, spilling everything he had, everything he was, deep inside.

———

Caleb stared at Nat in shock as the convulsions slowly faded. Afraid to believe. Afraid to move.

He felt good. More than good. The burning…it hadn't been in his stomach. It hadn't hurt. Or…it had but…the pain was so good.

Another spasm shot through him, and his cock twitched inside her once more, drawing a gasp from them both.

Nat trembled, and Caleb wrapped an arm about her, pulling her back slowly as he sat back on his heels, keeping her back pressed against his chest. He leaned into her neck, trembling with her, a hand moving up her body to cup her breast.

"Nat…" A deep shudder went through him when her body clenched around him, and he flexed inside, reveling at the sensations. At her moan.

His lips stroked her neck, his tongue slipping out to glide along her skin. Tears stung his eyes. Everything felt good. *Everything*.

He crushed her to him, burying his face in her hair.

"Are you okay?" he whispered.

She groaned with a small whimper but nodded.

"Did I hurt you?" he asked, his voice hoarse with worry.

"It hurt," she said with a shuddering breath, "but it felt good, too. More than good…"

He pressed her back to him with a shudder of his own.

"Was it…is my body…were you able to…do everything you wanted?"

Another groan left him, this time with a bit of a laugh.

"Nat…you're fucking perfect. I lost myself in you completely. I meant to hold back…I was trying not to hurt you but…" His lips brushed her skin, sending a shiver through her body, as he whispered, "You overwhelm me…"

She sighed with relief, leaning into him and closing her eyes. He held her close for a long while, unmoving, until he grew inside her yet again and she moaned, lifting herself carefully and sending sharp pangs of torturous pleasure along his thick length as she pulled herself off.

His stomach clenched at the scent of blood.

Turning her in his arms in a single movement that had her hands flying for his shoulders with a gasp, he pushed her down on her back, looking between her legs in horror.

"I *did* hurt you," he choked out, his eyes locked on the blood and semen on her lips and thighs, only for her to moan again and hit his shoulders.

"You're huge, Caleb! I mean, gigantic! It's just going to take my body time to get used to you. Could you *not* embarrass me in the meantime," she finished with a mutter, trying to close her legs and push him away. He ignored her, leaning down to kiss her wounded flesh softly, pain in his eyes.

"I'm sorry," he said hoarsely between tender kisses. "I'll be more careful next time." His kisses grew longer, softer, his tongue reaching out to massage her gently while she stroked his hair.

"I loved everything, Caleb," she whispered, and he looked up to see her staring up at the stars, her eyes glistening. "Everything. The way you touched me. The way you took me. I love the way you are. Who you are."

Her lashes fell to look at him, her eyes soft.

"You're my wolf. I love you. And I want you. All of you," she admitted with a touch of shyness.

Heat rushed through him, the rigid length between his legs twitching madly as the wolf within him surged. And the man. One mind. One body.

He pulled himself up until he hovered over her, his eyes roaming her face, before leaning down to touch his lips to hers. Her long legs wrapped around him, and he stilled against her when her hand snuck between them, positioning him against her somewhat battered entrance.

"Are you sure?" he asked, struggling to think. She only tightened her legs, pushing him into her body, and they both moaned as he sank into her depths.

They didn't speak again for a long while.

———

Caleb groaned, his heavy, muscular body collapsing on Nat's slender form, completely spent.

He didn't move when she suddenly gasped and tried to sit up.

"Ethan! We need to go check on him!"

"He's okay," he mumbled, barely able to form words. But guilt began stealing through him, and he leaned up on his elbows to look down at her. "The wounds I made weren't lethal. I was just...I saw the the rope, and one moment I was there thinking 'leash,' and the next I just...it's like my mind was gone. Everything was instinct."

His eyes fell, not wanting to meet the concern in hers. Not deserving it.

"But I didn't want to kill Ethan. Just...teach him a lesson," he muttered, the shame of it washing over him. Ethan had been doing everything to help him. His wolf should have been grateful. *He* should have been grateful.

"Caleb..." Her soft hand reached up to cup his cheek. "You have been fighting in the dark, with so much happening in your own body you couldn't possibly have prepared for."

His eyes returned to hers reluctantly, shame still heavy within them. Until they narrowed on her with a frown.

"And what were you doing here anyway? I told you to stay away! I barely restrained myself from hurting you far worse yesterday!" With every word, his outrage grew, and he reared up to glare down at her. "What the fuck were you thinking Nat! My mind was totally fucked, and you were almost—"

The memory strangled what was left of his voice, and he flipped them over, lying on his back and crushing her to his chest, his body shaking.

"I'm never again leaving you to deal with whatever happens by *yourself*. If I'm your mate, then you *don't* run from me," she said firmly. "Ever again! Promise me. Because *that* was the only danger I was in tonight. "

He finally released her enough for her to push herself back to stare fiercely at *him* this time while he looked up helplessly. Reaching his hand out to tuck her hair behind her ear, he shook his head, his eyes raw.

"You are the most stubborn, frustrating girl," he whispered.

At her smile, he sighed and sat up, pulling her close and tucking her head into his neck to stroke her hair, petting her gently.

She was so small. So fragile. Cuts all over her body. Blood between her legs. So very delicate and yet so strong, putting every bit of her softness at risk time and again to protect a *wolf*.

His mate. His fierce, beautiful mate with the kindest heart.

"I'll never run from you again." He spoke in solemn, hushed tones. "I promise."

Because he knew now that no matter how wild his wolf might be, he would never, ever hurt her again. They were bound together. He and his wolf. And both of them with Nat. He could feel it. And they would protect her. Forever.

He kissed her forehead once more before lifting her in his arms as he stood, his heart leaping when she cuddled closer, her long lashes fluttering closed.

His mate. His love. His choice.

They had both dared to reach for more than what fate had in store for them. And they had won.

He smiled against her hair and carried her back through the

woods, his old home still running through his veins. But it could never match the power of the home he'd built with Nat. It didn't matter if it was in a trailer. Or out under the moon. Or wherever they might go in the future.

They would always make their own fate. Together.

EPILOGUE

NAT FIDGETED with the skirt of her gown, the simple pink fabric draping her legs beautifully as she sat in the limo beside Preston. Caleb sat across from her, his gorgeous body filling out the rented tuxedo with his thick muscles, his eyes running down her body. Warm. Possessive.

A small sound came from her throat, and she turned to look out the window with anxious eyes. Why had she let him talk her into this!

Preston was worse than she was, staring pointedly out his own window, his arms crossed, and ignoring Ethan frowning at him from the seat across from them.

Pushy. Wolves were pushy! All of them! Well, it's not like she knew any wolves other than Caleb and Ethan—and Vick if you could count their brief encounter—but she didn't think it was *Preston's* idea to be coming out at prom.

Vick had completely disappeared after a short text to Ethan's father. She thankfully hadn't mentioned finding Caleb, and Ethan had somehow managed to keep it hidden from his father as well, in spite of his fears that he wouldn't be capable of it, so life had returned to normal for her and Caleb.

Well. A new normal. One where she could seldom walk comfortably. He was just so big! No matter how often he was inside her, she was always sore after. Not that she was complaining...

A blush crept over her, and Caleb reached a hand out to cup the back of her knee, stroking softly while he watched her, and she turned back to meet his heavy lidded gaze. Her heart quickened and her blush deepened at the unmistakable bulge growing between his legs. Nervous hands flew to her cheeks, the chill from her fingers cooling her growing heat.

At least they hadn't had to worry about any pregnancy scares. She'd been concerned at first, but a chat with Ethan revealed that his sister had thoroughly tested sex with humans and it seemed they were incompatible. Caleb had been deeply disappointed, and if she were honest, a part of her had been as well. It's not like they were ready for a child, of course, but one day she might have liked to have one.

Still. They could always adopt! Maybe they could even be foster parents one day. There were so many kids out there who needed adults that would actually care about them. Protect them. And who better to protect them than a wolf?

A wolf who was staring at her with eyes she knew were mentally undressing her right now piece by piece. She kicked his leg, and he grinned. Cocky as ever. God she loved him.

The limo pulled up to the curb and the driver exited to open the door beside her. Fuck. This was it. Were they just going to saunter inside like it was no big deal? What would everyone think!

Caleb didn't let her dwell on it, climbing out only to turn and scoop her into his arms, ignoring her tiny shriek with a very wolfish grin, and stalking toward the building. Oh god.

"Caleb," she said in a strangled whisper. "We can't just barge in with you holding me this way!"

"We can," he murmured against her hair, his pace not slowing.

"The teachers will throw us out! Or try to have us arrested or something!"

"Let them try," he growled. "We are getting our senior prom. And I want to dance with you."

She groaned into him when they reached the open door, tightening her arms around his neck and hiding her face.

Cool air brushed across her exposed shoulders as they stepped inside, the sounds of music and laughter and excited chatter wrapping around them. Nat peeked out to see a swathe of brightly colored dresses and black tuxes, with most students completely caught up in each other and not noticing them at all. At first.

Caleb joined the line of students waiting to get their prom pictures, and the couple in front of them glanced back. Nat squeezed her eyes shut once more when she saw their double-take.

And moment by moment, sound by sound, the area around them grew silent. A few hushed whispers floated above the music that swelled from the room beyond, and she felt Caleb draw a deep breath.

"I have an announcement!" He held her closer when she cringed into him. "We're in love."

Nat jerked up, coughing to the point of choking in her effort to clarify quickly only to see Caleb grinning at her.

"And we're not brother and sister! Or related! At all!" she cried out in a panic, but beginning to glare at him. He did that on purpose.

A few of the students near them looked around.

"Well, um, yeah. I mean, we kind of figured that out."

Nat frowned as she looked around at the general agreement

that began murmuring around the room, and Caleb smiled down at her happily.

"See? All that fuss for nothing."

She could see they hadn't been very good at hiding anything at all, evidently. Although she did think some of the expressions she saw seemed to be going along with the crowd's *I knew it all along* perspective more than might have been justified. But altogether, she really might have been making a fuss for nothing.

Her lashes lifted to Caleb. And she smiled happily, too. Until one of the chaperoning teachers approached, telling Caleb he couldn't hold her except on the dance floor.

Nat stopped him before he growled at the woman, but when he refused to put her down, an older man with a spark of humor in his eyes approached. Nat thought he looked a bit familiar but couldn't place him at first.

"I know it must seem like a dumb rule to you kids, but you have to think about old folks like us, trying to make sure you young ones don't get too crazy. Believe me, it's no fun being a rule enforcer."

That's where she'd seen him. The county sheriff. She'd seen his picture on the wall at the police station years ago when she'd run to them for help. And they'd returned her to the creep.

"Rules like giving a kid back to their mom's boyfriend and ignoring them telling you he was an abusive asshole?"

Caleb and the two chaperones looked at her in shock, and Nat forced her rapid breathing to calm down, her own anger taking her by surprise. Caleb recovered quickly, clenching her more tightly and turning cold eyes back to the man now staring at her with brows drawn in concern.

"No, I would never support a rule like that."

"Sheriff Douglas was an amazing sheriff, young lady, and if you—"

He halted the woman's tirade before the tension in Caleb's body snapped, still looking at Nat with deep, serious eyes.

"I've got things here," he said gently. After a brief exchange, and further reassurance from the sheriff, the woman hastened away.

He turned back to Nat, his tone grave.

"I retired five years ago. Did this happen under my watch?"

The anger that had flared up in her fizzed out instantly, leaving extreme awkwardness in its wake.

"Oh. No, I guess it would have been right after. Sorry…"

Caleb looked down at her in worry, but the sheriff shook his head, his lips drawn in a thin line.

"I know things were a bit chaotic for a while after I left. I didn't think they would have ever been that bad, though. To put a child in danger. That should never have happened. I may not be in office any longer, but I still have some sway. If you'll tell me more, I'll make sure those responsible are held accountable."

Nat swallowed. That would mean telling who the man was, the man whose body had been torn apart, which had thankfully been dismissed as an animal attack. And here she was, stirring things up again.

Ethan and Preston had wandered in at last, walking over to stand beside them, holding hands with their fingers interlaced and Preston looking everywhere but at Ethan.

"It was a long time ago." She tapped on Caleb to put her down, just wanting the sheriff to go away now. When he tightened his grip, she shot him a pleading look, and he relented with a sigh, setting her on her feet. "Anyhow, we'll wait for the dance floor so…" Go away.

The sheriff was opening his mouth to answer when Caleb and Ethan's heads snapped toward the door, and they shoved Nat and Preston behind them.

"What the fuck are you doing," Preston hissed, trying to get back around, only for Ethan to hold him back. Preston smacked his hand over his face peeking out around him from between his fingers.

Nat swallowed, the sheriff forgotten as she stared at the front door. And a moment later the ebony haired bombshell she'd hoped was gone for good stepped through the door. Wearing oversized sweats and what appeared to be men's slippers.

Vick tensed at the sight of the group of them staring at her, Nat's mouth agape, before gritting her jaw and stalking over.

The sheriff turned his gaze at last, and his eyes widened when Vick grabbed his wrist and slammed something in his hand.

"I counted," she bit out, looking up into his shocked face with fierce eyes and ignoring the rest of them.

They stared at each other a long moment before his eyes softened, and he gave a small nod.

"*Now*," she added, her eyes narrowing. His brows lifted with a helpless look, but he sighed with a slight curve of his lips. Glancing back at Nat, he hesitated, but turned to walk away at last when she avoided his gaze.

Vick's eyes followed him across the room before turning back slowly to them.

No one said a word.

"I'm not here to break up your little soirée." A delicate sneer touched her lips.

Ethan's brow was pulled together in intense confusion, his eyes wide on her clothes.

"If my clothes are bothering you, baby brother, I can take them off," she smiled slowly, her hands sliding to the hem of her shirt.

"Get out of here."

Caleb's voice was low. Guttural. And if Nat hadn't been watching so intently she might have missed the flash of fear in Vick's eyes. Fear or…was that hurt?

Nat hugged Caleb to her.

"I'm glad you're okay," she said softly. Hesitantly. Caleb didn't take his eyes off Vick and kept Nat firmly behind him.

Vick curled her lip.

"Save your concern for someone who needs it. I have no interest in wasting my time at a children's party."

She turned quickly, no less graceful or beautiful in her odd attire. But she stopped abruptly, her fists clenching, before turning her head to the side, her eyes down.

"You won't tell dad you saw me."

Tension held her body rigid as she waited for an answer.

"I...won't," Ethan agreed, his voice as confused as his eyes.

She didn't respond, but her body relaxed slightly. Her eyes lifted to look across the room for a brief moment, in time to see the sheriff walking back, and she clenched her hands again before moving in long strides toward the door. And then she was gone.

The four of them turned to look at each other.

"Can you let me go now?" Preston hissed, and Ethan finally let him move, frowning and lifting sad eyes when he jerked his hand away. "What? You said five minutes. It was five minutes!"

Caleb pulled Nat out of line and toward the dance floor, glowering at everyone who got in his way.

"I thought we were getting pictures?" Nat said a bit breathlessly when he pulled her into his arms.

"Later," he growled, pressing her to him. "I need to hold you..."

She sank into his arms, all the tumult settling as the tension melted away, and felt him start to stir against her. And she blinked. Blinked again.

"Caleb," she gasped, pulling back. "You're not hard!"

"I will be in a minute," he murmured, pulling her back and giving her a small glare when she smacked at him. Before going completely still. He stared down at her, their eyes mirror images of stunned relief.

"I'm not hard," he whispered before repeating it with a groan. "I'm not hard..."

And pulling her back, he began growing very, very hard.

"Fuck...I love you, Nat."

Letting herself melt into him completely, she closed her eyes, every last fear drifting away. College lay ahead, with all its new challenges. Marriage one day. Maybe they'd adopt or foster children. Or maybe they'd find careers they actually liked. She didn't know. She only knew they'd be together.

Fate might have had a different plan for them, but when she thought about what had been in store for each of them if they hadn't fought so hard to change it... Honestly.

Fuck fate.

———

Continue reading Ethan and Preston's story here:

An Unfated Mates Tale: Ethan & Preston

THANK YOU!

Fair reviews help so much, so please consider leaving one here, and thank you for your support!

https://Amazon.com/review/create-review?&asin= B09CZFHYK3

To get the latest updates, please sign up for my newsletter below. I take your privacy and time very seriously and will only send the most important announcements!

https://www.lexietalionis.com/subscribe

SNEAK PEEK: FLAMES OF LETHE

You may be interested in my other line, the *Lethe Chronicles*, for a more adult romance. However, whereas my *Unfated Mates* series is a collection of very sweet tales, my *Lethe* series has a deep darkness that can be very disturbing. Read with caution.

Flames of Lethe

Flames of Lethe, Chapter 1

She awoke on a hard bed of sand, the tender flesh of her breasts pressing into the rough grains beneath her. Stifling a groan, she shifted her body and opened one eye. And paused. Both eyes. Okay...weird. Pushing to her knees with a shake of her head, she rubbed her face and tried again.

The night blazed in a chaos of color. Twinkling golden sand stretched out to the horizon, emitting a soft glow that sparkled in random hues. Streaks of blue and violet raced across the sky to lose themselves in the depths of a starless void. And rising up into the violet ocean of night, above the warm blanket of golden light, was a massive moon that filled the sky, swirling in shades of red.

Blood pounded in her veins as her gaze locked on the sphere above her. *Calm down.* No panicking. Think! A nightmare? It didn't feel like a nightmare. Her breathing felt too real. Her hands buried in the sand. The crisp air hardening her nipples. She shivered, dropping her eyes.

Particles of sand clung to her flesh, illuminating the smooth pale skin beneath. Firm, full breasts swelled above a slender waist and well rounded thighs, while a small patch of brown curls provided her only cover.

Leaning forward and crossing her arms, she shook her head to let her hair cover her as she looked down. Nothing happened.

Her hand crept up to find baby soft hair no more than an inch or so in length all over. Who would have done this? Tears stung her eyes. Stop it. It was just hair. It would grow back. But her fingers clung to it as her gaze drifted to her right—to find a pair of sharp blue eyes watching her intently.

Christopher. Her mind went blank. Until he spoke.

"Josephine." The quiet, controlled tones drifted across the space between them.

A blood red glow filled her vision, the air around her growing thick and cloying. She heard nothing except the pounding of her heart and her rapid breathing, while a current coursed through her body. But as quickly as the sensations began, they vanished, leaving her quaking and struggling to focus.

Josephine. No, that was wrong. *Jo.* Her name was Jo. Exhaling slowly, she steadied herself and studied him.

He was naked as well, kneeling on one knee with an arm draped discreetly in front of him. His body was strong and lean with a light amount of golden hair on his gently muscled limbs and chest. Like her, his skin revealed no tan lines or other discolorations.

Her eyes began to wander lower, and she dragged them back

up to settle more safely on the hair on his head. It was the same length as hers, but it curled into soft blonde ringlets that danced about in tousled abandon atop a face unlined by age. It lent a somewhat boyish air to his otherwise sophisticated, sober appearance. A golden angel with a sharp jaw and soft, tender lips. Lips currently set in a grim line.

She met his eyes once more—and stopped breathing. They were narrowed and calculating. Her arms tightened around her, and the sensation of skin gliding on skin reminded her of just how much he could see.

Falling back in the sand, she pulled her knees to her chest, doing her best to cover herself. Not quite knowing where to look, she pretended to rub her forehead, hiding her eyes.

"Do you know...what happened to our clothes?" she mumbled, looking down to the left and right. She peeked back at him between her fingers when he didn't respond.

He stared at her a moment more.

"That isn't the most pressing concern right now," he said, turning his eyes away.

A shiver went through her. She didn't want to turn and look. *Stop being a baby*. Her head turned to follow his gaze.

The moon was impossibly large. And the color... A sickness rose inside her, and she unconsciously leaned closer to Christopher. He turned to her with a frown, and she stopped.

"Who are you?" he demanded.

She took a breath to answer. And nothing came out. It's a simple question, Jo. Answer him.

"Jo...I'm Jo..." she said, thinking furiously. He narrowed his eyes.

"I'm aware of your name." His voice was colder now.

"If you know my name, shouldn't you know who I am?" She wasn't doing anything wrong. Why did she feel guilty? Maybe because she was so stupid she couldn't remember the most basic information about herself. Come on, think!

"If I knew who you were, I wouldn't have asked the question." Okay. His voice was definitely veering toward hostile now. Her knuckles covered her eyes, rubbing. Stall stall stall!

"Well who are you?" Brilliant. Sit and hide behind her fists forever.

She could feel him staring at her.

"You don't remember me?" he asked.

"Your name is Christopher," she said tentatively, dropping her hands and giving him a questioning look. He stared a bit longer.

"Yes." He was very still, assessing her, before rising to his feet.

Jo quickly looked away, the blood rushing to her face—he seemed completely unconcerned with his state of undress. She couldn't very well keep sitting *now*, so she stood as well, trying to stay out of his field of vision and figure out how to cover herself. God this was awkward. She forced herself to breathe steadily, wanting desperately to match his composure and sure she was failing miserably.

She settled for wrapping her arms around her upper body to hide her breasts and pretending she wasn't entirely naked on her lower half. If she didn't look down, she could almost manage it. Thankfully he was about half a foot taller, so she could just keep looking up at him. She did so now, and followed his gaze to look around the horizon.

There was nothing but flat, oddly glowing sand everywhere. No plants. No rock outcroppings. No footprints or tire treads. Not even a sand dune.

"Please tell me you have some idea of what to do," she whispered. She may not remember who she was, but she was reasonably sure she had absolutely no survival skills. She only hoped he did.

He was silent a long while.

"Find water," he said. He looked at her once more, his eyes dropping down her body and back up in a single glance.

Her lips parted, and the heat climbed to her face as their eyes locked. She hadn't realized how close she'd been standing to him. His eyes grew dark, but she couldn't move. Couldn't breathe. The heat from his skin bled into her as she stared.

When he turned away at last, she closed her eyes weakly, drawing in ragged breaths as quietly as possible. Who was he? A shudder went through her, and her eyes opened once again to see he had started walking. She would just keep a nice comfortable distance between them. For all she knew, he had brought her here.

She looked around at the barren landscape. Okay, maybe that didn't make much sense. And she did remember him, at least. Enough to know his name. That was something, right?

Taking a deep breath, she stepped up her pace to walk close enough to talk. But not too close.

"Do you know where we are?" she asked.

"No." His voice was curt. She hesitated a moment but pressed on.

"Do you have any idea how we got here?

"No."

"Do you..."

She bit her lip. Did he remember anything? She couldn't very well ask him that without revealing herself. Oh well. If he thought she was stupid, so be it.

"I can't remember anything." Her voice sounded so small. It got him to look at her for a few seconds though.

When he turned back to walking without a word, she frowned.

"Do *you* remember anything?"

"No." His answer was so fast, she stopped, staring at his retreating back.

"But you knew my name," she pointed out, hurrying forward again.

"Yes."

Her lips pressed together.

"So you remembered something."

"And you remembered mine," he responded testily.

She exhaled.

"Do you remember anything *else?*"

"No." His pace never faltered. She rubbed her forehead and lapsed into silence.

They walked on and on, the only change the movement of the red moon drifting high above their heads. Jo tried an occasional question, but it always met with the same monosyllabic responses. Always the same—just like the sand. It was level everywhere, as if the wind never stirred. They saw no landmarks of any kind, and the sky was a deep emptiness, terrifying in its implications. She hoped that it was only the excessive light from the twinkling grains that prevented her from seeing the stars.

Don't think like that. She picked up a handful of sand as they walked, separating the glowing grains and tossing the seemingly normal grains of sand back on the ground. Eventually her hand was full of nothing but the luminescent sand, and she could see that individual pieces emitted slightly different shades. Together, they created a soft, warm light, like a weak incandescent bulb. So weird. But pretty.

"Do you think we're getting radiation poisoning?" she asked.

He glanced at her over his shoulder.

"Possibly."

The sand fell from her hands, and her arms wrapped about her once more.

So much for distracting herself. And her feet were really starting to hurt. Rubbing them with sandpaper all night couldn't have been any worse.

She stole a glance at Christopher.

"Are you thirsty?"

"No." To the point as usual.

"Don't you think that's…weird? We've been walking a long time," she pointed out.

"Yes." She stared dejectedly at his back.

"Would it kill you to make conversation?" she sighed.

"It might. Every time you open your mouth, your rate of dehydration increases." He didn't even bother looking at her. But her eyes lit up at the full sentence, and she stepped up her pace to walk beside him, covering her breasts with her arms.

"Okay," she acknowledged, "except I don't feel like I'm dehydrating. *At all.* I know I should be thirsty by now. I should be hungry. I should be at least *tired* by now. But I'm not. The only thing that lets me know that I've been walking all night is that my feet are raw."

He didn't bother acknowledging her.

"Are you tired?" she asked in exasperation.

"Yes, I'm tired of your questions," he snapped.

She groaned and dropped her head in her hands, coming to a halt. He was impossible. And she was in pain. She stood there for a few moments with her eyes closed, rubbing her temples. When she opened them again, he was a good ways in front of her. Her eyes fell to her feet glumly, wanting nothing more than to sit down and give them some relief, but Christopher wasn't slowing down. And the last thing she wanted was to be stuck out there alone.

Steeling herself against the pain, she caught back up and walked behind him in silence.

The night felt abnormally long. She hadn't counted the number of steps she had taken, but it had to be far more than what one could normally manage in a single night, even considering the somewhat rapid pace Christopher had set. And the moon that had risen in the sky now seemed to be moving back toward the horizon near where it had begun. Well that didn't make sense.

"Could we be walking in a circle…?" she decided to risk the

question.

"Our tracks are straight."

Jo looked behind them. He was right. She could see back a considerable distance, and their trail was a clean straight line. The perfectly level sand was good for one thing at least.

"How can a moon move that way?" she wondered aloud.

"I don't think that's the moon."

She frowned. What was it then? Another planet? But it was so huge in the sky—and to be that close to them at that size, wouldn't two planets just run into each other? Unless...

"Wait—are *we* the moon?"

"So it would seem."

She mulled this over in silence as she walked.

The night stretched on and on as the moon, as she'd decided to continue calling it, slowly disappeared below the horizon. Its absence left the sky completely blank, and fear crept over her. Although the entire desert floor was well lit from the sands, the soft illumination disappeared into the empty darkness above, a darkness so deep it threatened to swallow them. She shuddered and walked closer to Christopher, no longer wanting to stop, regardless of the pain.

But when the first glow of dawn began peeking over the horizon hours later, she breathed a sigh of relief. Darkness or no, she was ready to begin crawling rather than walk another step. The night had been impossibly long. Yet she wasn't tired—she was just sure her feet had lost a layer of skin. And she still wasn't thirsty.

She looked over at Christopher in desperate hope. "Can we sit down now? Just for a few minutes?"

Christopher considered the question, looking toward the horizon blooming softly with pink tendrils. But he stopped at last, and she groaned in relief as she threw herself to the ground, lying on her back and hugging her knees to her chest to keep her feet off the abrasive sand.

She couldn't walk another step—she would just lie here and die instead. Tightening her arms around her legs and tucking her head into her knees, she rocked back and forth, whimpering and whining and laughing at herself. Christopher's movement beside her drew her attention, and she glanced up to see him lower himself to the ground and sedately brush the sand from his feet.

"You're so respectable," she groaned at him, all her worries eclipsed by the sheer relief of being off her feet. "I bet you always wore a suit and tie."

His irritated glance only made her groan more. She rolled over on her side facing him, her knees still tight against her chest. How could he be so unaffected? A sigh escaped her as she stared at him, but he ignored her, stretching out his legs in front of him and leaning back with his hands in the sand. She couldn't help envying his consistent composure. How on earth did they know each other? Something told her they didn't move in the same circles. Her eyes began drifting over his body.

God, he was appealing, despite his complete unwillingness to have any sort of discussion with her at all. He still seemed intimidating, but with the dawn peeking over the horizon, that had faded a bit. She wanted to lean up on an elbow to watch him, but…she wasn't completely crazy. Instead, she would just enjoy the ability to stare at him since he seemed so uninterested in her. Her lips rested against her knee as her eyes glided over him, down the muscles of his chest, across the soft ripples of his abs, and finally…

Christopher put his knee up and glared at her. She blinked rapidly, feeling like a child who'd been caught with her hand in the cookie jar. The heat flamed in her cheeks as she cringed into her legs as far as she could, her eyes peeking out over her knees.

"Sorry," she said in a tiny voice.

His face was stony, but his eyes blazed. He tore his gaze away angrily and sat staring in front of him.

Fuck. What was the proper decorum when walking around

naked with a relative stranger? Squeezing her eyes shut, she rolled back over onto her back, keeping her knees tight against her chest. Whatever it was, it probably didn't include ogling someone. She wanted to groan again but restrained herself. Maybe if she just stayed in the sand with her eyes closed, it would all go away, and when she opened them again, she'd be back home in bed.

The light grew brighter behind her closed lids, and she opened them with a sigh as the sun finally broke over the horizon. And all her thoughts evaporated.

———

Searing heat hit her all at once, blinding, tearing into her, through her, ripping into her flesh and burning the very screams erupting from her lungs. The flames devoured her, eating through her skin, her muscle, through her very bones. Dragging her into the earth, pulsating and relentless, ravaging even the air around her until screaming was no longer possible. And still it went on.

There was no escape. No moment of peace. Death withheld its comfort. Impossible agony. Torment. An eternity of anguish in every moment, savage and merciless.

And the day went on. Hour after hour, without pause. There was nothing else. No thoughts. No feelings. There was only pain. Endless pain.

———

Jo lay trembling violently in the sand, barely registering her restored body around her. Emptiness surrounded her. A coldness as deep as the heat of the flames that had torn her apart. She curled into a ball on her side, wrapping her arms around her knees, gripping her shaking body with all her strength.

She wanted to cry. To scream. To break down into terrified tears. Everything was gone. Everything was over. Whatever this was... She choked back the tears. No. If she started, she might never stop. And she didn't want Christopher to think even worse of her.

Christopher.

She jerked up to her knees and her heart pounded in an odd rhythm when she saw he was lying beside her, whole and perfect again. He was on his stomach, his face in his arms, and very still. Too still... Her heart stopped.

She reached out her hand tentatively, touching his shoulder. He tensed immediately, and she pulled back, releasing the breath she had been holding.

"Christopher..." she whispered. He didn't move. "Hey... it's...it's over now. We're..." she glanced at his short blonde curls and down at her own body. "We're back to...normal." Whatever that was. He still lay unmoving.

She knelt beside him, uncertain what to do. Finally, she reached her hand out once more, ignoring when he tensed, and began slowly stroking his back.

Soothing. Soft. Gentle. And with every touch, she felt her own tension melt away, moment by moment. She hummed softly, a melody from another time coming to her, and she kept stroking. Bit by bit she felt him relax under her hand, his breathing returning to normal. Her eyes closed, the touch of her hand on his skin lulling her into a cocoon of warmth and safety until she wanted nothing more than to stretch her body out beside his and press herself against him. Tears stung behind her lids. She shook her head and drew a shuddering breath. No crying. Just drift away.

She focused on the feeling of her hand against his skin, tracing the line of his muscles up to his neck and back down the center of his back. Her fingers splayed as she moved back up, gliding across the contours, feeling them ripple beneath her fingers. His breathing seemed to stagger, and her nipples grew hard, the night air around her feeling empty. She shivered.

"You can take your hand off me." His voice was acid.

Her eyes flew open, and she snatched her hand away.

The muscles tensed in his back as he pushed himself up, not looking at her. He kept his back to her and sat for some time, still and silent.

Jo gripped her hands in her lap and looked down at them with wide unseeing eyes, trying to get her breathing back under control. She felt...she didn't know. It was confusing. Her body began shaking again, and she dug her fingernails into her palms, trying to control it. But the shaking didn't stop.

She looked over at Christopher, still sitting as before, his body turned completely away from her.

"Do you..." *Do you feel what I'm feeling?* She couldn't ask that. "Do you think...this is Hell?" she whispered.

His head moved slightly, but he didn't answer.

"Please talk to me." Her voice was husky. "I'm...I feel like... like I know you. But..." her throat was getting blocked by tears, and she focused on breathing for a moment.

"What is it you want me to say," he asked bitterly. "I don't know anything more than you do."

She heard his disgust at being reduced to her level. But also hopelessness.

"Then..." Then what? What should they do? She drew in a deep breath. Actually, figuring out what to do wasn't the challenge. "We should run," she urged.

He turned his head slightly towards her but didn't look back.

"Run." Contempt laced his voice. "Run where."

She started to crawl around to face him, but he turned his body from her, so she stopped. Releasing a breath, she sat on her knees beside him. He had his knee up, an arm draped across it, and he turned further away from her. She ran her hands through her hair.

"Run as far as we can tonight and hope we finally find some shelter," she said in a single exhale. When he didn't acknowledge her, she continued. "So that we aren't out here when the sun comes up again," she explained awkwardly. He again refused to respond.

She wanted to both cry and shake him in frustration. Instead, she grabbed his shoulder and before he could react, slid around in front to face him.

His hand flew to her wrist to pull it off of him, his jaw clenched, his eyes burning into hers. He held her firmly, and they stared at one another, breathing heavily. And she didn't need to look down to suddenly realize why he'd been so intent on turning away.

She blinked rapidly, swallowing. But neither of them moved. She could feel the heat of his hand on her wrist, gripping her tightly, almost painfully.

"I...we—we're all we've got out here," she said, her voice a bit hoarse as she tried to keep her eyes on his. "Can't you just... talk to me?" His grip seemed to grow even tighter, and his eyes grew dark.

"Why would I want to talk," he whispered viciously, "to *you*."

She jerked as if he'd slapped her.

She didn't even realize she was crying until he shook her.

"Stop it!" He was furious. But she couldn't. She was still staring at him but his image was blurred now. Silent sobs shook her shoulders as she struggled with herself. She wanted to be strong. She was trying so hard to be strong.

Christopher pushed her away from him roughly and stood up, walking away a few steps and turning his back to her again, his muscles rippling with tension. Jo put a hand to her mouth, nausea threatening to choke her, as her body trembled from the effort to control her tears.

They stayed that way for a long time. Until her tears were no longer flowing and she sat staring numbly at the sand between her knees.

"We should go." Christopher's voice was low and calm as he turned to face her again. Jo couldn't bring herself to respond.

She climbed to her feet, wiping the sand from her body, and wrapped her arms around herself, waiting with her head down until he finally turned to go. Then she waited a bit longer before following. He looked over his shoulder at her impatiently.

"Are you trying to keep us from finding shelter as long as possible?"

She just stared at him.

He didn't move, his eyes narrowing, and she looked down again. But she walked forward until she was beside him, keeping her arms around herself.

He turned to walk again, not looking at her. And they walked in silence.

Who was he? The burning seemed to have jarred her mind just enough to bring a single memory of him to the surface. Only one. It was so small—the briefest image. She remembered his eyes. He was looking at her, and it was different. He had been… alarmed. Worried. No, it wasn't quite worry. It was too strong for worry. There was deep pain there. Grief.

She pushed at the memory, trying to see beyond it—anything. But nothing more came to her. And she couldn't reconcile it with how she'd felt when he first spoke. Or the way he seemed to feel about her now. Had she done something to him? Nothing made sense.

He suddenly exhaled in a short burst.

"You shouldn't touch me."

Her eyes jerked to his as the heat rushed to her face. He didn't look over.

"Sorry," she said, her voice small.

"You don't know who I am."

She glanced at him again.

"Do you?"

He didn't respond, and her eyes fell back to the sand in front of her.

"I do have memories." His voice was so quiet, she wasn't sure she was hearing him correctly. "Just pieces. Nothing that makes any sense."

She hesitated.

"It's the same for me," she said at last. "It's like trying to remember a dream. I just can't seem to hold onto anything." Her arms wrapped around her more tightly. "But...I know that I know you. More than just your name although...nothing very clear. But it feels...I...I don't know..."

"I remember you, too." His voice was dark.

"What...what do you remember?" she asked, looking over when he didn't answer. His closed expression revealed nothing.

"I told you: nothing that makes any sense."

Irritation laced his voice again, and she lapsed into silence.

They walked a good distance before he glanced at her, his eyes a bit wary.

"You were right about running. If there is any shelter to be found, we're just prolonging our pain if we walk."

She blinked at him but nodded.

His eyes dropped down her body, but he turned forward again quickly.

"Go ahead," he said.

She hesitated. In front? Feeling his eyes on her the whole time?

"No, you can go first."

He rubbed his brow.

"I can't keep an eye on you if you're behind me."

She frowned. He wanted to keep an eye on her?

"That's okay. I'll be fine."

He shot her a frustrated glance.

"I'm not going first."

"Well neither am I!"

He looked away, his jaw twitching, and she stared at him uneasily.

"If I have to run ahead, I will be turning around to check on you. Frequently. Do you really want me seeing your body. Running." He didn't look at her.

Jo's face filled with heat. She glanced down. Her breasts were new, firm, and not exactly small. And probably really...bouncy.

She swallowed and reached a hand back to feel behind her. How bouncy would that be? He jerked his head further away from her.

"Have you heard of peripheral vision," he snapped.

The heat in her cheeks increased, and she snatched her hand away. She looked down again. Maybe if she... She put a hand over each breast. Yes. That would be supportive. And it would hide her. She could run this way.

"I'll just run like this," she said looking up.

He turned his head toward her again irritably and froze. Her eyes flew down at his expression, worried she'd missed a nipple. No. They were hidden. Her hands seemed a little small against her breasts though.

"It's the best I can do," she said, starting to look up at him again only to freeze as well, her eyes locked on the now rigid length between his legs.

They stood that way for some time before Christopher finally raised his eyes to hers. Then he reached out without expression and wrapped his hand around her upper arm before turning and pulling her into a run alongside him. He let her go once he'd established the pace, never once turning back to her. And she kept her eyes on the sand in front of her.

The night flew by as they flew over the sparkling sands, and the red moon rose and set. But still they found nothing.

Flames of Lethe

ABOUT THE AUTHOR

Lexie Talionis is the pen name of a formerly very bored professor with a PhD in business who published in academic journals and developed a curious case of narcolepsy at the mere mention of having to read yet another academic paper.

But she will stay up all night slaving over heart-wrenching scenes of love, dreaming of the day readers will share in the trauma...and a few laughs along the way to the happy ending she promises to always deliver.

Thank you for sharing in my crazy daydream. :)

https://linktr.ee/LexieTalionis

Milton Keynes UK
Ingram Content Group UK Ltd.
UKHW041312180124
436258UK00006B/460

9 781737 800378